Praise for Edward Marston's
THE RAVENS OF BLACKWATER

"Marston draws a resonant and historically accurate picture of life during the period, creating lively and appealing protagonists as well as believable deep-dyed villains."
—*Publishers Weekly*

"William's henchmen find themselves adjudicating land claims, investigating murder, and reuniting lovers in this interesting look backward."
—*The Washington Times*

"Mr. Marston writes an engaging story which illustrates the tensions of post-conquest England in a bright and lively way."
—*Deadly Pleasures*

By Edward Marston
Published by Fawcett Books:

The Elizabethan Mysteries:
THE QUEEN'S HEAD
THE MERRY DEVILS
THE TRIP TO JERUSALEM
THE NINE GIANTS
THE MAD COURTESAN
THE SILENT WOMAN
THE ROARING BOY

The Domesday Books:
THE WOLVES OF SAVERNAKE
THE RAVENS OF BLACKWATER
THE DRAGONS OF ARCHENFIELD

THE DRAGONS OF ARCHENFIELD

Edward Marston

FAWCETT CREST • NEW YORK

A Fawcett Crest Book
Published by Ballantine Books
Copyright © 1995 by Edward Marston

http://www.randomhouse.com

Library of Congress Catalog Card Number: 96-96971

ISBN 0-449-22545-3

This edition published by arrangement with St. Martin's Press.

Manufactured in the United States of America

First Ballantine Books Edition: January 1997

10 9 8 7 6 5 4 3 2 1

To my father,
a wild man from Wales,
and
to all the boyos back home

Mae hen wlad fy nhadau

Their Lord they will praise,
Their speech they will keep,
Their land they will lose,
Except Wild Wales.

—TALIESIN

Welsh Border 1086

ANGLESEY

Chester

Cardigan
Bay

POWYS

Shrewsbury

Hereford
BRYCHEINIOG
ARCHENFIELD

DEHEUBARTH

MORGANNWG

Bristol Channel

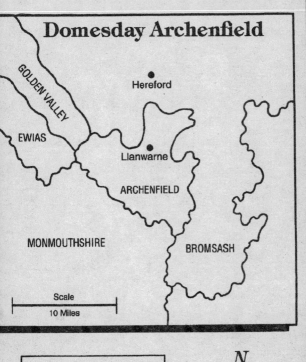

Domesday Archenfield

GOLDEN VALLEY

EWIAS

Hereford

Llanwarne

ARCHENFIELD

MONMOUTHSHIRE

BROMSASH

Scale
10 Miles

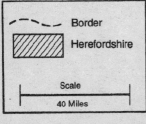

- - - Border

/// Herefordshire

Scale
40 Miles

N

Prologue

H E WAS COMING DOWN THE HILL WHEN THEY
struck. The ambush was so sudden and so unexpected that it threw him into a complete panic. Warnod
had been riding along in the fading light of a warm
evening with a reflective smile on his face and a feeling
of deep satisfaction coursing through his whole body.
The visit to Hereford had been a delight in every respect.
As his horse picked its way along a track through the
woodland, Warnod sat back in the saddle and savoured
each detail of his outing. It had been worth all the effort.
He would cheerfully have ridden ten times as far for a
taste of such happiness.

The first arrow jerked him out of his reverie. It came
whistling murderously from the gloom and shot across
his path before thudding into the trunk of a sycamore. A
second arrow was much closer, passing within a foot of
his shoulder before spending its fury deep in the undergrowth. Warnod did not wait for a third missile. His heels
kicked hard and the horse was soon plunging down the
hill in a mad gallop. Heart pounding and mind ablaze,
Warnod ignored the bushes that lashed out at his legs and
the branches that scratched angrily at his face. Hoofbeats
drummed behind him in a terrifying rhythm. Fond

thoughts of Hereford were wiped savagely away. Survival was paramount.

Warnod was less than a mile from home, but it seemed an impossible distance away. He might never even reach it. The thunder of pursuit was getting louder and louder. They were gaining on him. Not daring to look over his shoulder, he strained his ears to work out how many horses were behind him. Six? Eight? A dozen? Far too many riders for him to fight off. Warnod had only a dagger at his waist and that was more for ornament than protection. He had no chance against a gang of armed robbers.

Riding hell for leather, he took his mount through a grove of alders with reckless unconcern and came out into open country. He was a more visible target now. The chasing pack fanned out across the field as they closed in on their quarry. Warnod swung his horse toward the deepest shadows in search of cover. He cursed his luck and berated himself for being caught so hopelessly off guard. His instinct for danger had been blunted by the visit to Hereford. On the journey home, he had felt supremely safe and with good reason.

Archenfield was no longer the turbulent frontier zone that it had once been. It was a more peaceable community. Lying in the south of the county, cradled by the Wye and its serpentine tributary, the River Monnow, it was an area with rich soil and lush pastures. By force of arms and strength of purpose, the Normans had imposed a stability on the district. Archenfield was a portion of Wales that now belonged irretrievably to England. An air of resignation had descended on the indigenous Welsh population. They had come to terms with Saxon settlers and with Norman overlords. Violent attacks from across the border were things of the past—or so Warnod had believed until that moment.

Was he the victim of a Welsh raiding party? Or were these men fellow Saxons with a grudge against him? Warnod had no time to speculate. The riders had spread out in an arc behind him now, and seemed to be about to encircle him. Finally and miraculously, his house came into view. The low clump of buildings beside the trickling stream offered the only hope for him. His old mare was no match for the horsemen at his back. If he tried to ride on to the village beyond, he would be caught before he got close enough to raise the alarm. Warnod's home was his promise of salvation.

He kicked a final spurt out of his animal and urged it on with harsh commands. Warnod was trembling with fear now. His head was aching, his mouth was dry, his hands were clammy, and his face was lathered with sweat. The last hundred yards were a protracted agony for him. The hounds of hell were on his tail. Somehow, he forced himself through the ordeal to reach the beckoning safety of his home. Reining in his horse, he leaped from the saddle and ran to the door of the house. He pushed it open, dived inside, slammed the door shut behind him, then dropped the stout wooden bar into place. They would need a small battering ram to get at him now.

Panting hard, Warnod yelled out in the darkness.

"Elfig! Hywel! Close the shutters!"

But his servants were nowhere to be found. His voice echoed through the empty house with rising desperation.

"Elfig! Hywel! Where *are* you!"

Warnod stumbled quickly through the murky interior of the building and saw that the narrow windows had already been shuttered. They could not fire their arrows at him through the apertures. The house was secure. He could take some comfort at last. Relief flooded through him, but it was cruelly short-lived. Loud banging on the door made him start with fright. He had not escaped their clutches after all. They were going to smash their way in to get at him.

Groping his way through the gloom, he felt along a wall until his hands closed gratefully on the hilt of his sword. The weapon instilled some courage in him. They would not take him without a fight. Now in his thirties, Warnod was still strong and fit. He would defend himself with honour. Ridiculously outnumbered, he would at least make sure that he killed some of his adversaries before he was himself cut down. He would die with a bloody sword in his hand like a true Saxon thegn.

The house was a long, low structure divided into bays. Its walls were solid oak, its roof thatched, and its floor was sunk into the earth. The door was reinforced with extra timbers, but it could not indefinitely withstand such an unremitting assault. Sooner or later, they would batter a way into his home. Taking a stance at the door, Warnod held his sword ready and waited for the first sound of splintering wood.

It never came. Instead, the hammering ceased altogether and an eerie silence followed. Had they given up and retired from the scene? Were they looking for another mode of entry? He ran to a window and peered through the tiny crack. Nobody was in sight. He moved to a window on the other side of the house and applied his eye to a split in the wooden shutter. There was still no sign of life. Warnod's spirits rose. Had he escaped his enemies? Was he being spared? Could he dare to relax?

The answer was immediate. A new and appalling sound broke through the silence and shattered any foolish hopes he may have had. It was the helpless cry of an animal in great pain and it grew in volume and intensity until it was quite deafening. Unable to get at their human prey, they were slaughtering the cow in the byre. Warnod was outraged. His first instinct was to rush to the aid of the creature, but that was clearly what they were tempting him to do. He would be casting aside his own chance of survival in a forlorn attempt to save an already doomed cow.

A last pitiable groan of protest was followed by a ragged cheer from the crude butchers. Hooves and feet approached the house. Warnod went back to a window and peered through the crack again. Five figures came into view, but it was too dark to identify them. Four were on horseback, the fifth on foot. It was this last man who attracted Warnod's attention. Selecting a spot some thirty yards or so from the house, he knelt down and—using his sword like a spade—began to dig away the turf. Warnod was utterly mystified.

Another man joined the others from the direction of the byre, lugging a heavy wooden pail and spilling some of its contents along the way. Warnod was even more confused. A hole in the ground and a bucket of water? What strange game were his tormentors playing? One of the horsemen looked up at the house and gave a signal to unseen accomplices. A hideous crackle soon went up as they set fire to the thatch.

Warnod shuddered with horror. They were going to burn him alive!

He rushed to the door and flung the bar aside. Better to die fighting against overwhelming odds than to be eaten

5

up in the flames. But he had no choice in the matter. When he wrenched at the door, it would not open. He realised in a flash what had happened. The men had not been trying to hammer a way into the house. They had been boarding up its one exit so that he would be trapped inside.

Hacking wildly at the door with his sword, he felt the first wave of heat hitting him like a body blow. It made him stagger back. He looked around for another means of escape and dived at a window, flinging back the shutter in the hope of being able to squeeze through the narrow gap. But the window frame had also been boarded up from outside. His home had been deliberately turned into his coffin.

The thatch was a raging inferno now and he had to dodge the sparks that showered down all over the floor. The walls of the house were also alight so that he was surrounded by a hissing rectangle of flame. Smoke attacked his eyes and lungs. Scorching heat buffeted him to and fro. The sword fell from his hand as he lumbered around in the brilliant light. Jeers of delight came from the watching men. They had set a cunning trap and he had fallen into it.

Warnod saw that now. They had not meant to ambush him at all. He had been allowed to escape so that they could drive him back to a house already prepared for him. To serve their malign pleasure, he would be burned to a cinder. The heat was now overpowering and the smoke all but blinded him. Lurching across to the window, he summoned up all his remaining energy to shout his defiance at them, but the words died in his throat. What he saw through the greedy flames robbed him of all power of speech.

Everything was lit up by the repulsive glow of the fire. The man who had dug at the turf stepped back to admire his handiwork. He had cut a shape in the ground, inches deep and some two yards in length. The profile was crude but instantly recognisable. The man with the pail poured its contents on to the bare earth and Warnod saw that it was not water at all. By the glare of the blaze, he watched the thick scarlet liquid that plopped from the bucket stain the ground, which had been exposed by the digging. It was the blood of the slaughtered cow.

All resistance now left him. His tunic, his shoes, even his hair caught fire. The pain was indescribable. Overcome by smoke and roasted by the surging heat, he collapsed in a heap on the floor, taking with him the memory of what he had seen carved in the ground and enriched with fresh blood.

It was the emblem of Wales.

Y Ddraig Goch.

The Red Dragon.

Chapter One

HEREFORDSHIRE GAVE THEM A WET WELCOME. FOR the last few hours of their journey, a steady drizzle fell on the little cavalcade and severely dampened their spirits. A stiff breeze added to their discomfort, hurling the rain into their faces, plucking at their bodies, and unsettling the horses. Progress was slow and tedious over the muddy ground. Their chosen route offered no protection from the elements.

Ralph Delchard was glistening all over with moisture.

"A curse on this rain!"

"It will soon ease off," said Gervase Bret.

"Not before it has soaked us to the skin."

"Take heart, Ralph. Another mile and we are there," Gervase raised a finger to point. "Look ahead of you. The castle is within sight. We shall have food, shelter, and a warm fire there."

"If we are not drowned before we reach the place!" Ralph was in a petulant mood. "This is madness, Gervase. Why on earth did we bother to come to Hereford? It will take us the best part of a week to get there and back, yet our duties will be discharged in a couple of days at most. What, in God's name, are we *doing* in this rain-sodden county?"

"Obeying orders."

"Ha!"

Gervase smiled. "We are on the king's business."

"The business of a conqueror is conquest. I should be leading my knights in battle against the Welsh, not dragging them through this quagmire to wave a few mouldy documents under someone's nose."

"Those documents are important," argued Gervase. "They help to bring silver into the royal coffers. War is costly. You cannot raise an army without money."

Ralph was scornful. "Peace unnerves me. I am a soldier born and bred. Put a sword in my hand and I come alive."

"Even in *this* weather?"

The drizzle seemed to thicken and the breeze blew it even harder into their faces. Ralph Delchard pulled his cloak more tightly around him. He was a big, boisterous, well-built man with a vigour that had not been sapped by middle years. His face was raw-boned but handsome, with an authority in the eyes and the upward tilt of the chin. Having borne arms at the Battle of Hastings, he was a Norman lord with the pride of a victor still burning deep inside him.

At the same time, he was capable of laughing at himself.

"No, Gervase!" he said with a chuckle. "I am no rain warrior. Give me dry weather on the battlefield. Sunshine shows off my armour to the best advantage and puts me in the right frame of mind to kill. It is a wonderful feeling."

"I will take your word for it, Ralph."

"Have you never wanted to meet a man in armed combat? To test your strength and skill against a worthy adversary?"

"Never."

"Come, Gervase. You dissemble."

"Never, I swear it."

"Even you must have a spark of aggression somewhere."

"If I do, I seek to contain it."

"Supposing you were pushed to the limit?"

"Words are the best weapons to resolve a quarrel."

"And if Alys were in danger?" asked Ralph, teasing his young companion. "If some brutish Viking were molesting your beloved, would you stand calmly by and try to talk him out of it? Alys would not thank you for that."

"It is not a fair question."

"Every man can be roused to kill. Even you."

"At least I would take no pleasure in it."

Gervase Bret was uncharacteristically sharp with his friend. As a rule, he took Ralph's good-natured mockery in his stride, but it had caught him on a raw spot this time. Betrothed to Alys, he was constantly being sent away from her, and the absences were increasingly difficult to bear. Gervase was a slender man of medium height with the studious air of a Chancery clerk. An astute lawyer, he had a boyish innocence that made him look much younger than his twenty-five years and a mature intellect that made him seem decades older. He and Ralph made an effective team and he did all he could to avoid friction between them.

His apology came hard upon the irritable rejoinder.

"I take that back, Ralph. I spoke harshly and hastily."

"There was a grain of truth in what you charged."

"Mention of Alys provoked me."

Ralph grinned. "Alys would provoke any man. She is very beautiful and you are very fortunate. I worship the lady. If the truth be told, I called up her fair name out of envy."

"Envy? Of whom?"

"You and Alys. No matter how hard the rain or how cold the wind, thoughts of her will keep you dry and warm. And while *you* trudge through the mud of this godforsaken place, Alys waits in Winchester and dreams of nothing but her wonderful Gervase." Ralph shrugged. "Love is truly a blessing. Lose it and you feel excommunicated from life."

Gervase was surprised to hear such serious comment from his friend. Ralph Delchard was normally such a jovial and extrovert character. It was true that he became soulful after too much wine, and had even been known to break into maudlin song, but he rarely talked about the problems in his private life. His wife had died years before trying to bring their only child into the world and the boy soon joined his mother in the grave. A contented man had been cut completely adrift. Interest had waned, purpose wilted. Ralph usually hid those painful memories behind a whirl of action.

"Have you never thought to marry again?" asked Gervase.

"Nobody could replace Elinor."

"Many ladies would like the opportunity to try."

"Then that is what they may do!" said Ralph with a chortle. "Let them come, one and all. Save for battle, there is no greater pleasure than wenching. I can tell you now that I look to find a comely lady or two in Hereford to take the sting out of this interminable journey. What else are women for?"

Gervase bit back a reply and took a deep breath. "I will not rise to the bait this time."

"Then I'll not dangle it before you." He leaned across to Gervase and lowered his voice. "Many have taken Elinor's place in my bed; none will ever oust her from my heart."

"So it is with me and Alys."

Ralph nodded. He became suddenly brisk and barked out a command, slapping the rump of Gervase's horse with the palm of his gauntlet and spurring his destrier into a canter that brought loud protest from the two riders directly behind him. Canon Hubert and Brother Simon were spattered in even more mud as a fresh volley was thrown up by the flashing hooves. Hubert was a round, fat, self-satisfied prelate with an endless supply of red-cheeked, righteous indignation. Seated on a donkey that was all but invisible beneath his bulk, he ordered Ralph to slow down, then blustered impotently when his own mount quickened its pace to catch up the others. Brother Simon was a Benedictine monk buried deep in his black cowl, a laconic and emaciated man who had chosen the skinniest horse in Christendom to match his ascetic tastes. Clinging to the pommel of his saddle as his horse lunged forward, Simon bounced along precariously and prayed for all he was worth.

They were twelve in number. Eight men-at-arms from Ralph's own retinue rode in pairs behind the holy men and towed the sumpter horses after them. An escort was vital on such a long journey. Like their lord, the knights wore helm, hauberk, and sword, and rode upon trained warhorses. Four of them carried a lance and four had bows slung across their backs. Necessary escorts on the long trail from Winchester, they would be able to lend force and status to the work of the commissioners.

Ralph Delchard, Gervase Bret, Canon Hubert, and

even the unsoldierly Brother Simon knew the value of a military presence while they were about their business. The men themselves hoped for some action and adventure in Hereford. It had been a tame, uneventful ride so far and they had exhausted all their crude jokes about the adipose canon and the spectral monk. With their destination rising up before them, they goaded their horses into a steady canter.

As they approached the city from the southeast, Gervase also felt a glow of anticipatory pleasure. Their work would not be too onerous, but it promised to be full of interest. He glanced across at Ralph and called out above the jingle of harness and the thud of hooves.

"Who will greet us this time?" he asked. "What creatures await us here?"

"Creatures?"

"Yes, Ralph. We met with wolves in Savernake Forest and ravens in the Blackwater Estuary. What does Hereford hold?"

"The most dangerous animals of all, Gervase."

"Dangerous?"

"More savage than wolves, more sinister than ravens."

"What are they?"

"The worst foe that any man can encounter."

"Wild bears?"

"No, Gervase," shouted his friend. "Churchmen!"

As they walked side by side into the choir, the noise was ear-splitting. Carpenters, woodcarvers, stonemasons, and smiths seemed to be everywhere, filling the cathedral with the most unholy sounds and adding unbearably to the din by raising their coarse voices above it. The visitor was profoundly shocked. He watched a block of stone

13

being winched up to the top of a pillar by a giant of a man who was whistling at his trade as if completely unaware that he was on hallowed ground. God's work was being done by mindless heathens.

Idwal turned an accusatory glare on his companion.

"This is sacrilege!" he exclaimed.

"No," said the other calmly. "Burning the cathedral to the ground was sacrilege. That, I have to remind you, was the work of your compatriots from across the border. Rebuilding is an act of faith. Bishop Robert has decreed that the work be advanced as swiftly as possible."

"By this crew of noisy infidels?"

"They are skilled craftsmen, Archdeacon."

"But wherein lies their skill?" demanded the irate Welshman. "In taking the Lord's name in vain? In turning His house into a fishmarket? Listen to that appalling sound!"

The dean was imperturbable. "Building is a noisy occupation," he said easily. "No man can carve solid oak or chisel rough stone in silence. And the fellows must talk to each other or how else can they know what is needed and when?" He put a hand on the other's shoulder and eased him toward the transept. "Let us step outside and leave these good men in peace."

"Peace!"

"The rain may have stopped by now."

Dean Theobald was a tall, slim, dignified man of fifty in canonical robes. He moved with a stately tread and towered over the little Welshman beside him. Conducting his visitor back out into the fresh air, he took him far enough away from the building work for the clamour to subside to a distant hum. Idwal was clearly going to be a troublesome guest.

"How is Llandaff?" Theobald asked politely.

"Quiet!"

"Your cathedral church was not razed to the ground."

"Indeed not," said Idwal, "but it has suffered many other humiliations. I see it as my mission in life to right some of the terrible wrongs that have been inflicted upon us."

"Wrongs?"

"I mention but one. All else follows from this." He flung back his tattered lambskin cloak and drew himself up to his full height. "A Bishop of Llandaff should not have to kneel to an Archbishop of Canterbury."

"Lanfranc is a great man."

"The good archbishop may be three parts saint and one part human being, but that does not entitle him to hold sway over the Welsh nation. Llandaff had a church when Canterbury was still overrun by miserable pagans. The bright light of Christianity shone upon Wales centuries before its rays deigned to touch Kent."

"An interesting argument," said the dean tactfully.

"You will hear it in full before I leave Hereford."

Theobald groaned inwardly. "I feared that I might."

Idwal was the Archdeacon of Llandaff Cathedral in South Wales. A small, wiry, animated man in his late thirties, he had a manic glint in his eye and a combative nature. His piety and intelligence were not in doubt, but they were allied to a fierce patriotism. There was a flamboyance about his language and gesture that seemed incongruous in someone so shabbily dressed. His shoes were almost worn through, his hat was shapeless, and his cloak looked as if it had been dragged through every patch of mud on the long road from Glamorgan.

Dean Theobald had a reputation for being able to get on amicable terms with almost anyone, but he sensed that

15

he might have met his match in Idwal. There was something about the voluble Welshman that made the hairs on the back of his neck stand up in alarm. Welcoming the archdeacon would be nowhere near as pleasant as bidding him farewell.

"How long will you be with us?" he asked.

"As long as it takes," said Idwal.

"A couple of days? A week?"

"We shall see."

"There surely cannot be much to detain you here," said Theobald, probing for enlightenment. "If your bishop has sent you on a tour of your native country, you will not wish to spend much time on the wrong side of the border."

"Christianity knows no frontiers."

"That is certainly true."

"Besides, I could not come so close to your cathedral without paying Bishop Robert the compliment of a visit. Part of my work is to forge closer links with other dioceses. Since we regard whole areas of Herefordshire as essentially Welsh in spirit and inclination, this was an obvious port of call."

"It pleases us to offer you hospitality."

"The priests in Archenfield spoke well of your work."

"That is reassuring."

"Hardly," said Idwal with a wicked cackle. "All it means is that you do not interfere with their ministry. The churches in Archenfield are part of the diocese of Llandaff. They look to a more ancient and distinguished see for their spiritual guidance. You understand now why I feel I have a bounden duty to pay my respects to you. The Welsh have left large footprints all over this beautiful county."

Theobald sighed. "Not only footprints, alas!"

"Why do you say that?"

"A man was murdered in Archenfield last evening. Close to the village of Llanwarne."

"Llanwarne!" gasped Idwal. "But I spent an hour at the little church there yesterday afternoon."

"Had you stayed until evening, you might have witnessed the tragedy. From a distance, that is. The victim was burned to death in his own home. The flames could be seen for miles."

"Dear Lord above!" Compassion brought tears into the wild eyes. "Poor man!" he said with quavering voice. "What a dreadful way to die! May his soul rest in peace! Burned alive! I break out into a fever whenever I read the story of Shadrach, Meshach, and Abednego going into the fiery furnace—and they came out unharmed. But this unfortunate creature! The suffering he must have endured! My heart goes out to him. Tell me who he was that I may include him in my prayers."

"A Saxon thegn. Of no real consequence."

"He deserves our sympathy as much as any man," said Idwal. "Death makes us equal partners of one nation. To perish in the flames is like going to hell. Let us hope the ordeal took this noble Saxon to heaven." He remembered the earlier remark and blinked in astonishment. "But what has a murder in Llanwarne got to do with Welsh footprints?"

"Something was carved in the turf outside the house."

"What was it?"

"The signature of the killers."

"In what form?"

"A red dragon."

For the first and perhaps the only time in his life,

17

Idwal was rendered speechless. Theobald savoured the phenomenon.

By the time they clattered into the city through St. Owen's Gate, the travellers had slowed to a gentle trot. The drizzle had faded away, the wind had dropped, and the sky was visibly clearing. They were able to relax and take the measure of the place. Compared to Winchester, from which they had set out on their assignment, Hereford was small and compact. Less than a thousand people lived in a city that had a curiously cosmopolitan flavour. Apart from native Saxons and newcomers of Norman stock, it housed Welshmen, Bretons, Flemings, even a Dane or two. Frenchmanne Street lay to the north of the city as did Jews Street. The bustling market was truly a meeting place of nations. Haggling was done in many tongues.

Ralph Delchard had been duly impressed with the fortifications. It was now thirty years since the Saxon ramparts had been stormed and pulled down by Welsh raiders. The ferocity of the attack had left castle and cathedral in ruins and the whole city in a state of shock. Norman expertise had been brought to bear upon the defences. The earthwork that encircled Hereford had been raised higher and made stronger, while the ditch that fronted it had been deepened. Pierced by six gates, the city walls had also been reinforced.

A large motte and bailey castle was raised on the site of its hapless predecessor. Perched on the River Wye so that it could act as a moat on the southern side, the castle was protected on its other flanks by Norman thoroughness. As he led the others into the courtyard, Ralph threw an admiring glance at the high, solid walls all around them, and at the massive stone building set up on the mound ahead of them and screened by an additional wall. A few guards patrolled the ramparts. Other soldiers practised their swordplay. The clang of steel showed that the armourer was busy in his workshop. Ralph felt at home.

"Welcome to Hereford, sirs!"

"Thank you," said Ralph.

"I am Corbin the Reeve."

The figure who greeted them beside the stables was a fleshy man in his forties with a smile that seemed more of a mask than an indication of genuine pleasure at their arrival. Seated astride a chestnut stallion with handsome trappings, Corbin wore a tunic and mantle of the finest cloth and cut. His hat was trimmed with sable. Gold rings congregated on both flabby hands. The reeve was evidently a man who liked to display his wealth.

Ralph performed the introductions, then dismounted as an ostler came to take his horse. Gervase and the men-at-arms followed suit. Canon Hubert and Brother Simon remained in the saddle. While the others lodged at the castle, they would be offered accommodation at the cathedral. Corbin also stayed mounted so that he could look down at his visitors from a slightly exalted position. His manner was lordly.

"I trust that your business can be despatched with all due celerity," he said. "You catch us at a difficult time and we would not be diverted from our duties any longer than is necessary."

"Our work takes precedence over all else," said Ralph.

"That is a matter of opinion, my lord."

"It is a matter of fact," added Hubert coldly. "We have not ridden all this way for the benefit of our health or for the uncertain joy of making your acquaintance. A royal

19

warrant sends us here. We will not leave until we have obeyed its commands to the letter."

"May I know what those commands are?" asked Corbin.

"Of course," said Ralph. "When we choose to tell you."

"Nothing will be achieved without my assistance," warned the reeve. "I am here to offer help, but I cannot do that if you preserve this mystery about your needs and intentions."

Ralph bristled at his tone. "Our immediate needs should be obvious to the naked eye," he said. "We have ridden long and hard through unkind weather. Rest and refreshment would not come amiss. Show my men where they are to be housed and provide someone to escort Canon Hubert and Brother Simon to the cathedral. They are not horsemen and the journey has been an act of martyrdom for them."

"Indeed it has," agreed Hubert.

"Suffering ennobles the soul," murmured Simon.

"Only in certain circumstances."

"If you say so, Canon Hubert."

The reeve looked at the four of them with mild disdain.

"This is a mean embassy," he observed. "When the first commissioners visited Hereford, they included Bishop Remigius of Lincoln, with a clerk and two monks in attendance, and three barons of high standing supported by a troop of men-at-arms. They were shown all that there is to be shown about the disposition and ownership of land in this county. What is the purpose of this second visit and why does it carry less weight?"

"Your horse will carry less weight if you bandy more words with me," said Ralph irritably. "Find a servant to guide my colleagues to the cathedral and see my men bestowed in their lodgings. Do you not recognise an order when you hear one?"

Corbin glowered down at him for a second before manufacturing a smile of appeasement. He clicked his fingers and waved his hands. When the soldiers were taken care of and the two ecclesiastics were led away by a servant, Ralph and Gervase were themselves taken to the living quarters in the main building. The apartment which they shared was small but serviceable, and it offered them a fine view of the Wye through its arched window. The beds were soft and other small touches of comfort recommended themselves to the weary travellers.

When they had changed out of their wet clothing, they went down to the hall to find Corbin the Reeve waiting for them. Food and drink had been set out at the end of the long oak table and a fire was crackling nearby. Their host waved them to the bench and hovered in the background as they slaked their thirst, Ralph choosing wine, but Gervase preferring the local ale. Corbin had already helped himself to a cup of wine and he drained it before taking up the conversation again. His tone was now noticeably more conciliatory.

"I would be friends with the king's officers," he said.

"Then master the laws of friendship," suggested Ralph through a mouthful of chicken. "Or avoid my sight."

"How may I be of service?"

"Do you really wish to know?"

"Let me tell you," said Gervase quickly, heading off the obscenity that he knew was about to tumble from Ralph's lips. "We will be in session at the shire hall early in the morning. Four witnesses must be summoned before us."

21

"Do you think you could manage that?" mocked Ralph.

"Tell me their names and they will be there."

"The first is well known to you, I think," said Gervase.

"Who is he?"

"Ilbert the Sheriff."

"Why do you need to question him?"

"That is a matter between us and the sheriff himself," said Ralph, pouring more wine from the jug. "Your job is simply to bring him to the shire hall at the appointed time."

"Then it will not be tomorrow."

"It *must* be tomorrow," insisted Ralph.

"The sheriff is indisposed. Who is your next witness?"

"A man called Warnod," said Gervase. "He holds land in Archenfield and is at the heart of our enquiries."

"Then your journey has been wasted."

Ralph stiffened. "Is this Warnod indisposed as well?"

"Completely."

"Then I will have to send some of my men to bring him before us by force. *Nobody* has the right to ignore our summons. Neither earl, nor bishop, nor reeve." He turned to glare at Corbin. "We will start with this indisposed sheriff of yours. Ask—nay, tell in round terms— this Ilbert to present himself at the shire hall at nine o'clock in the morning."

"That will not be possible, my lord."

"*Make* it possible!"

"The sheriff is too busy hunting."

"Hunting!" Ralph's face turned puce. "Ilbert dares to chase game when he is called by royal commissioners? Give us no more of **this nonsense!** The king's business will brook no delay." He banged the table with an angry fist. "We will see the sheriff at nine o'clock and this Warnod at noon. Arrange it. Do you hear me? About it now, man! Arrange it!"

"Only God could do that."

Ralph was on his feet. "Do you still obstruct us?"

"Let him speak," said Gervase, easing his friend back down onto the bench. "There has to be a good reason why the first two men we seek are not available."

"An excellent reason," said Corbin.

"Yes!" sneered Ralph. "Ilbert must go hunting!"

"It is his duty, my lord. But his quarry is not deer."

"Then what is he after?"

"Murderers," said Corbin. "The men who killed Warnod."

There was a long silence as Ralph and Gervase absorbed this startling piece of information. The reeve gave a brief hearsay account of what had happened in Archenfield on the previous evening. It altered matters considerably. The Saxon thegn who was such a pivotal character in their inquiry had been summarily removed from the scene on the very eve of their arrival. The timing of his death could surely not be a coincidence. He was being silenced before he could speak to the commissioners.

The reeve was enjoying their discomfort. Two of the four people they sought would not be able to present themselves at the shire court on the morrow. Corbin relished his role as the bearer of bad news, believing that he had already drastically shortened their stay in Hereford. Suppressing a smirk, he leaned forward with his palms spread wide.

"Whom else do you wish to examine?"

"Richard Orbec," said Gervase.

"And do not dare to tell us that *he* is indisposed," growled Ralph. "Do not find an excuse for him."

"No, no," said Corbin. "Richard Orbec will be there."

"Call him for nine o'clock," decided Ralph.

"Call them both at the same time," said Gervase.

The reeve raised an eyebrow. "Both?"

"Richard Orbec and Maurice Damville."

"Together?"

"That is what we require."

"Richard Orbec and Maurice Damville . . . *together*?" Corbin spluttered with amusement. "That is not practical. It is not wise. It is not safe."

"Why not?" yelled Ralph.

"The sheriff will have another murder on his hands."

"Indeed, he will!" he said, leaping to his feet again. "And you will be the victim if you do not stop sniggering in our faces and obstructing the course of law. God's tits, man! We call four witnesses and you cannot produce one of them."

"You may have Richard Orbec alone," said the reeve.

"What about Maurice Damville?"

"He, too, may be questioned on his own."

Gervase was puzzled. "Why not both men together?"

"Because they are sworn enemies," explained Corbin. "I would not put them in the same town, let alone in the same room. They despise each other with a deep and lasting hatred. Richard Orbec and Maurice Damville never meet, but they are at each other's throats. And it will take more than your eight men-at-arms to break them asunder." A smirk played around his thick lips. "Do you still wish me to invite them to the shire hall at the same time?"

Chapter Two

THE CASTLE AT EWYAS HAROLD HAD BEEN BUILT BY Osbern Pentecost over fifteen years before the Normans had invaded Britain. It stood at the confluence of the Dore and Monnow rivers, staring out at the looming grandeur of the Black Mountains and guarding the road from Abergavenny. Like all the castles on the Welsh Marches, it was both a springboard for attack and a safe retreat in the face of retaliation by superior forces. Heavily refortified in the wake of the Conquest, it was now being further strengthened. Like its counterpart in Hereford, it was a typical motte and bailey structure, in this case making use of a huge natural mound that faced the higher ground to the north.

Maurice Damville hauled himself up into the saddle of his destrier and adjusted his helm. When he felt ready, he held out a hand and snarled an order. The waiting squire gave him the lance and stepped smartly out of the way. Everyone else in the bailey watched from a safe distance. Damville was a dangerous and unpredictable man at the best of times. When he was mounted on his warhorse with a weapon in his grasp, he could be lethal. The slaves who had been carting the ashlar remembered only too well what had happened to one of their number who had dared to question a decision made by his Norman lord. Maurice Damville had run him through with a sword out of sheer malice.

The castellan of Ewyas Harold was a tall, rangy man in his forties with a sinewy strength that he enjoyed showing off. Naked force had conquered the land on which the castle was built and he exemplified it. His keen spurs made the animal rear before breaking into a canter across the bailey. Standing directly in his path, his adversary was strong and unafraid. The rider gritted his teeth and dipped his spear. When his horse ran straight at the mark, he pulled back his arm, then thrust home the weapon with awesome power—straight through the heart of his enemy. An involuntary groan of fear came from the slaves by the wall, but the soldiers acclaimed their master with shouts and laughs of approval.

No blood had been spilled this time, but it was still an impressive killing. The corpse was no more than a hauberk that had been stuffed with straw and set up against a stout post in the middle of the courtyard. Such was the violence and timing of the attack, however, the mail had been pierced as if it were paper, the lance had gone deep into the wood, and the post had snapped in two with a loud crack. Even in the best armour, a human being would have been impaled to the ground by the vicious force of the thrust.

Damville reined in his horse and swung its head round to view the devastated target. When he glanced across at the slaves, they went straight back to their work of unloading the stone slabs from the cart so that they could be hoisted up to reinforce the wall around the bailey. Damville was a hard taskmaster but they had to obey him. He was a law unto himself on that stretch of the Welsh border. They felt deeply grateful that one of them had not been lashed to the post in place of the straw soldier.

Dismounting with a grunt, Damville tossed the reins to a servant and beckoned his steward across. Huegon was a much older man with greying hair and a lined face. He had been standing near the main gate with a stranger. Damville removed a gauntlet and flicked a thumb at the newcomer.

"What does he want?"

"He brings a message from Hereford," said Huegon.

"Who does he serve?"

"Corbin the Reeve."

Damville gave a derisive snort. "Send him on his way with a dusty answer. I read no letters from that fat-gutted fool."

"Corbin has his faults," said the other, "but he is certainly no fool."

"No," admitted his master. "Perhaps he is not. Any man who can feather his nest the way that the greedy reeve has done must have some intelligence. Or native guile. I would not trust the fellow to tell me what day of the week it was. That big, oily face of his is a map of deceit." He waved a dismissive hand. "Despatch the message unread. That is all the reply that Corbin deserves."

"But the letter is a summons."

"A summons!" Damville was insulted. "For me!"

"Sent on behalf of royal commissioners," said the steward. "What its nature is, I do not know, and neither does the fellow who brought it here post haste. All he can tell me is that it is a matter of urgency. I think you should know what this letter betokens. Read it."

"I am too busy."

"Then let me glance through it on your behalf."

Damville scowled, but he soon saw the wisdom of the

27

advice. To spurn a letter from a despised reeve was one thing; to ignore a summons from officials on the king's business was quite another. He gave a curt nod and Huegon collected the message and brought it across to him. Tearing it open, Damville read swiftly through its contents with growing irritation.

"I am called before them tomorrow!" he growled.

"For what purpose?"

"They do not tell me. That is what enrages me most."

"Why have they come to Hereford?"

"In connection with this royal survey."

"The Domesday Book?"

Damville was furious. "Call it what you will, I'll have no more dealings with it. When the first commissioners came to the county, I went before them and gave all the evidence that was asked of me. What more do they want?"

"There is only one way to find out."

"I will not be sent for in this manner, Huegon."

"If they are here by royal warrant—"

Maurice Damville turned away with an imperious gesture. The last thing he needed at that point in time was to be questioned before a tribunal in Hereford. It would be a blow to his pride and take him away from more pressing matters. Pacing up and down, he weighed his anger against the more moderate response of his steward. Huegon was a wily man whose advice was invariably sage, but Damville was minded to disregard him on this occasion. He stopped abruptly in his tracks, snatched off his helm, and glared at the messenger through black eyes. His question was hurled like a spear.

"Did you see these commissioners arrive?"

"Yes, my lord," said the man, nervously.

"How many did they number?"

"Four."

"With men-at-arms at their back?"

"Eight, my lord."

Damville was contemptuous. "Only eight swords to enforce this demand! They'll need ten times that number to get me to Hereford tomorrow." He took a menacing step towards the now trembling messenger. "Nobody can command my presence at such short notice. Tell them that I am in no mood to oblige them. Away with you!"

"Not so fast, sir!" interceded Huegon, catching the man by the arm as he tried to scurry away. "Wait for a proper answer. This was but spoken in jest."

Anxious to quit the place, the messenger agreed to stay while further discussion was held, but it would not take place in the bailey. Damville was already striding purposefully towards the motte, mounting the rough stone steps that led up to the tower and sweeping in through the door. Huegon went after him but waited until they were in the hall before he spoke. Maurice Damville was easier to handle in private. A gaping audience such as he had in the bailey always brought out the worst in him.

The old man closed the door of the hall behind him.

"Your reply was ill-considered," he said quietly.

"So was their summons."

"They have been sent by the king."

"That is my main objection to their presence. I will not have every inch of my land poked at and pried into by King William. I endured it once, but not again. These royal commissioners will hear nothing from me."

"Do you not wish to hear anything from them?"

"Why should I?"

"Because they come from Winchester."

Damville's expression changed visibly. His temper

29

slowly subsided to be replaced by a calculating curiosity. He ran a hand across the lower part of his lean face.

"What can they tell us?"

"Whatever you wish to get out of them. They come from court. Their news is fresh." He lowered his voice to a persuasive whisper. "Take me with you and let us meet their enquiries with a show of obedience. They will the sooner be sent on their way. As long as they are in Hereford their presence is a hindrance and may advantage your foe."

"Orbec?"

"If you are summoned, the likelihood is that he will have to bear witness as well. Richard Orbec disputes your land. Will you let him put his case to these commissioners while you stay sulking here?"

Damville crossed to the fireplace and spat into the flames. He brooded for several minutes before turning to face the steward. Mastering his rage, he nodded.

"I will go."

"It is politic."

"Orbec will only tell them more lies."

"That would not be the end of it," said the old man. "If he attended their tribunal and you did not, they would wish to know the reason why. They would come looking for you here and that is to be avoided at all cost."

Maurice Damville allowed a sly smile to lighten his features. In repose, his face had a kind of brutal charm. Fair hair swept back from a high forehead and the clean-shaven chin was square and strong. He reached out to slap his companion on the shoulder.

"Where would I be without you, Huegon?"

"Still toiling in Normandy."

"You always give good counsel."

30

"But you do not always pay heed to it."

"True," said Damville, accepting the mild rebuke. "This time, I will. Let us satisfy these commissioners and pack them off to Winchester. But not before we have used them to strike a blow at Orbec. That would content me most." He walked the steward back to the door. "Send word that I will present myself at the shire hall at noon tomorrow. When my business is finished, I will return here with all speed."

"Unless you have a reason to linger in Hereford."

"What?" Damville saw the twinkle in the old man's eye and grinned. "I had almost forgotten that."

"Would you rather I had not reminded you?"

Maurice Damville's laughter echoed through the hall.

Gervase Bret knelt at the altar rail and offered up his prayers. Work on the cathedral had stopped for the day. Alone in the building, he was able to commune with his Maker in silence. Gervase was a devout but sometimes erratic Christian. Educated in a monastery, he had been imbued with a love of study and prayer, and was on the point of taking the cowl himself when more worldly concerns pressed in upon him. Something of those concerns threaded their way into the words that he was now sending up to heaven.

Gentle footsteps moved over the paved stones behind him. Dean Theobald was surprised to find a stranger on his knees in an attitude of such deep prayer. Genuflecting before the altar, he moved to the shadow of a pillar and waited patiently until the visitor was about to leave.

When Gervase rose and turned, he was met by a smile of welcome. Theobald had had time to guess at whom he might be.

"Gervase Bret, I believe?" he said.

"You know my name?"

"Canon Hubert spoke of you. He also spoke of one Ralph Delchard but, from his description, I did not look to find your colleague so accustomed to taking his place at an altar rail." They shared a polite laugh. "I am Dean Theobald and it is a privilege to have Canon Hubert and Brother Simon in our community for a short while."

"They will be grateful guests."

"Yes," agreed Theobald. "I am not sure that the same may be said of another whom we have under our roof at the moment, but it is our duty to extend Christian fellowship to all. Even those with more eccentric modes of belief." He took Gervase out through the door before stopping to look at him properly. "Why did you come to the cathedral?"

"To pray."

"But why here? The castle has its own chapel."

"I would be mocked if I was seen going into it."

"By this Ralph Delchard?"

"Yes," said Gervase tolerantly. "He pretends to deride the Church, but I know that he worships God in his own way."

"That is what I tell myself about Archdeacon Idwal."

"Archdeacon Idwal?"

"An unworthy remark," said Theobald, repenting at once. "Please ignore it. But what do you think of our cathedral?"

"It will be quite beautiful when it is finished."

"That will not be in our lifetime, alas! Bishop Robert initiated the rebuilding six years ago and you see what little progress has been made since then. The work is painstakingly slow and fearfully expensive."

"It will be worth it."

"We believe so. It will never compare with Winchester or with Canterbury, of course, but we feel that God will not be displeased by our humbler creation." He gestured with his hand. "Would you care to take a proper look around?"

Gervase accepted the invitation without hesitation. Not only was he genuinely interested in the cathedral and its operation, he warmed to its friendly dean. There was an unforced dignity about the man which was very appealing. But Gervase had another reason for touring the precincts with his amenable host. No important event in the county escaped the attention of the church. It was the common storehouse in which every scrap of information, rumour, or scandal was routinely placed. Theobald could be extremely useful.

"We were alarmed to hear of this murder," said Gervase.

"It has shocked us all profoundly. Warnod did not deserve such a grisly fate."

"Who was he?"

"A thegn from Archenfield," said Theobald. "His father was a wealthy man in the reign of King Edward. Warnod was set to inherit nineteen manors. But most of the land was taken from him after the Conquest. Warnod was left with only the vestiges of his estate."

"That much I knew. The man was the one of the subjects of our enquiry. Some of the land which legitimately remained in his keeping was also expropriated. The name of Maurice Damville came into the reckoning on that account."

"It would, I fear!"

"Richard Orbec, too, is implicated."

Theobald smiled ruefully. "Never one without the other.

Maurice Damville and Richard Orbec dispute everything out of force of habit, as you will very soon discover."

"What manner of man was this Warnod?"

"An honest, God-fearing fellow who never complained at the blows that rained down upon him. And there were plenty of those, I can tell you."

"Apart from the loss of his inheritance?"

"That was but the start of it," said the dean with a sigh. "Warnod was ill-starred. His first child died of a terrible sickness, the second was drowned in the Wye. He and his poor wife were distraught. Just as they were getting over those tragedies—if any human being can ever fully do that—the wife herself was killed when she was thrown from a horse. It was a most unhappy household."

"And yet he bore these tribulations?"

"With great courage."

"Did he have many enemies?"

"None that I can name. But then I did not know him very well myself. What I tell you is merely what I have heard in the last twenty-four hours." Theobald shrugged. "I cannot fathom the reason for the murder. Warnod was well respected. With every reason to hate all Normans, he came to terms with our arrival far better than most. Then there are the Welsh."

"Corbin the Reeve told us of the red dragon."

"A hideous epitaph to leave behind."

"It seems like a clear message."

"I am not so sure."

"Why not?"

"Because, by all accounts, Warnod rubbed along extremely well with his Welsh neighbours." He glanced involuntarily towards the refectory. "I could use some of his talent in that direction myself."

"Perhaps he offended them in some way."

"Far from it. Archenfield is still largely inhabited by people of Welsh descent. Warnod even went so far as to learn the rudiments of their language."

"And yet they burned him to death."

"That has not yet been proved."

"Corbin seemed to feel that it had."

"Our reeve is rather prone to summary judgments."

"How else do you explain the red dragon?" said Gervase.

Theobald shook his head. "I cannot, Master Bret. Nor can I explain the strange treatment of the two servants."

"Servants?"

"In Warnod's house. Elfig and Hywel."

"A Saxon and a Welshman."

"Living under his roof without undue discomfort."

"Were they trapped in the bonfire with him?"

"They were both spared," said Theobald, "but they have rather different tales to tell."

"In what way?"

"They were seized at the house by a gang of men. Bound and gagged, they were dragged a hundred yards away so that they could not warn their master on his return."

"Wherein lies the difference between the servants?"

"Elfig was beaten senseless. Hywel was unharmed. Was it a case of Welshmen relenting with one of their own?"

"Not necessarily," argued Gervase. "The Saxon may have resisted the attackers and been punished for his boldness."

"Hardly. Elfig is a frail old man. They are not at all sure that he will survive the attack."

"And the other servant? Hywel?"

"Still young and virile."

Gervase was baffled, but he had no opportunity to ask any further questions. They were close to the refectory now and their conversation was rudely interrupted by the sounds of a violent quarrel from within. Dean Theobald blenched. The college of regular canons maintained the most strict decorum. Voices were never raised within the cathedral precincts and disputes were never allowed to become acrimonious. Theobald moved to quell the disturbance. Pushing open the door of the refectory, he sailed in with Gervase Bret at his heels.

"Dyfryg!" shouted Idwal.

"Ethelbert!" roared Canon Hubert.

"Dyfryg was a holy man."

"So was Ethelbert."

"He was King of the East Angles. Offa had him killed when Ethelbert came here to marry his daughter."

"Miracles resulted. That is why Ethelbert was made a saint and why this cathedral is dedicated to him."

"It should honour St. Dyfryg instead!"

Both men became aware of the presence of Theobald at the same time, but they reacted in opposite ways. Hubert was immediately contrite, abandoning the argument with the testy Welshman and mouthing his apologies for his loss of control. Idwal was completely unabashed. Two new faces simply meant two more people with whom to debate the merits of St. Dyfryg.

"Let us have *your* opinion, Dean Theobald," he said.

"My opinion is that you are both guests here and should not seek to violate the peace of our community."

Idwal chuckled. "It was a friendly discussion. Canon Hubert and I were just exchanging views on the nature of sainthood. Bishop Dyfryg was *born* in Ergyng—Archenfield, as you insist on calling it. His ministry touched much of this county. Why is this not the cathedral church of St. Dyfryg?"

The two combatants were sitting either side of the long oak table that ran down the length of the refectory. Half-eaten meals and half-drunk mugs of ale showed that everyone else had fled from the scene. Brother Simon had gone with them, unable to stop the fierce argument and unwilling to be drawn into it. Idwal the Archdeacon was a small man with a powerful presence. His truculent scholarship had cleared the room.

"Well?" he demanded. "What is your view, Theobald?"

"I have given it," said the dean crisply. "Excuse me while I have private conference with Canon Hubert."

"They're running away. I won the debate!"

"I will speak with you in due course, Archdeacon."

On that icy note, Theobald took Hubert out of the refectory, convinced that the only way to end the dispute was to separate the two men, and wondered how soon he could assist their Welsh visitor back across the border. Gervase Bret was left alone with Idwal, who, now divested of his filthy cloak, was still wearing his mean travelling apparel. His hat had been removed to reveal straggly hair.

The mad eyes switched their beam to Gervase.

"And who might you be, young sir?"

"Gervase Bret. Travelling with Canon Hubert."

"That shameless bigot?"

"He has his redeeming features."

"So do we all." Idwal swallowed the dregs of his ale and appraised the newcomer. "Gervase, eh? And what do *you* know about St. Dyfryg?"

"More than you would imagine."

"You have actually *heard* of him?"

"Of course. He was a monk who helped to spread

Christianity in this area. His first foundation was indeed in Archenfield."

"The Welsh call it Ergyng."

"Dyfryg may have known it as Ariconium, its Roman name."

"That is where he did much of his apostolic work," said Idwal wistfully. "I traced his holy footsteps through the area only yesterday."

Gervase pricked up his ears. "In Archenfield?"

"I visited all the churches there."

"Including the one at Llanwarne?"

"I spent an hour with the priest in the afternoon."

"A man was murdered less than a mile from there."

"Unhappily, it is so," said the Welshman, "and I have already included Warnod's name in my prayers. Elfig, too, for the old servant lies grievous sick from his beating."

"What did you *see*?" asked Gervase.

"Nothing. I left the village by four."

"You may have noticed something of significance without even realising it. The men who burned Warnod's house were in the area well before he returned to his home." He came to sit opposite Idwal. "Rack your brains, Archdeacon. Piece it together again in your mind."

"I will try."

"Tell me exactly what you did in Archenfield."

"First of all, I called it Ergyng. . . ."

Gervase suppressed a smile.

Ralph Delchard had much to keep him occupied at the castle. Having inspected the lodging assigned to his men, he gave them their orders for the morrow and warned them not to carouse too long or too wildly in the city that night. He then explored the whole building to familiarise himself with its layout and appreciate the finer points of its construction. It was good to have high stone walls around him. A soldier by training and instinct, Ralph knew from personal experience that Norman success in subduing the English—and keeping the Welsh and Scots at bay—depended largely on their skill at building castles.

His stroll eventually brought him to the main gate. Two guards were talking idly but, at his approach, separated to take up sentry positions. Ralph saw the opportunity to gather some intelligence. He chatted casually with them to win their confidence, then tossed a name into the conversation.

"What can you tell me of Richard Orbec?"

The two soldiers exchanged a glance. The bigger of them, a broad-shouldered man with a gruff voice, answered for both.

"He is a power in this county."

"I know that from the size of his holdings," said Ralph. "What of his character, his likes and dislikes, his reputation? Describe the man to me."

"Richard Orbec likes to keep himself to himself," said the guard. "He rarely stirs from his estates unless someone is unwise enough to trespass on his land or his patience. Slow to rouse, he is a ruthless man when his temper is up. I have known him to ride the length of the county to punish some insult or affront to his dignity."

"A proud man, then. Strong, aggressive."

"And lonely."

"Does he have no wife and family?"

"None, my lord. Some say he has a religious streak, and he has certainly been generous towards the cathedral. Parts of the choir were rebuilt with Richard Orbec's money." He traded another look with his partner. "Others take a darker view of his dislike of women."

Ralph saw the cold snigger in the eyes of both men.

"Maurice Damville also interests me," he said.

"Treat him with caution, my lord."

Ralph was peremptory. "I will treat him as I think fit. If he proves quarrelsome, he will find that the King's writ runs in Herefordshire as in every other county." He relaxed a little. "The two men are not the best of friends, I hear."

"True, my lord," said the soldier, with a grim chuckle. "The sheriff spends much of his time keeping them apart. Richard Orbec and Maurice Damville have too many old scores to settle."

"Damville sounds to be hot-tempered and violent."

"None more so. He is also a famous lecher in these parts. He keeps his wife and family in Normandy so that they may not interfere with his sport. They say he has bastards all over the county. In fact . . ."

The man's voice trailed away as he looked through the open postern gate. Two figures were walking quickly towards the castle. When Ralph saw the first of them, he immediately lost interest in the men's gossip. A tall, graceful woman was bearing down on them in an elegant gunna of white linen and a blue mantle. Her wimple enclosed an oval face whose soft beauty was enhanced by a sense of anxiety. The small, thin girl beside her, in meaner attire, was evidently a servant and claimed no more than a cursory glance from Ralph.

He crossed to the gate to offer a polite welcome.

"May I be of service to you?" he said.

"Has the sheriff returned?" asked the woman.

"I fear not."

"When is he expected?"

"Nobody seems to know," he said. "Perhaps I may be able to help you in his stead. My name is Ralph Delchard, sent here by royal warrant that makes the sheriff answerable to me as long as I am in Hereford. Step inside and we will find somewhere with a measure of privacy. I can see that you have come on a matter of some urgency."

The woman hesitated before responding with a fleeting smile. Ralph's blend of gallantry and easy authority was reassuring. She allowed him to take her hand as she stepped through the gate. Both of the guards gave the newcomers a nod of recognition. When Ralph led the two women across the bailey, the servant girl walked a few paces behind them. He spoke to her mistress with respectful curiosity.

"May I know your name?"

"Golde, my lord."

"You live in the city?"

"At the west end of Castle Street," she said. "It is the merest step away."

"I wondered why the guards seemed to know you."

"They have seen me here many times. I have business in the castle that makes me a frequent visitor, though I have come on a different errand this time."

Ralph did not press her for details. They would come when they were away from public gaze. Instead, he chatted amiably about his first impressions of the city. Only when they reached the tower did his manner change. He opened the door of the solar and gestured for her to go in.

Golde met his eyes and saw the frank affection in them. He saw an answering flicker of interest that was replaced by a look of concern, but she signalled her trust by asking her companion to wait outside. Ralph followed her into the room and closed the door behind him. He waved her to a chair, but she preferred to stand.

"May I call for some wine?" he said.

"No, thank you."

"Can I offer you any other refreshment?"

"I have simply come in search of information."

"About what?"

"There are rumours of a cruel murder."

"Why do they arouse your interest?"

"Because the name I heard whispered was Warnod."

"You know the man?"

"I know of him," she said carefully. "And I would be glad to learn the truth of the matter. Marketplace gossip can often be misleading. I hope to hear that Warnod may not have been the victim of this crime."

Ralph heaved a gentle sigh. "Then your hope is likely to be dashed, I fear."

"Can you be certain?"

"Warnod was killed last evening by unknown assassins."

"How?"

"The details might distress you."

"*How?*" she insisted.

"He was barricaded into his house and burned alive."

Golde winced but quickly regained her composure. Ralph was struck once again by the haunted beauty of her face. In his opinion, Saxon women did not usually compare with the ladies of Normandy, but here was a startling exception. Still in her twenties, she had the look of someone well acquainted with adversity yet able to meet it with a brave heart. Though apprehension had brought her to the castle, what Ralph now caught was a sense of her innate resilience. Expecting bad news, she had adjusted to it with remarkable control.

"Are you sure you would not like something?" he asked.

"No, my lord."

"The wine is tolerable."

"I do not drink wine."

"Neither do most people around here," he complained in jocular tones. "They prefer the local ale. It is beyond belief. They could have the finest wine from Normandy yet they drink this disgusting English ale." He saw a half-smile. "What is the joke? Have I said something comical?"

"No, my lord."

"Do you despise our taste for wine?"

"It is not my place to do so."

"Then why did you smile even now?"

"That comment about disgusting English ale."

"It is flat, evil-smelling, and revolting to look at. I loathe it. But why should that amuse you?"

"Because I brew the ale for this castle."

Ralph goggled. *"You!"*

"For castle and cathedral," she said proudly. "It is a worthy occupation and I have yet to receive a complaint. My husband was the most successful brewer in Hereford and I inherited his business when he died. Do not be amazed, my lord. Many of the best brewers in the city are women."

"I do not doubt it," he said, covering his embarrassment with a chuckle. "And I was not condemning *your* ale. It has a quality all of its own, I am sure, but I was raised amid the vineyards of Normandy. Wine is nectar to me."

Golde smiled to show that she was not offended by his remarks. In the brief moment when their eyes locked, he saw a vulnerability which had not been there before. It was as if their discussion of ale had thrown her off guard.

He stepped in close to her to take advantage of the moment.

"What really brought you here this evening?" he said.

"I wished to make enquiry."

"Is this Warnod related to you in some way?"

"No, my lord."

"A friend, perhaps? A customer for your ale?"

"He is . . . known to me. That is all."

"It would take more than that to fetch you in search of the sheriff," he suggested. "Warnod is known to many people, but they are not all queueing up at the castle gate to learn the details of his murder. I think you have a more serious reason. Confide in me and I will not betray you."

She turned away. "I will take my leave."

"Wait," he said, touching her arm to stop her. "This is important to me. I am part of a commission sent to look into abuses that have come to light in this county. Warnod was to have been called before us. His evidence would have been crucial. His death is an inconvenience, to say the least. I wish to see if it is in any way linked to our arrival here, so anything—anything at all—that you may tell me about Warnod will be of value." He took his hand from her arm. "Please, help me. If this man means something to you, help me to find his killers."

Golde bit her lip and looked up at him, wrestling with her conscience and wondering how far she could trust him. Ralph met her gaze and waited until the words eventually slipped quietly from her lips.

"Warnod was a friend," she confessed. "When he was riding back to Archenfield, he was on his way home from a visit to my house."

Chapter Three

Richard Orbec rose before dawn and went straight to the tiny chapel. Its simplicity was striking. Four bare stone walls enclosed an area which could accommodate no more than a mere handful of worshippers. The gold crucifix that stood on the little altar was the only concession to luxury. Wax candles burned on either side of it. There were no windows. It was more like a monastic cell than a chapel of a Norman lord.

Orbec knelt on the cold paving slab in an attitude of submission. He remained alone in the dank chamber for the best part of an hour. Nobody dared to interrupt him. Morning prayer was a solitary vigil that he never neglected. Members of his household had learned to stay well clear of their ascetic master during his devotions.

Breakfast was a hasty meal of bread and wine. Orbec then changed into his hauberk in readiness for the journey. He summoned Redwald, the manorial reeve.

"Is all ready?" he asked.

"Yes, my lord."

"You have the documents?"

"In my satchel," said Redwald, patting the leather pouch that was slung from his shoulder. "I have brought everything that may be asked for, my lord, and much that may not. Nothing has been left to chance."

"Good."

Richard Orbec was a stocky man of medium height with dark hair and a swarthy complexion. Unlike most Normans, he kept his hair long and wore a beard. When driven to anger, his green eyes would blaze and his face would take on an almost satanic quality. Most of the time, however, he was placid and personable. Still in his thirties, he moved with an athletic grace.

"Who else is called before the king's tribunal?" he asked.

"I do not know, my lord. But I can guess one name."

"Damville?"

"You will be able to renew your dispute with him."

"I would rather do that with a dagger than with a pile of documents," said Orbec, ruefully, "but this way may prove just as effective. We caught him on the hip when we appeared before the first commissioners. Let us do the same with this new tribunal."

"It may not be quite so easy, my lord."

"Why not?"

"Huegon is a wily steward and a persuasive advocate."

Orbec smiled. "That is why I put you up against him."

A big, shapeless, ungainly man in his forties, Redwald's distinguishing feature was a long drooping moustache falling from beneath a broken nose. As the manorial reeve, he was responsible for the administration of his master's estates in the county and he had given good service.

In employing a Saxon reeve, Orbec followed many of his countrymen in choosing an official with a sound working knowledge of the area and its inhabitants. Where

Orbec differed from his compatriots was in talking to Redwald in the latter's native tongue. An intelligent and cultured man, Orbec spoke a number of languages and had mastered the complexities of Anglo-Saxon with comparative ease. It earned him respect in the Saxon community and open derision from fellow Normans.

Richard Orbec saw the practical advantages. Peasants on his estates could say nothing in his hearing that he did not fully understand. By the same token, he could converse with Redwald in a wholly Norman gathering in a language totally beyond the comprehension—and beneath the dignity—of all but his reeve. These were valuable political assets.

"Maurice Damville has been quiet of late," Orbec noted.

"It may be the calm before the storm, my lord," warned Redwald. "He is not a man to be trusted."

"Come what may, I am prepared for him."

"If he rides to Hereford, he will have men at his back."

"So will I, Redwald. They are saddled and waiting even as we speak." He saw the anxious look on the reeve's face. "Do not be alarmed. They'll behave themselves. They'll not seek a brawl with Damville's knights." His manner hardened into cold resolution. "Unless they have cause."

"That is what I fear."

Orbec grabbed his helm. "Let us be on our way."

They left the house and mounted the waiting horses. Six men-at-arms were also in attendance, complaining noisily about having to get up so early to travel to Hereford, but secretly looking forward to a few hours of pleasure in the city. Richard Orbec called them to order with a curt command and the eight of them set off at a canter.

The manor house itself was large and capacious. Built

of stone and of Norman design, it was an impressive dwelling that offered far greater comfort than a draughty castle. At the same time, however, the house was well fortified. It was surrounded by a deep ditch and a substantial mound that was in turn topped with a palisade. Entry to the property was over a timber drawbridge across the ditch. Orbec made sure that the drawbridge was kept in good working order.

Standing on a hill, the house commanded a superb view of the Golden Valley. It looked down on a scene of tranquil beauty. From its source above Dorstone a few miles to the north, the River Dore gargled happily with pebbles in its throat and meandered down to the point where the valley opened out into meadows and cornfields.

Richard Orbec found it at once inspiring and restful.

"I love this part of the county," he said. "It reminds me so much of Normandy. Orchards, mills, cattle, sheep. It is just like the land around Bayeux."

"Not quite, my lord," said Redwald. "You have no Saxons on your estates in Normandy."

Orbec laughed. "A small price to pay for this beauty." He became serious. "Nobody must take this away from me, do you hear? I am relying on you, Redwald. This is *mine*!"

"Yes, my lord."

"I would kill to keep it. Save me that trouble."

"I will do my best."

"Confound these royal commissioners yet again."

"They are not the real enemy."

"No," said Orbec. "Damville is. Defeat him soundly."

"He has strong weapons at his disposal," warned the reeve. "He will not easily be routed. Maurice Damville has the fire of ambition inside him."

"So do I, Redwald. And mine burns even brighter."

48

*   *   *

Corbin the Reeve did not improve on acquaintance. He irritated Gervase Bret, he annoyed Canon Hubert, and he even bored the normally over-tolerant Brother Simon. But it was Ralph Delchard who was the chief victim of the reeve's supercilious manner, and he was in no mood to put up with it.

"Tell a plain tale in plain terms, man!" he howled.

"That is what I am doing, my lord."

"Then why am I being driven slowly mad?"

"Show a little self-restraint," advised Corbin with a condescending smile. "We will get there the sooner."

"Damnation! Can you not answer a simple question?"

"When I am not impeded."

"I'll impede you with the point of my dagger in a moment," threatened Ralph. "Give us the tidings without any more ado, you blockhead. They are germane to our enquiries."

"I am fully aware of that, my lord."

They were in the shire hall, about to begin their examination of the witnesses. A trestle table had been set up with four chairs behind it. On the opposite side of the table, chairs and benches were arranged in jagged rows. The hall itself was long, low, and narrow. Its thatched roof housed a veritable colony of spiders and mice. Having fought their way in through the small windows, the shafts of daylight lost their nerve and met for safety in a central position, abandoning the rest of the room to shadow. The place had a musty smell.

Gervase Bret took over the questioning of the reeve.

"Has anything new transpired about the murder?"

"Indeed," said Corbin, tapping his chest with a

beringed finger. "I made a point of speaking with the sheriff's men who returned from Archenfield last night."

"What did they say?"

"They were in a foul mood. So, I hear, was the sheriff."

"Why?"

"They made little headway. Ilbert was peeved. Our good sheriff can get extremely peeved when given provocation."

"Do you give him anything else?"

Corbin was affronted. "Ilbert Malvoisin and I are close friends, my lord. We work so ably together because we are well-suited by temperament."

"Hell's teeth!" yelled Ralph. "There are *two* of them!"

"Enough prevarication," snapped Canon Hubert. "Tell us what the sheriff's men said. Are the killers apprehended?"

"Not yet."

"Are their identities known?"

"Vaguely."

"Is there any likelihood of an early arrest?"

"Probably not."

"This news is not news at all."

"There's more, Canon Hubert," said the reeve with a smirk of self-congratulation. "I drew the information out of the men by skilful means. I have the trick of it."

"Teach it to us!" whispered Brother Simon. "Then we may at last draw the information out of you."

Ralph guffawed, Gervase smiled, and even Canon Hubert let his lip tremble at this unexpected sign of a sense of humour under the black cowl. Brother Simon retreated at once into anonymity but his wry comment had hit its target. Corbin the Reeve was stung into disclosing his tidings.

"They reached Llanwarne to find the house destroyed

and Warnod burned to a cinder. Nothing remained. The man and his abode were wiped out."

"Even the outbuildings?" asked Gervase.

"Everything," said Corbin. "Not a stick remained standing, not an animal was left alive. Except one."

"What was that?"

"The red dragon."

"But it was merely carved in the turf."

"I know, Master Bret," he said, "but many people came running when they saw the fire blazing and they all avowed the same. The creature *moved*. The red dragon came to life!"

"Arrant nonsense!" said Ralph, exploding with contempt. "How can a hole in the ground take on flesh and blood? Those who came running to the scene must have been drunk or crazed or both. Show me a man who saw a real dragon and I will show you an idiot or a barefaced liar!"

Corbin was not deflected. "Their testimony was precise. We have the word of a dozen men or more, including the priest from the church at Llanwarne. In the crackling flames, the beast appeared to stir from its slumber."

Ralph was sceptical. "When the sheriff and his men got to Archenfield, was the dragon still dancing around the field? Or did it simply *appear* so?"

"I speak but as I heard, my lord."

"Did anybody see the assassins?"

"They saw, but did not recognise in the dark."

"Those flames must have lit up the whole area," argued Gervase. "If they saw the red dragon come to life, they must surely have noticed how many riders were fleeing and on what sort of horses. Also, in what direction they headed."

"These things were, indeed, noted."

"Well?" pressed Hubert.

"Ten men on Welsh ponies. Riding toward the border."

"I'm surprised the dragon didn't gallop after them," said Ralph. "If I did not feel so appalled at the wretched fate of this man, Warnod, I would laugh at this confusion. Is there no firm evidence in this case?"

"Ilbert the Sheriff is collecting it."

"From credulous fools who see phantom creatures?"

"From frightened people, my lord," said Corbin, taking an indignant step toward him. "There have been consequences. Warnod had two servants, Elfig and Hywel."

"I know," said Gervase. "The old Saxon was beaten by that murderous crew and the young Welshman was spared."

"He was not spared for long."

"What do you mean?"

"Elfig died from his wounds yesterday," explained Corbin. "His friends were so incensed at the injustice of it that they set upon Hywel. The Welshman now lies beaten. His kinsmen did not let it end there."

"What have they done?" said Ralph.

"Assaulted those who attacked Hywel. Much blood has flowed and it has not all come from that slaughtered cow. The whole district is up in arms." He flung back his mantle and put his hands on his hips. "Now you will see why Ilbert the Sheriff is not able to come before you today. He is not just trying to solve one murder. He has to prevent several others from taking place in Archenfield."

Ilbert Malvoisin was a big, solid man who sat foursquare in the saddle of his horse. When he saw yet another fight

52

break out, he called to his men in a voice like a clap of thunder.

"Stop them!" he ordered. "Pull them apart."

Watched by a knot of peasants, two youths were wrestling on the ground with ferocious vigour. They were not armed, but their hands had become deadly weapons. If the fight was allowed to continue, only one of them would get up alive.

"Knock their heads together!" boomed Ilbert.

Four soldiers descended on the combatants, dragging them apart before dashing their heads together. The two youths were dazed. Already covered in blood, they were panting from their exertions and glaring wildly at each other. The Saxon youth was fair-haired and brawny, the Welsh, dark and wiry. When the two of them lunged at each other once more, the soldiers held them in iron grips.

"Who started this brawl?" demanded Ilbert.

Half-a-dozen voices piped up, but he silenced them with a wave of his hand and pointed at the two antagonists.

"*You* tell me."

"He insulted our nation," said the Welsh youth.

"They killed Warnod," argued the young Saxon.

"They attacked Hywel."

"And who beat old Elfig to death?"

"He said that all Welshmen were murdering barbarians."

There were loud complaints from the onlookers, all of them Welsh and proud of their heritage. Ilbert quelled the noise at once.

"Silence!" he roared. "Let there be an end to this! We do not yet know who burned Warnod alive in his house. When we do, we will arrest them and bring them to account."

"Not if they are safe across the border," shouted the Saxon youth. "They strike and flee—like all the Welsh."

The accusation produced a fresh outbreak of protest, but it quickly faded as the sheriff pulled his sword from its scabbard and held it aloft. Since there was no longer an earl in the county, Ilbert Malvoisin was the most powerful man in Herefordshire. He could bring down all manner of ills upon them, if he chose, and they would have no court of appeal. Welsh eyes smouldered, but tongues were stilled for the moment.

"What would you have me do?" he said. "Take these two hot-blooded fools back to Hereford with me and throw them into the castle dungeons? Three months in the dark among the rats would cool their tempers, I fancy. Is that what you wish?" His swordpoint swung to the Saxon. "Is it?"

"No, my lord," said the youth.

"Will you swear to keep the peace?"

There was a reluctant nod of acceptance. Ilbert turned his attention to the other combatant, who was bleeding more profusely, but seething with a deeper rage.

"What of this wild young Welshman?"

"I have a score to settle with him, my lord."

"I have already settled it."

"You will not stay in Archenfield forever."

"Do you dare to defy the sheriff?" hissed Ilbert. "It is the castle dungeon for you, then. Pinion the rogue."

"Stay, my lord," said an elderly man, breaking clear of the group to run across. "This is unjust. Why should my grandson be punished when the other youth goes free?"

"Because that is my decision."

"This is Archenfield, my lord," pleaded the other. "We are allowed to live by Welsh customs here."

"Some of your customs are not to my taste," said Ilbert with a glance at the dragon carved in the turf nearby.

"Your grandson will learn some manners in Hereford. If you wish to join him there, obstruct me further." The old man stepped back. "Away with the whole pack of you!"

The onlookers dispersed with mutinous mutterings. The Saxon youth glowered at the prisoner before trotting off towards the wood. Ilbert Malvoisin took another look at the mythical beast which had sparked off all the unrest.

"Cover it up!" he ordered. "Bury that red dragon under the earth again. It has caused enough trouble already."

Richard Orbec was punctual. He arrived at the shire hall at the appointed time. Four of Ralph Delchard's men-at-arms were on sentry duty outside the building to keep curiosity at bay and ensure privacy for the day's deliberations. They recognised Orbec by common report and stood aside. As the newcomer swept into the hall with Redwald lumbering beside him, they found four more soldiers on duty.

Corbin the Reeve grasped another opportunity to insinuate himself into the action.

"Welcome back, Richard," he said. "Prompt as usual."

Orbec flicked him a neutral glance. He clearly had far less respect for the reeve than the latter had for him. Corbin introduced the commissioners one by one and polite greetings were exchanged. The visitor presented Redwald to the tribunal. He and his reeve were then offered seats. The four commissioners sat behind the table. Brother Simon had a quill poised in his hand to act as scribe.

Corbin was still a large and intrusive presence.

"We will not keep you from other duties," said Ralph.

"I have made myself available to you, my lord."

"We will call you when we need you."

"I prefer to remain," said Corbin, lowering himself onto a bench. "I will be a silent observer. You have my word."

Ralph conferred briefly with the others. They elected to endure Corbin's trespass in return for his undoubted value as a source of information. He would be a useful point of reference in the debate with Richard Orbec, and with Maurice Damville. Whatever his shortcomings— and they had counted many—the reeve was exceedingly well-informed about personalities and events in and around Hereford.

As leader of the commission, Ralph Delchard spoke first. He tried to put their first witness at his ease and thus off guard.

"I know Orbec well," he said, amiably.

"Do you?"

"I was born and brought up in Lisieux."

"Most of my estates in Normandy are near Bayeux."

"A beautiful town," said Ralph. "Would you not rather trade its charms for this ale-swilling city of Hereford?"

"No," said Orbec, simply. "I prefer it here."

Ralph was appalled. "You prefer England to Normandy?"

"I prefer peace to discord."

They knew what he meant. Twenty long years of Norman occupation had imposed a measure of harmony that was lacking in the duchy from which the invaders came. Baronial feuds were rife in Normandy, and much violence went unchecked and unpunished. To a man wearied of the endless strife, life in the Golden Valley could indeed seem like a glorious escape.

"I hope that we do not destroy your peace," said Ralph.

Orbec was blunt. "I will not permit it."

"It is we who dispense any permission," said Canon Hubert, pedantically. "You are under scrutiny, my lord."

"On what account?"

"Several matters need to be raised," noted Ralph as he glanced down at the document in front of him, "but one in particular dominates all others. Archenfield."

"What is the problem?" asked Orbec. "I hold land in the hundred of Archenfield, it is true, but Redwald here will show you the charters which support my claim."

"Maurice Damville also has claims upon that land."

"False claims."

"That remains to be seen."

"It *was* seen, my lord. By your predecessors."

"Yes, my lord," added Redwald, responding to a nudge from his master. "The first commissioners rejected the testimony of Maurice Damville and found in our favour."

"That was before a third claimant appeared."

"A *third*?" Corbin was surprised. "This is news to me."

"Why did he not come forward before?" said Orbec.

"Because he was prevented from doing so."

"By whom?"

"By someone who stood to gain by his absence."

Orbec raised an eyebrow. "Is that an accusation against me?"

"Only you will know that, my lord," said Ralph.

"Who is this third claimant?" pressed Corbin.

"You took a vow of silence," chided Hubert.

The reeve held up his palms in apology, then put three fingers to his lips by way of a promise not to interrupt again. He watched intently from his bench.

"May *I* know the name of this man?" said Orbec, calmly.

"You already do."

Ralph's gaze was searching. He was finding the witness

extremely difficult to fathom. Richard Orbec gave nothing away. His manner was relaxed and his face expressionless. Ralph could see the soldier in his bearing, but there was much more to the man than that. Deep secrets lurked behind those green eyes.

Orbec made his first mistake. Assuming that he was in the presence of men who spoke exclusively in Norman-French, he addressed his reeve in Anglo-Saxon.

"We must both tell the same story, Redwald."

"Yes, my lord."

"I'll not yield a square yard of Archenfield."

"Nor shall you."

"I have not built up my estates to see them cut down as they were in Normandy." Orbec was adamant. "That will never happen again. Take note."

"I do take note, my lord," said Gervase Bret in the same tongue. "I note that you are as proficient in this language as I am, yet without my advantage of a Saxon mother."

Orbec was duly startled. Ralph was exasperated.

"We will not conduct this examination in gibberish."

"Saxon is a fine language," said Gervase, slipping easily back into Ralph's own tongue, "but I believe you will hear no more of it in this hall." He looked at Orbec and got an answering nod. "I felt it only fair to warn you, my lord," he said. "Be fair with us in return."

"I will be."

"To return to the subject of dispute," said Ralph. "The land concerned runs along the border between Archenfield and the hundreds of Ewyas and Golden Valley. It amounts in all to a total of . . ." Exasperation showed again as he consulted the document in front of him. "Why must they confuse me with all these carucates and

58

numbers of ploughs? The hide is the simplest measurement of land."

Gervase came to his aid. "The total area is just under a thousand acres. Use that as a round figure."

"We can account for every acre," asserted Redwald.

"So can Maurice Damville," countered Hubert.

"Not to mention our third claimant," said Ralph with a grin. "Is the name of Warnod familiar to your ear?"

"It is," admitted Orbec with a noncommittal shrug. "I believe that the land under discussion once belonged to his father. But Warnod is hardly a claimant. The poor man was murdered at his home in Llanwarne."

"His kinsmen will inherit his land," said Gervase, "and they will contest this claim on Warnod's behalf."

"He has no kinsmen in this county," said Orbec, firmly.

"Can you be sure?"

"Certain of it."

"Then he may have willed his holdings to another."

"That, too, would produce no third claimant."

"Why not?"

"Because we cannot know who the beneficiary is unless we have sight of a will," argued Orbec, "and that went up in smoke when the house was burned. Along with this supposed charter that legitimates his claim to my land. The name of Warnod does not belong in this dispute at all. No will, no charter, no claim."

"The charter survived, my lord."

"How do you know?"

Gervase picked up a scroll of parchment from the table. "Because I have it here in my hand."

Orbec was visibly shaken. "How did you come by it?"

"The document was sent to Winchester."

"By whom? Not Warnod, I'll wager. He would never trust a Norman tribunal to find against a Norman. Another hand is at work here. Who sent that document to the Exchequer?"

"We have no idea," said Ralph, blithely. "It is one of the things we came to Hereford to find out."

The brewhouse was at the rear of the premises, attached to the house by a short and aromatic passageway. There was no way to keep all the fumes out of the house itself, but Golde had done her best. A thick curtain hung in front of the door and absorbed some of the pungent odours of her profession. Rushes and herbs inside the dwelling acted as a further barrier against the pervasive smell of ale.

When Golde came in, the girl was in exactly the same spot with exactly the same distraught look on her face. Golde put a consoling arm around her sister's shoulders and lowered her onto the wooden stool in front of the fire. The house on Castle Street was not large, but it was always warm and impeccably clean.

Golde knelt on the flagstone to hold her sister's hands between her own. She squeezed them gently.

"Spare yourself, Aelgar," she said, softly.

"How can I?"

"You were not to blame."

"But I was, Golde. I was."

"You punish yourself for sins you did not commit."

"I will never forgive myself."

"Aelgar!"

"I helped to kill the one thing I held dear."

"That is not true."

"What life is left to me now?"

"A good life. An honest life."

"Bereft of all joy. My hopes are shattered."

"Rebuild them, sweet sister."

"Nobody could rebuild after such a loss."

Golde became wistful. "I did."

It was Aelgar's turn to offer condolence. She bent forward to kiss her sister's forehead. Both of them let tears run freely for a few moments. Golde then controlled her pain and stood up. As the elder sister, she had to be strong enough for both of them.

She looked down at Aelgar and let out a long sigh.

"What a cruel blow too much beauty can be!"

"I feel as if I want to scratch it away out of spite."

"That is not the way, Aelgar."

"Then what is? What is? Teach me, please."

The entreaty brought Aelgar to her feet. She was a few inches shorter than Golde and years younger. Barely nineteen, she still had the bloom of youth on her cheeks. She wore a plain gunna of green linen and a white wimple. The heart-shaped face was distorted by grief and striped with concern, but its essential loveliness shone through. Golde had the more mature charms, but few men noticed her when Aelgar was present. The latter's innocent beauty was almost overwhelming.

Golde took her sister by the shoulders.

"Watch and pray," she advised.

"I have done little else."

"Hold fast to your memories. Let them stay you."

"They only pluck at my entrails, Golde," said the younger woman. "I dare not sleep for fear that those memories will haunt me afresh. I must *know*," she said with sudden intensity. "I must find out the truth."

"In time. In time."

"Now, Golde. I have a right to be told."

"Yes, Aelgar," conceded the other. "Who has a better right than you? I will go to them again."

"Take me with you!"

"Stay within and mourn in private."

"But I have questions of my own to ask."

"Put them to me. I will seek the answers."

Aelgar's intensity drained slowly out of her. She dropped to the stool again and stared into the flames with a wan expression on her face. Her voice was distant.

"The worst is over, Golde. I fear nothing now."

"I do."

"What?"

Golde took her sister's hand again and kissed it.

"What do you fear?" asked Aelgar.

"Him."

Maurice Damville led the charge. The shepherd was herding his flock on the lower slopes when the riders came over the crest of the hill. Damville and his knights could not resist the temptation. Spurring their horses into a frenzied gallop, they tore down the incline with battle cries and obscenities mingling on their lips.

The sheep scattered in a mad panic and the old shepherd was knocked flying by the flank of a passing destrier. They pursued the fleeing animals for a few minutes, hacking at them to frighten or wound rather than to kill. When the cavalcade reassembled again, the flock was spread over half a mile or more.

Damville's sport was not yet over. On the plain ahead of them was a small farm with a cluster of rickety outbuildings. A fresh-faced Saxon girl came out of the byre with a wooden pail filled to the brim with milk. She was

62

no more than fifteen, but her hair was the colour of straw and her skin shone in the morning sunlight. Her bare arms were splashed with milk. One glance was all that Maurice Damville needed.

He kicked his horse into a canter and bore down on the girl. Too frightened to run, she stood rooted to the spot until he brought down an arm to scoop her up and carry her off. The pail was dropped and its contents seeped into the grass. Urged on by whoops of envious delight from his men, Damville rode behind the cover of some bushes before he dismounted. The screams lasted for several minutes.

In one swoop, the girl lost her milk and her maidenhead.

Two hours in the shire hall had taught Richard Orbec some respect for the commissioners. They could not be deceived or fobbed off. Ralph Delchard was a stern inquisitor. Gervase Bret was a perceptive lawyer. Canon Hubert was relentless in pursuit of the truth. Orbec and Redwald put their case with skill, but it was severely weakened by the appearance of a charter which seemed to grant the land in question to Warnod.

When Gervase had displayed the document and allowed the two men to inspect it, he made way for Canon Hubert to take over the questioning. The latter used a different method of attack. He bestowed a flabby smile upon Orbec.

"You have been a most generous patron of the Church."

"I think I know my duty," said Orbec.

"Your gifts go beyond the limits of duty," continued Hubert. "Dean Theobald was kind enough to conduct me around the cathedral. Your endowments are writ large in stone and timber. God will reward you for this munificence."

"It pleases me to hear you say that, Canon Hubert."

"You have, I am told, a private chapel at your house."

"I do."

"Consecrated by no less a person than Bishop Robert."

"He deigned to visit my abode and grace my table."

"Gratitude took him there," said Hubert. "If all the marcher lords had your belief in Christianity, we should have far more churches and far less castles." He leaned across the table to purr his question. "Why have you done all this?"

"Because I felt moved to do so."

"Yes, but from what motives?"

"Does it matter?"

"Profoundly."

"I donate money and the cathedral is restored." Orbec was dismissive. "That is all there is to it. The ceiling of the nave will look just as beautiful, whether my reasons for meeting its cost are shallow or meaningful. People will admire that ceiling many years after my reasons have followed me into my grave."

"You are trying to evade my point," said Hubert. "But you raise an ethical dilemma about means and ends. Does a good result justify a bad reason? It does not, my lord. It never can. The church would rather be poor and honest than flourish on riches that have been wrongfully acquired. Reasons and results must be cohere."

"My wealth is sinful. Is that what you're telling me?"

"I merely seek to establish a motive. Why?"

"Because I am a good Christian."

"Whence comes this goodness, my lord?"

"From the same source as your own."

"I wear my reason for all to see," said Hubert, indicating his attire. "Is yours so shameful that it must be kept hidden?"

"I came here to discuss my holdings," said Orbec with vehemence. "My spiritual needs are not relevant here."

"But they are," insisted Hubert, "because they help to establish your character. A man who seeks only to serve the greater glory of God is unlikely to seize land that is not legally his or to indulge in some of the corrupt practices that our investigation has uncovered. Good men do good works from pure motives."

Richard Orbec weighed his words carefully.

"Then I am not a good man, Canon Hubert," he said, quietly. "No soldier is or can be a good man."

"That is nonsense!" protested Ralph.

"Men put on armour to kill."

"To defend themselves from being killed."

"A soldier is a violation of the sixth commandment. 'Thou shalt do no murder.' What else is a battle but an act of slaughter? You may dress it up in fine words and shower it with incense to make it smell the sweeter, but there is no disguising the truth. War is ritualised murder."

"Not if it is a just war!" argued Ralph.

"The two words insult each other."

"A man is entitled to fight for his rights."

"Not with a sword and spear."

"I have great sympathy with your view," said Canon Hubert, with a sidelong glance of reproof at Ralph. "Conquest will always contain the seeds of evil."

"The same may be said of the Church," growled Ralph.

"That is blasphemy!"

"It is cold fact, Canon Hubert. Holy men march behind soldiers and reap the benefits of our labour. The Church's one foundation in this country is the Battle of Hastings."

"No, my lord," said Hubert, complacently. "You fought and we sought reconciliation with God. That is why the bishops in Normandy drew up the Penitential Ordinance that was confirmed by the papal legate, Bishop Ermenfrid of Sion."

Richard Orbec rose involuntarily from his seat.

"Take special note of the first article in that decree," he said with unexpected passion. "Whoever knows he has killed in the great battle is to do one year's penance for each man slain. Remember that. Each man slain."

"You are too young to have fought at Hastings," said Ralph.

"There are other battles. With other deaths."

Orbec's mien had altered completely. Dignity and self-possession had been supplanted by wild agitation. But it was his expression which alarmed the others. The green eyes were hot coals of fire and the bearded face was twisted with hate. Even Ralph Delchard was taken aback at first.

They were looking into the face of Satan.

Chapter Four

IDWAL THE ARCHDEACON SPREAD HIS OPINIONS EVENLY throughout the cathedral. During his short stay, therefore, he contrived to infuriate everyone to the same degree. His arrogance and his outspokenness were devastating. Robert Losinga, Bishop of Hereford, a man renowned for his learning and revered for his Job-like patience, found the scholarly Welshman too great an affliction to bear. His command to the dean was simple.

"Rid us of this tumult!"

Theobald went off to implement the order from on high. It would be a delicate task. The laws of hospitality were being breached and Christian fellowship was being negated, but their visitor had brought it upon himself. He had caused more upset than a swarm of bees during a choir rehearsal. The dean should feel no compunction in directing him to the road out of Hereford.

"Good morning, Archdeacon," he said.

"*Bore da.*"

"You slept well?"

"Fitfully," said Idwal. "Fitfully. I was much distracted by some remarks you made about the Holy Eucharist. I will take issue with you on that account."

"This is not a convenient time for debate," said the

67

dean, hastily. "Let us postpone our discussion until a more fitting moment. During another visit, perhaps."

"Yes, I intend to come back here soon."

"When you have the whole of Wales to visit?"

"I have met with such friendship," said Idwal. "A man should always make a determined effort to see his friends."

Theobald swallowed hard. "Yes, of course."

They were in the half-built cathedral cloister, picking their way among the slabs of stone. Two canons darted out of the way as they approached, fearful of being drawn into another conversation with the evangelical Celt. Idwal was wearing his grubby lambskin cloak. Theobald's hope rustled.

"You are dressed for travelling, Archdeacon," he said.

"My life is one of perpetual motion."

"You are *leaving* us?"

"Unhappily, yes."

"Today?"

"Within a matter of hours."

"This is sad news indeed," said Theobald, rejoicing inwardly. "We looked for a longer visitation."

"My plans have been upset and I have been compelled to change my itinerary slightly."

"I wish you God speed!"

Theobald could not believe his luck. Having racked his brains to find a diplomatic means by which he could evict the little Welshman, he was instead being confronted with a voluntary departure. It was the clearest example of divine intervention that Theobald had met in a long while and he offered up a silent prayer of gratitude.

A gust of wind blew and a noisome vapour attacked his nostrils. He realised, with disgust, that it was the archdeacon's cloak which was giving off the stink.

"Must you wear this common lambskin?" he asked.

"I like it."

"Surely, a man in your position could well afford a richer fur? One that imparted more dignity and status to its wearer."

"What had you in mind, Dean Theobald?"

"Sable, beaver, or fox skin."

"They are such shifty animals," said Idwal. "Their skins might do for English bishops and abbots but I am a plain man and therefore content with lambskin."

"At the very least, you might wear cat skin."

"That would be an abomination."

"Why?"

"I have often heard the *Angus Dei* sung," said the Welshman, "but I shudder at the thought of a *Cattus Dei*!"

His cackle reverberated around the cloisters.

"I will hold you back no longer," said Theobald, even more anxious to speed the parting guest. "Convey our best wishes to Bishop Herewald when you return to Llandaff."

"But I will come back here first."

"Here?"

"In a day or two at most."

"You said even now that you were quitting Hereford."

"The city only, not the county. I merely travel back to Ergyng once more."

"To Archenfield, you mean? Why?"

"To solve a murder."

"How are you implicated in that?"

"By birth, Dean Theobald," said the other. "A man is killed and the blame is placed on my nation. You cannot expect me to stand idly by while such injustice occurs."

"What will you do?"

"Find the real culprits and exonerate Wales."

"Oh."

"Ample reward then awaits me."

"Reward?"

"Yes, Dean Theobald," said Idwal, slapping him familiarly on the shoulder. "You, Bishop Robert, this cathedral. It calls to me. I cannot wait to cross swords with you all in debate once more."

Theobald shuddered as the stench of the lambskin hit him.

The interrogation of Richard Orbec was long and probing but it yielded no firm results. His manors in Archenfield gave him a substantial holding that was second only to the King's demesne in that part of Herefordshire. Ralph Delchard and Gervase Bret questioned his right to that land, while Canon Hubert's opinion was clouded by the fact that the rent from the estate went towards the re-building of the cathedral.

Brother Simon was a mute witness, but Corbin the Reeve was brought in on a number of occasions to clarify certain points relating to people and procedures in the county. It was left to Redwald to summarise his master's position.

"The carucates under review are worked by sub-tenants who know only one landlord," he said, turning to Richard Orbec. "He sits before you. We have a legal charter to enforce that claim and sub-tenants who will attest it upon oath." He glanced down at the table. "You have shown us a charter, but its legality remains in doubt and its contents are, in any case, no longer relevant. Warnod is not here to press his claim and neither is anyone else on his behalf."

"They may be," said Gervase.

"When?"

"When we find them," added Ralph.

There was no more to be said. The first session with Richard Orbec was over. Maurice Damville was due in the shire hall at any moment and it was politic to keep them apart. A brawl between two witnesses would achieve nothing. Ralph gave Orbec and Redwald leave to depart and they bade farewell.

"Do not stray too far," Ralph warned.

"Why not?" said Orbec.

"We will need to call you again."

"In order to give me an apology, I trust."

Richard Orbec strode out with Redwald at his heels.

Mindful of the presence of Corbin, the commissioners spoke with glances and nods. All had come to the same conclusion. There were two Richard Orbecs. One was a rich and respectable Norman lord who led a solitary life in the Golden Valley, and who made generous donations towards the restoration work at the cathedral. The other Richard Orbec was a more disturbing figure, a malevolent being with wild eyes and a heart full of malice who would not have scrupled to put the torch to Warnod's house with his own hand. The commissioners were not certain which of the conflicting personalities was the true man.

"Stand aside and let me in, you dolts!"

There was no such problem with Maurice Damville. What they first saw was the essential character of their next witness.

"Nobody dares obstruct my path with impunity!"

Pushing the men-at-arms aside, he stormed into the hall with Huegon a few paces behind him. When Damville reached the middle of the room, he paused to appraise the four men who sat behind the table ahead of him. Bluster made way for courtesy. He gave the commissioners a polite nod and adopted a conciliatory tone.

"Maurice Damville at your service!"

"Thank you for coming at such short notice," said Ralph. "It is much appreciated."

He introduced the other members of the commission and they in turn were introduced to Huegon. Ralph was interested to observe Corbin's reaction. The reeve had been almost obsequious towards the first witness. With the second, he was much more wary. Maurice Damville unsettled him.

When the visitors took their seats, Ralph outlined the problem which they were addressing. A thousand acres of land was caught between rival claims. Damville's jaw tightened at the mention of Richard Orbec, but he said nothing. Schooled by Huegon on the journey to Hereford, he left the argument to his steward. The old man had a more persuasive touch.

"I am glad to know that royal commissioners can admit their mistakes," he said, pleasantly. "Some sharp-eyed clerk at the Exchequer has clearly been through the evidence collected by your predecessors and found it wanting. You have come here to repair that deficiency."

"That is precisely our task," agreed Ralph.

"Then you will need to peruse our documents."

"All in good time, my friend. Gervase is our lawyer. He will need to examine your claim word by word."

"Before I do that," said Gervase, taking his cue, "it is only fair to warn you that the case is altered since your first appearance in this hall."

Huegon smiled. "You are ready to tear up Richard Orbec's fraudulent charter?"

"We are obliged to consider a third claimant."

72

"A *third*?"

"Warnod of Llanwarne."

Huegon remained impassive, but Maurice Damville's mouth twitched with irritation. The two men conversed briefly in whispers. There was much shaking of heads before the steward answered for both of them.

"We do not know the man."

"His father was a wealthy thegn before the Conquest."

"A familiar story," said Huegon, easily. "On our arrival here, he was dispossessed. Like most of the other Saxon nobles."

"Not entirely, it seems," said Gervase. "These manors in Archenfield were confirmed in his name and yet his son did not inherit them. We would know the reason why."

"Start your questioning with Warnod."

"That may be difficult," said Gervase.

"He was murdered two days ago," explained Ralph. "We have many talents in our armoury but communing with spirits is, I fear, not one of them."

"If the man is dead, his claim is void," said Huegon.

"That is what his killer would like us to believe."

Damville bridled. "You dare to suggest that I was involved in the murder of this man?"

"No, my lord," said Ralph. "I merely remark that his absence is of signal benefit to you at this moment."

"That is equally true of Richard Orbec," said Huegon.

"The point was not lost on us."

Canon Hubert had been watching Damville throughout. He was hiding behind the smooth and plausible tongue of his steward. Nothing of value would be elicited in a formal debate. Huegon was too practised at throwing a defensive ring of words around his master. It was important to lure Damville himself into the conversation.

73

Hubert touched Ralph's sleeve for permission to intervene. The latter gestured for him to speak.

"One thing puzzles me, my lord," said Hubert. "You seem to me to be a strong-willed and sensible man. When you see what is in your own best interests, you doubtless pursue that course remorselessly."

"I will not deny it," said Damville.

"Then why quarrel so bitterly with your neighbour?"

"What neighbour?"

"Richard Orbec."

"I do not consider him as such," said Damville, crisply. "His land adjoins mine, it is true, but that is a circumstance to drive us apart rather than bring us together."

"Even though amity would advantage you?"

"Amity?"

"Richard Orbec is a fellow Norman to the east," said Hubert. "I need hardly remind you that a hostile country lies directly to the west of your castle at Ewyas Harold."

"Wales has been quiescent for years," said Huegon.

"That situation could change. Perhaps it already has. In that event, would it not be more sensible for you to make common cause with your strongest neighbour?" Hubert studied Damville's reaction. "Adversity can unite the worst of enemies."

Damville scowled. "Orbec is more than my worst enemy."

"Do you dispute his title to this land out of hatred?"

"We have a charter," resumed Huegon, trying to shift the debate back to legalities. "You will see that it predates the counterclaim made by Richard Orbec."

"But not the one made by Warnod," said Gervase.

"He is no longer in the reckoning."

"Perhaps he is," said Ralph, thoughtfully. "While we

74

sit haggling over charters in a musty shire hall, the man who is the key to this dispute lies in Archenfield. Or, at least, his ashes do. I submit that we suspend our enquiries here and move them to the place where they will have more meaning."

"Is that wise, my lord?" said Hubert, uneasily.

"It is practical."

"Yes," agreed Gervase. "We would have an opportunity to view the land and see for ourselves what makes it so attractive to rival claimants."

"It is settled," said Ralph. "We go to Archenfield."

"You will be able to meet the sheriff there," said Corbin, helpfully. "Ilbert sent word that he would need to spend at least a day or two more in the area."

"An additional reason to make the journey," decided Ralph. "The sheriff can not only give us fuller details of the murder itself. He can act as a witness in our investigation."

"In what way?" asked Huegon. "Ilbert Malvoisin has no connection with the disputed land."

"We believe that he may," said Gervase.

Ralph wound up the proceedings with an apology to the two men for bringing them so far for such a short session. He asked Huegon to surrender the relevant charter so that Gervase could study it at his leisure and pronounce upon its authenticity. The steward looked for approval from his master, but was instead taken aside for an animated discussion. The two men walked a few yards away. Corbin inched forward to try to catch their whispers, but the commissioners waited patiently.

After several minutes, Huegon came back to the table.

"Our charter is no longer valid," he announced.

Ralph was astonished. "You admit it is a forgery?"

"We withdraw it unconditionally."

"On what grounds?"

"We do not wish to contest Richard Orbec's claim."

"Give us your reason, man."

"My decision is reason enough," said Damville, coming forward to look from one man to another. "We have wasted each other's time. Your work is done. I cede the land to Orbec. If he wishes to dispute it with a dead man, that is his business. Keep the name of Maurice Damville out of all future deliberations."

He stalked towards the door with Huegon at the rear.

"You cannot yield up a thousand acres on impulse," said Ralph. "That is rank stupidity."

"It is what I choose to do," said Damville, pausing in the doorway. "It may seem rash to you, but I have learned to trust my impulses. They have never betrayed me yet."

"You cannot just walk away like this!"

"I can and I will. I am weary of the whole affair!"

Before Ralph could protest, Maurice Damville and Huegon went out through the door. The session was definitively over.

It was market day and the streets were thronged with people as Golde made her way towards the shire hall. Brewing ale in such large quantities was a demanding business, but she had to leave it to her assistants that morning. Blood was thicker than alcohol. Her sister's needs took priority over the fermentation of the ale. Aelgar was not the most robust girl at the best of times. Recent events had made her almost frail and defenceless. Golde had to be both mother and sister to her.

When she reached the shire hall, they were just coming out. Corbin the Reeve was talking airily with four men. She recognised Ralph Delchard at once and guessed the others to be his fellow commissioners. Two of them set off in the direction of the cathedral and a third—the youngest of them—towards the castle. Golde stepped in to accost the others.

"Forgive this intrusion," she said.

"No intrusion at all, dear lady," said Ralph with smiling gallantry. "It is a pleasure to see you again. Corbin is not unknown to you, I take it."

"We are acquainted," said the reeve, coldly.

"Has the sheriff still not returned?" she said.

"No."

"He is still investigating this murder?"

"What business is that of yours?" said Corbin.

"I merely ask out of curiosity."

He was brusque. "It is not my duty to provide tittle-tattle for the ale-wives of Hereford."

"But it *is* your duty to be polite to a lady," chided Ralph. "Since you cannot do anything else properly, at least try to rise to that." He beamed at Golde. "Forgive his bad manners. Ignorance walks hand in hand with petty officialdom."

"I am no petty official!" asserted the reeve.

"Let us step back into the hall," suggested Ralph as he offered Golde his hand. "It is too noisy out here in the street. And we are delaying Corbin from important work like counting up taxes in the name of the King."

He gave the reeve a wink then escorted Golde back into the building. His men-at-arms had left now and the two were quite alone. Ralph gave himself the pleasure of taking a proper look at her. She was as appealing as at their first encounter. A clear-eyed woman of independent means and independent spirit. Even in her plain working apparel, she had a charm that he found quite irresistible.

"If there no more news?" she asked.

"The killers are still at liberty," he said. "Warnod's death has ignited passions in Archenfield. There has been much unrest. The sheriff, we hear, is hampered in his search. He has to keep Saxons and Welsh from coming to blows."

"Two days have passed. Ilbert the Sheriff must have learned *something* by now."

"Assuredly, he has. But the only channel of information that we possess is that egregious reeve of yours." Ralph rolled his eyes. "Getting news out of him is worse than squeezing blood from a stone. It is frustrating."

Golde was deflated. "Is there nobody who can help?"

"Only Ilbert the Sheriff."

"But he is in Archenfield."

"We will be there ourselves before the day is out."

"You go to Llanwarne?" she said, eagerly.

"To a place not too far distant from it."

"Take me with you, my lord!"

"What?"

"Let me ride beside you," she implored. "I will be no bother to you or to your companions, I swear, but I simply must go to Archenfield."

"Why?"

"To see for myself!"

Ralph was struck by the intensity of her plea. It brought her face close to his own and he could see the supplication in her eyes. Her breath was soft and sweet, her fragrance bewitching. A wave of envy washed over him.

"He was indeed a fortunate man."

"Who?"

"Warnod."

"Fortunate!" she exclaimed. "To end his life like that?"

"To have someone like you to mourn him, Golde."

"Warnod was . . . a good man."

"Of that there is no doubt."

"He was kind and generous."

"You would not love any man who was not."

She gave him a curious stare, then backed away slightly.

"I fear that you mistake me, my lord."

"The man left your house that night, did he not?"

"I admitted as much."

"Why else should he ride so far to visit a beautiful widow?" She turned abruptly away. "I do not mean to offend you, Golde. You ask an extremely large favour of me. I am entitled to know your reason for doing so."

"If I tell you, will you take me?"

"I will consider it," he promised.

She swung round. "Warnod did not come to my house to call on me, my lord. But on another. It is for her sake that I make these enquiries."

Ralph's interest quickened. "Then he was not . . . ?"

"He was not and never could be."

"That puts the matter in a very different light," he said, stroking his chin. "My companions will not like it, I warn you now. Gervase will see you as a distraction. Canon Hubert will view you as an abomination. And Brother Simon is so terrified of any woman that he will disappear into his cowl like a snail going back into its shell."

Golde was thrilled. "Does that mean you will take me?"

"What is my reward to be?" he teased.

"As much ale as you can drink."

"That is a punishment, not a reward!"

"Then all I can offer is my heartfelt thanks."

Golde came close again and looked up into his face with a gratitude that was fringed with real affection. Life as a widow had accustomed her to the unwanted attentions of many men, but Ralph Delchard was different. She trusted him. It would not be a pleasant ride to Archenfield and grim tidings would await her there, but she could withstand the pain all the more easily with him to support her.

"One last question, Golde."

"Yes, my lord?"

"This other person whom Warnod came to see."

"Well?"

"Who is she?"

Golde searched his eyes and found what she needed. He would not betray her confidence. There was the merest hint of polite lechery in his gaze, but there was also a store of integrity and understanding.

"Who is she, Golde?"

"My sister."

Aelgar knew that it was him as soon as she heard the horses clatter past the side of the house. A sword was used to bang on the front door. The servant girl came in from the brewhouse.

"Do not answer it!" ordered Aelgar.

"Why not?"

"Bolt the door!"

"Who is it?"

"Do as you're told and bolt the door!"

Aelgar was so rarely angry that the girl knew she was in earnest. The servant ran to bolt the door as instructed.

She then cowered in a corner as the banging became louder and more insistent. The door was shaking.

"Come on out!" roared a man's voice.

"Say nothing!" Aelgar hissed to the servant.

"I want to see you, Aelgar. Come on out."

"Perhaps you should go in, my lord," said another man. There was crude laughter from outside the door.

Aelgar looked around desperately for a means of escape. She could run to the brewhouse, but they could find her just as easily in there. Her only hope lay in remaining so still that she convinced them that the house was empty. She gestured to the frightened servant to keep silent. The girl put both hands over her mouth and crouched down even lower.

Aelgar's strategy did not work. She herself backed slowly up against a wall and sat on the floor. There was a tapping on the shutter above her head. It was a gentle noise like the sound of a bird fluttering in a cage. Aelgar slowly rose to peer through the window and almost fainted with shock. The lean face of Maurice Damville was grinning at her.

"Come to me, my darling!" he coaxed.

"No!"

"I only wish to talk to you."

"Go away!"

"Open the door."

"Leave me alone."

"I have brought a present for you, my pretty one."

"I want no presents."

"Here it is," he said. "In my hand."

But when his hand came up to the window it was only to grab at her through the narrow space. Aelgar jumped back in the nick of time and the sinewy fingers were left grasping thin air. She snatched up the broom that was lying against the wall. It was made of birch twigs lashed tightly together. Aelgar swung the broom at the hand and produced a howl of pain.

More crude laughter came from Damville's soldiers.

"You'll pay for that, you little vixen!"

Her courage deserted her. Terrified that she had now provoked him, Aelgar dropped the broom and ran to the ladder that was angled up into the roof. She scrambled up the rungs and tucked herself under the thatch so that she was not visible through the window.

Damville cursed and banged on the door again, but the timber held. The jeers of his men finally made their master burst into laughter. Here was no nubile milkmaid who could be taken on a whim. Aelgar had quality and spirit. She needed to be stalked by a more cunning hunter. He knew that the prize would be more than worth the effort.

"Good-bye, my darling!" he called. "I must go."

"Thank God!" she sighed.

"But I'll be back for you soon."

The hooves clacked off down Castle Street and were soon swallowed up in the general hubbub of market day. Aelgar had survived the visit this time, but there would be another.

Maurice Damville would not endure refusal for long.

"No, no, no!" protested Canon Hubert with crimson jowls shaking. "I refuse to countenance this act of madness."

"Your disapproval is noted," said Ralph, cheerfully.

"You visit two of the plagues of Egypt upon us."

"A woman and a Welshman?"

"Yes," moaned Hubert. "The woman will lead you astray and the Welshman will talk the ears off my donkey."

He was not happy with the travel arrangements. It was bad enough to be wrested away from the relative comfort of the shire hall and from his accommodation at the cathedral. Canon Hubert was now being forced to share the journey with an urgent widow and an eager archdeacon. It was Purgatory.

Brother Simon was at least prepared to compromise.

"The archdeacon is fit company," he said, exhausting every last drop of Christian charity at his disposal, "but the woman is not. Let us take one without the other. I would sooner bear the pain of endless theological argument than the discomfort of a female presence. Women terrify me!"

"Has lust never found its sly way into that celibate body of yours?" mocked Ralph. "Embrace sin gladly, Brother Simon. Give yourself some pleasure to repent."

"Heaven forbid!"

Gervase Bret did not even bother to offer an opinion on the subject. When Ralph made a decision, he held firm to it regardless of opposition. Golde would ride with them to Archenfield in the company of Idwal the Archdeacon. Gervase was the only man in Hereford willing to befriend the roving ambassador from Llandaff, who, hearing of their journey to Archenfield, was quick to attach himself to them. Gervase alone foresaw Idwal's value. In an area that was predominantly Welsh, they would need a skilful interpreter.

When they finally set off, they were fourteen in number. Ralph led the way with Golde at his side on a palfrey. At the rear of the column were Gervase and Idwal, the latter riding a Welsh pony and still wearing his malodorous cloak. Canon Hubert and Brother Simon rode in the very middle of the cavalcade, thus occupying an intermediate station between sinful thought and sacerdotal torture. While Simon watched the woman up ahead through apprehensive eyes, Hubert cocked an ear to catch the latest ramblings of the man he privately referred to as the Celtic imbecile.

Gervase was intrigued by the garrulous Welshman.

"Do you always travel alone, Archdeacon?"

"No, Gervase. God is always at my side."

"But you take no companions? No priests or deacons?"

"I prefer to seek friends along the way."

"You are more likely to encounter foes."

Idwal chuckled. "Not in Wales. I am too well-known and too well-respected. I can ride from Caerleon in the south to Caernavon in the north with not a hand raised against me. I need no protection from my own countrymen."

"But you are not in Wales now, Archdeacon."

"I am, Gervase. Spiritually."

A snort from up ahead told them that Canon Hubert had caught the last remark. His donkey chose that moment to relieve itself without breaking its stride. It seemed to Hubert an apt comment on the lilting lunacy behind him.

Untroubled by harsh criticism from man and beast, Idwal was in full flow on the subject of the red dragon. His face was turned in the direction of his native country and his voice took on a declamatory note.

"Long centuries ago," he chanted, "Merlin prophesied the future struggles of the Welsh people. He revealed to our great chieftain a stone chest hidden at the bottom of a lake."

"Would that chieftain's name be Vortigern?"

"Indeed, it would. Vortigern himself. Lord of the Britons, as the Welsh were once called. Vortigern commanded that the stone chest be opened and out of it came a white dragon and a red dragon. Immediately, they began a fierce battle. At first, the white dragon drove the red one to the middle of the pool, then the red one, provoked into fury, drove the white one hither and thither."

"What did it signify?" asked Gervase.

"Merlin explained that. The red dragon signified the Britons, the white, the *Saeson*, as we call them."

"The Saxons."

"Red for Wales, white for England. 'Woe to the red dragon,' exclaimed Merlin, 'for her calamity draws nigh, and the white dragon shall seize on her cells. Then shall the mountains be made plains, and the glens and rivers overflow with blood. The *Saeson* shall possess almost all the island from sea to sea, but afterward our nation shall arise and bravely drive the *Saeson* out of their country.' Thus spoke Merlin and thus it came to pass."

"There is no mention of the Normans in that prophesy."

"They are just a more monstrous white dragon."

"And will the red dragon arise and drive them out?"

"In time, my friend. In time."

"What of the emblem left by Warnod's killers?"

"They were not true Welshmen," insisted Idwal.

"A red dragon was carved in the turf."

"It was an insult to us and not a portent."

"How can you be so sure?"

"Because my heart tells me so," said Idwal, punching his chest. "We are a proud people, Gervase, and we cherish our warrior history. Our nation will arise one day

85

to reclaim the land that the white dragon has taken from us. But we will not send ten callous assassins to burn one man to death in his home. With banners held high, we will come in all our glory under a new and courageous Welsh prince."

"And who will that prince be?" wondered Gervase.

Idwal fell silent, but his face was shining with joy.

In the shelter of some trees, two horsemen watched from a hill almost half a mile away. They could see the column wending its way along the track in the afternoon sunshine. Even at that distance, they could recognise Ralph Delchard, sitting upright in his saddle and talking with a female companion. Canon Hubert and Brother Simon could also be picked out, black-clad figures among the glinting helms and hauberks. One of the men at the rear had to be Gervase Bret.

The bearded rider turned to his companion.

"What do they want?" he said.

"I do not know, my lord."

"Follow them."

"I will."

"Take three men and trail them every inch of the way."

"Yes, my lord."

"Send me reports of everything they do and everywhere they go. If they so much as set foot on my land, I wish to be informed instantly. Is that understood?"

"Clearly, my lord."

"I'll permit no trespass. By anyone!"

Richard Orbec threw a last, hostile glance at the procession below before swinging round to canter off in the opposite direction. His peace was being invaded.

* * *

Ilbert the Sheriff had imposed a form of a truce on Archenfield, but he had neither the men nor the time to maintain it indefinitely. The district was sparsely populated with its inhabitants scattered over a wide area. There was no way that he could subdue every corner of it. The situation was profoundly aggravating.

"I've a mind to ride back to Hereford and let them get on with it!" he said. "If they want to kill each other, they might as well go ahead. In a week or so, when it's all over, we'll simply come back and bury the dead."

"It might not end there, my lord sheriff."

"I know. More's the pity!"

"Welsh passions run deep. This argument may spread."

"We must contain it," emphasized the sheriff. "It must not cross the border at any cost or we are doomed." He heaved a rueful sigh. "Which task is worse? Keeping the Welsh and the Saxons apart in Archenfield? Or preventing Maurice Damville and Richard Orbec from fighting a duel?"

"Both are equally onerous."

Ilbert the Sheriff was standing near the little church in Llanwarne with the captain of his men-at-arms. They had been counting the cost of one night's villainy in the area. In the wake of Warnod's death, his old servant, Elfig, had expired from his beating, and his Welsh servant, Hywel, had been viciously attacked. Five more people from each community had been seriously wounded and several had suffered minor assaults. Three prisoners had been trussed up for the return journey to Hereford.

Warnod's house was a pile of debris in the distance.

"Will we ever find his killers?" said the captain.

"We have to find them," asserted the sheriff. "It is the only way to lay this whole business to rest. There must be a reason why Warnod was singled out for attack. If we dig deep enough, we will uncover it."

"In the meantime, my lord sheriff?"

"Keep the patrols for a day or two more."

"The worst of it seems to be over."

"Thanks to our show of strength," said Ilbert. "It is the only thing these people understand. Superior force. By acting swiftly, we stamped out the flames of civil strife. We may take due credit for our ruthless efficiency."

Congratulations were premature. No sooner had the sheriff spoken than voices were raised nearby in a derisive cheer. Ilbert and the captain ran to their horses and leaped into the saddles. The shouts gave them direction, but it was the smoke which guided them to the exact spot. It curled up into the clear sky like a giant finger that beckoned them on.

Everyone had fled from the scene when they arrived, but their purpose was vividly evident. A fire was crackling merrily. Sitting in the heart of it was a large red dragon, crudely fashioned from wood and daubed with dye. Several arrows had been shot into the beast to speed its symbolic death.

Ilbert the Sheriff and his captain watched with horror. The red dragon did not submit quietly to its fate. As its wooden frame began to crack and blacken, a sudden burst of flame roared from its mouth and made the two men jump back in alarm. At the very moment of its demise, the red dragon came back to life with fiery defiance.

Wales had been awakened.

Chapter Five

CADWGAN AP BLEDDYN ASCENDED THE DAIS AT THE end of the hall and sat on the throne with an imperious air. His subjects were ranged around him in strict order of rank and position. As prince of Powys, he held sway over a border region that stretched from mid-Wales all the way north to Gwynedd, and he was eager to extend the frontiers of his territory. His crown bestowed both power and prestige. The court enabled Cadwgan to put them ostentatiously on display.

Like all Welsh princes, he kept a mobile court, shifting the seat of power according to caprice or necessity. He had come as far south as Elfael for this occasion. The court itself comprised a group of timbered buildings within an enclosure. Occupying the central position, the hall was by far the largest structure, long and wide with its roof timbers supported by thick oaken pillars. It was filled with members of his household, minor princelings who had come to pay homage, and a few privileged guests. Cadwgan provided generous hospitality for them all.

He was a compact figure in a long gown that trailed to the floor. His mantle was held at the shoulder by a gold brooch in the shape of a dragon. The circlet of gold around his brow bore the same motif. Dark, brooding, and bearded, he was of medium height, but exuded such a sense of innate strength that he seemed much bigger than his physical dimensions. His eyes roamed the hall with sovereign arrogance to drink in the respect and fealty of the assembly.

Power was a precarious commodity in a country as unsettled as Wales. It was far easier to acquire than to hold onto for any length of time. Dynasties were built on shifting political sands. Cadwgan knew the unwritten laws of kingship by heart. His first duty was to protect his title at all times. To this end, those who stood closest to him were always elite members of the *teulu*, his military retinue. A bold warrior himself, he knew how to select the best men to protect him.

He summoned the captain of his royal bodyguard.

"Goronwy!"

"My lord?"

"Come close for private conference."

Goronwy smiled with anticipatory delight. He was a tall, slender young man with dark hair and complexion. His face was too squashed to be handsome, but there was a vitality in his eyes and manner, which saved him from being thought of as ugly. Goronwy wore light armour. Sword and dagger were at his belt.

Expecting good news, his smile broadened into a grin.

"Can the day be named, my lord?"

"Not yet, Goronwy."

"But all has been arranged."

"Something has upset those arrangements badly."

Goronwy's face clouded. "An accident?"

"Of a kind. It must be looked into speedily."

"Send me, my lord. It is my wish and my duty."

"No man would be more appropriate," said Cadwgan with an affectionate hand on his arm. "You are my brother's son and royal blood flows in your veins. Let it boil until this matter has been settled. Show no mercy. Hound them."

"What has happened?"

The tidings were not for common usage. They were whispered to the young man in the soft consonants of the Welsh language. Goronwy was momentarily crushed. He recovered at once and his temples pounded with rage. He listened carefully to his orders, nodding throughout and rubbing his palm against the handle of his sword. The news had roused him to a pitch of fury. Goronwy was eager to be on his way.

"What of the men responsible for this crime, my lord?"

"Bring them to me."

"Alive or dead?"

Cadwgan's words were like soft caresses on the ear.

"Bring me their heads. They will suffice."

Ralph Delchard sent word ahead of their approach. Ilbert the Sheriff was highly displeased to hear that they were coming. He had more than enough on his hands without the burden of peripatetic royal commissioners. They could not have arrived at a worse time. At the very least, they would be a gross encumbrance.

Controlling his temper, he rode a few miles north to meet them in the hope of heading them off before they penetrated too deeply in Archenfield. He did not wish to have anyone looking over his shoulder while he was about his business. His methods were necessarily cruel at times. He wanted to apply them without criticism or hindrance.

His annoyance was markedly increased when he saw the cavalcade. The presence of Golde made him seethe. When Ralph introduced himself and his companions, the sheriff's gaze never left the woman for more than a split second. For her part, Golde maintained a dignified silence; head up, eyes downcast.

Idwal pushed forward shamelessly to claim attention.

"I will help you solve this murder, my lord sheriff."

"Will you, indeed?" said Ilbert, wincing at the sound of yet another Welsh voice. "What makes you think that?"

"I am an advocate for my nation."

"We have too many of those at work already."

"Show me the place where the crime occurred."

"I am too busy pursuing my own enquiries," said the sheriff, testily. "I have no time to waste on the burblings of a wandering scholar like yourself."

Idwal blenched. "I am neither burbler nor wandering scholar," he said in a querulous voice. "Herewald, Bishop of Llandaff sent me on a mission throughout Wales."

"Then attend to it."

"I am needed here first."

"Not by me, Archdeacon. I want no interfering churchmen getting under my feet. This is unholy work. Avoid."

The sheriff's abrupt manner threw Canon Hubert and Brother Simon into a quandary. Delighted to see Idwal being rebuffed so sternly, they were yet witnessing open disrespect of a man of God. The Church of Wales was, in their opinion, a lower order of creation than that in which they had been called to serve, but it still merited the courtesy of a kind word. Torn between applauding and upbraiding the surly sheriff, Canon Hubert managed no more than a bout of meaningless spluttering.

Golde was next to take up the questioning.

"Has anyone been arrested for the murder?"

"Not yet."

"But you know who the killers were?"

"We believe so."

"Do you know why they chose Warnod as their target?"

The sheriff was blunt. "I can no more answer that question than tell why you should ask it. Do you not have work enough in Hereford brewing your ale that you should ride about the countryside to interrupt my work?"

"That is too harsh a reply for a man," said Ralph, tartly. "Let alone for a lady who has asked her question politely. We realise that you are jaded by your obvious failure to make any progress with your investigation, my lord sheriff, but you should not take out your frustrations on an innocent party such as our delightful guest here."

Golde thanked him with a smile, but Ilbert fumed.

Canon Hubert tried to mollify him somewhat. Nudging his donkey forward, he spoke on behalf of the whole commission.

"My lord sheriff," he said. "You will wonder, no doubt, why fourteen sane people who could find a better lodging in Hereford are instead riding all the way to Archenfield."

"It baffles me," said Ilbert.

"Warnod brought us here. He is one of the main pillars that holds up our work. Take him away and it collapses."

"Then you are standing in the ruins, Canon Hubert."

"Ruins can be rebuilt—your own cathedral is a case in

point." Hubert was precise. "We need to know every-thing we can about the deceased—his character, his pos-sessions, his way of life. Most of all, we need to know who killed him and for what reason. Our deliberations cannot proceed without this crucial information."

"Does Golde form part of the commission?" said Ilbert with heavy sarcasm. "Or is she merely here to provide ale?"

"That remark is very unbecoming," scolded Ralph. "The lady is here at my personal invitation. Offend her with your boorish comments and you offend me."

Ilbert bit back a rejoinder as he met the unyielding gaze of Ralph Delchard. He decided that nothing would be served by antagonising the commissioners. It was in his interest to satisfy their demands and send them swiftly on their way. With a visible effort, therefore, he set aside his personal feelings and sounded a note of appeasement.

"I beg the lady's pardon," he said with rough courtesy. "Her appearance in such company as this took me by sur-prise and robbed me of my manners. It was unworthy of me."

"Thank you, my lord sheriff," said Golde.

She was poised and he was relaxed, but the look that passed between them was full of unresolved tensions. Ralph wondered what Golde had done to ruffle the sheriff.

"May we now ride on to Llanwarne?" she suggested.

"Yes," urged Idwal. "My countrymen have need of my peculiar gifts. I have to vindicate the red dragon."

"If you know how to tame it," said Ilbert, grudgingly, "you may yet be welcome in Archenfield."

"Ergyng."

"Call it what you will."

"No man alive could stop me."

Ralph was eager to press on. "Shall we set forward?"

"Hold there," said Gervase. "Can we not make better use of our numbers here? The sheriff does not want all fourteen of us treading on his tail. While some ride on to view the place where Warnod died, others might strike off west to find the holdings that are the cause of the dispute. That way we get fuller value out of the daylight hours remaining."

"Sage advice," agreed Ralph. "I'll on to Llanwarne with one party, Gervase. Take four of my men and anyone else who wishes to go with you. Survey those controversial acres that Richard Orbec is so determined to keep and Maurice Damville is so willing to cede on impulse."

The sheriff's ears pricked up. "Damville giving in to Orbec?" he said in disbelief. "Can this be true?"

"I will explain as we ride along," said Ralph. He turned to Canon Hubert and Brother Simon. "The road forks here. Archdeacon Idwal and Golde will accompany me. Which route will you choose?"

The choice was made for them. Hubert seized the chance to pluck out the Welsh thorn in his flesh, while Simon was able to rid himself of the alarming proximity of a beautiful woman. They elected to ride with Gervase. He was more amenable company in every respect.

Ilbert the Sheriff led the way south at a trot with Ralph Delchard beside him. Though the talk was of Richard Orbec and Maurice Damville, another person kept wafting her way into Ralph's mind. Golde was at once behind him and before his eyes. The journey from Hereford had enabled him to become more closely acquainted with her and there had been a deepening affection on both sides. Ilbert Malvoisin complicated the relationship between the two of them. Ralph sensed a rival.

Gervase Bret, meanwhile, veered off to the west with his six companions. The sheriff had given them directions and they rode at a brisk trot. The landscape was breathtaking. They passed through undulating countryside with wooded slopes, rich pastures, golden cornfields, and plentiful streams that trickled playfully along. When they paused to water their horses at one of those streams, they looked around to admire the scenery.

Gervase was particularly struck by the copse of silver birches on a rise ahead of them. With the sun hitting them directly, their trunks gleamed like so many soldiers massed for a battle. He did not realise that some of those armoured figures were not made of wood.

Activity was brisk at the castle. Maurice Damville had returned to Ewyas Harold and was inspecting progress on the walls of the bailey. Fearing severe punishment if they were deemed to be slacking, his slaves laboured with frenetic commitment. Masons had reinforced the battlements with slabs of stone dressed to shape, but rougher boulders were now being winched up or brought by hand. They were being piled at strategic points along the battlements.

Damville strutted along with Huegon beside him.

"We will need more skins of oil," he said.

"Order has already been given, my lord."

"Braziers, too," added Damville. "Hot coals and boiling oil are worthy accomplices. See that fuel is provided."

"The storehouse is full," said Huegon, pointing to one of the timber buildings in the courtyard below. "The castle is well-supplied with all our needs. Food, wine, water, hay for the horses, and fuel for the braziers."

"There is only one thing missing, Huegon."

"My lord?"

"Women!" Damville laughed. "Fuel for my bed!"

"Ewyas Harold may not be the ideal place for the fairer sex at this moment," said Huegon, tactfully. "Ladies have their function, it is true, but they must take their turn behind more pressing matters."

"A fair, fat wench is a pressing matter in herself."

"There will be ample time for sport."

"One name will head all the others."

"One name?"

"Aelgar."

"The Lady of the Brewhouse."

"She is more than that, Huegon," said Damville with a wistful smile. "Aelgar is an English rose in full bloom. My hand itches to snap her stem. Have you ever seen such fine eyes, such full lips, such a trim shape? I tell you this girl has bewitched me. I could almost believe I was in love."

"Hereford lies a long way off yet, my lord."

Damville accepted the covert reproach in his steward's gaze. Huegon was, as usual, correct. In the short term, the pleasures of the chase had to be forsaken. They could be enjoyed at a later date. To postpone a delight was to intensify its quality. Damville was content.

His mind swung back to more immediate problems.

"Did we handle the royal commissioners aright?"

"We did what was needful, my lord."

"It grieved me to give Orbec that land *gratis*."

"What is given can as easily be taken back."

Damville chuckled. "I'll have the whole of his

demesne in my grasp. His house I'd destroy, but I'll let his chapel stand as a privy." He looked down over the battlement. "If only Richard Orbec were at my door right now."

"He way well be so in due course."

"I will be ready for him, Huegon."

Grunting noises made Maurice Damville turn. Two slaves were struggling to carry a large boulder between them. They dropped it onto a waiting pile then hurried off. Damville swooped on the missile and picked it up without effort. Heaving the jagged stone over the battlement, he let out a wild cry of triumph.

"Richard Orbec!"

With an awesome thud, the boulder sank deep into the ground.

The messenger was waiting for him as he came out of the tiny chapel. Richard Orbec was bareheaded and wore only a tunic. His mind was still exercised by the febrile thoughts with which he had wrestled before the altar. It took him a few seconds to collect himself.

"Well?" he said.

"They are heading this way, my lord."

"The whole commission?"

"Three only," said the man. "Their leader rode off towards Llanwarne with the sheriff, taking four of his men-at-arms with him. The others escort the three who travel towards your demesne."

"What speed do they make?"

"Slow but steady. An hour will get them here."

"They must be stopped," said Orbec, decisively. "When they sit behind a table in Hereford, commissioners with a royal warrant have some power. It turns to vapour when they dare to encroach on my property. A show of force will teach them their place. Have twenty men armed and ready to ride."

"Yes, my lord. How will I deploy them?"

"I'll lead them myself," said Orbec. "If I speak directly to these interlopers, they will more readily understand the danger that they court." He glanced guiltily back at the chapel, then moved quickly away. "Fetch my sword and armour! We leave immediately!"

They were shocked when they saw the scene of devastation. Warnod's house had been reduced to ashes. Only a few charred timbers remained to show where he had once lived with his doomed family. Golde let out a gasp of horror and brought her hands up to her mouth. Idwal sighed with compassion. Even Ralph Delchard was initially jarred. He walked around the perimeter of the house.

"What could one man do to deserve all this?" he said.

"The blameless often suffer the most in this world," observed Idwal, darkly. "Thank heaven his suffering is over!"

"There were no witnesses, my lord sheriff?"

"None that will come forward," said Ilbert.

"An inferno like this? Think of the noise, the light."

"Everyone was struck deaf and blind."

"By fear."

"Or by agreement," said the sheriff. "I begin to wonder if they were all part of the conspiracy. The Welsh will always protect their own."

"I deny your accusation with every breath in my body!" said Idwal, quivering with indignation. "Do not tie this crime around the necks of my compatriots when you do not have a shred of evidence to do so."

"You forget the red dragon," argued Ilbert.

"That is something I will never forget!" affirmed the archdeacon. "But you have no proof that this emblem carved in the ground was put there by a Welshman. It could just as easily have been hacked out of the earth by a Saxon, Norman, or Breton. The shape of a dragon is not unknown to them."

"Idwal has a point," agreed Ralph, pensively.

"Remember the servants," said Ilbert. "Elfig and Hywel. One beaten, one spared. One now dead, one alive. One scourged for his nationality, one saved by it."

"He was not saved for long," said Ralph, "if reports that we hear are true. This young servant is your most valuable witness. What has he vouchsafed?"

"Nothing beyond the fact that he was bound and gagged."

"Did you not question him with sufficient vigour?"

"I used every threat I could to loosen his tongue."

"To no avail?"

"Hywel is beyond us, my lord. He speaks only Welsh."

"Then he is not beyond me," said Idwal, confidently. "Where is the lad? Let me speak with him at once."

"He was severely wounded by the attack upon him."

"Then I will medicine his injuries while we talk."

Ralph Delchard encouraged the idea. The softer arts of a Welsh archdeacon might succeed where the rough questioning of a Norman sheriff had failed. When Ilbert finally accepted this, they mounted their horses and rode off towards the village itself. Hywel was being cared for in a fetid hovel that belonged to his uncle. Idwal and Ralph were admitted to the dwelling. The former was at home in the mean surroundings, but the latter coughed as the stench hit his throat.

Hywel lay on a makeshift bed of straw. He was a sturdy youth with dark hair and a tufted beard, both still clotted with blood. One eye was hideously swollen, the other was ringed with a black bruise. A fresh scar had baptised his forehead and there were scratches all over his face. His tunic had been torn to expose gashes and bruises all over his body. One of his hands was swollen to twice its normal size, but it was his right leg which had suffered the worst damage. Broken in two parts, it was bound tightly with strips of cloth to a wooden splint.

When the youth tried to move, he was clearly in agony.

"Rest, rest, Hywel," soothed the archdeacon in Welsh. "We have not come to hurt you. I am Idwal of Llandaff. When I passed through here two days ago, your body was sound and your mind untroubled. What miseries have befallen you since!"

Hywel said nothing. He glanced resentfully at Ralph.

"He comes as a friend," reassured Idwal, inspecting the injuries as he talked. "Who set this leg for you?"

"The priest," mumbled the youth.

"He was done his work well," noted the other. "Mark that, Hywel. The Church repairs what men break asunder." He clicked his tongue. "But he might have bathed your wounds with more thoroughness. Bring water!"

An old woman, who had been huddling with alarm in a corner, got up and scurried out. Idwal continued to soothe the patient with soft words before offering up a prayer for him. When the old woman came in with an earthenware pot, he took it from her and used the hem of his own garment to dip in the water. Squeezing it out, he knelt beside Hywel and bathed his face and hair with gentle strokes. Ralph did not understand a word, but he was intrigued by the way that Idwal was slowly winning the confidence of the wounded servant.

"Tell me what happened, Hywel."

"I have told my story many times."

"Tell it once more to me," coaxed Idwal. "Men came to the house and bound you. Is that not true? Did you chance to get a close look at any of them?"

"They took me from behind, when I was chopping wood."

"You are a strong lad. Did you not struggle?"

"There were too many of them."

"Did you not cry out for help?"

"They gagged me and blindfolded my eyes."

"Then you were still able to hear their voices."

"No," said Hywel, recalling memories that were branded into his young mind. "They said nothing. All I heard was poor Elfig's screams as they beat him. And the crackle of the flames much later."

"How much later?"

"An hour or two at least. I cannot be sure."

"What else did you hear?"

Hywel shuddered. "Their shouts and jeers as the house burned down. But they were too far away for me to pick out their voices."

"How were you released?"

"By my kinsman. He was roused by the noise."

"And what did you see when you were untied?"

"The house in flames and ten men riding off."

"Nothing else?"

"The red dragon. *Alive!*"

Idwal attended to the wounds for a few minutes and

102

translated what he had so far heard for Ralph's benefit. The latter suggested the next question and the archdeacon rendered it back into his own language.

"Where had Warnod been when he returned home?"

"To Hereford."

"Why?"

"He did not say."

"What sort of mood was he in when he left Llanwarne?"

"Happy."

"Was he a kind master, Hywel?"

"Yes."

"How did he treat you and Elfig?"

"Well."

"Did he have many enemies in Ergyng?"

"None that I know of."

Idwal bent in close. "Who do you think killed him?"

The boy's one visible eye filmed over with tears. He was still deeply distressed about the fate of his master and shaken by the savage beating he had been given. Desperate to help, the youth had no more information to offer. After going through some of the details a second time, Idwal thanked him and promised to call on him again to tend his wounds and to offer succour.

Ralph Delchard stepped quickly outside the hovel and gulped in fresh air. Golde was some distance away, locked in conversation with the sheriff. His manner seemed much less hostile towards her. Idwal came out of the house and gave Ralph an account of everything else that the youth had said.

"I still do not spy a Welsh hand in this," argued Idwal.

"Nor do I," said Ralph.

"Why?"

"Because this attack was planned. They knew that

103

Warnod was away from his house and they knew when he was likely to return and by what route. No random band of killers from over the border would have had that intelligence."

"Why burn him alive when they could have cut him down?"

"They wanted to send a signal."

"To whom?"

"Everyone."

"All that is signalled was an outbreak of violence."

"Exactly," said Ralph. "Then there was the red dragon."

"A false trail."

"Not necessarily."

"Hywel was feverish. He did not see that dragon alive."

"In his mind's eye, he did."

"What do you mean, my lord?"

"He is Welsh."

The remark sent Idwal into a burst of invective against Saxons and Normans alike. Ralph did not hear him. He was too busy looking in the direction of the border.

"Who are the most dangerous men in Wales?"

"Look elsewhere for your murderers, my lord."

"I ask but in the spirit of enquiry," said Ralph. "I know little of the Welsh beyond the fact that they are fierce soldiers. I fought against them near Chester many years ago. They were bloody encounters with no quarter given."

"Praise the Lord! We have always had brave warriors."

"Brave warriors need great leaders."

"We have had our share of those," observed Idwal with pride. "I could recite a long list of immortal heroes. In recent memory, Gruffydd ap Llewelyn was the most

104

famous. Prince of Gwynedd and Powys, and lord of all Wales. A mighty man on the battlefield. You may yoke the name of Gruffydd ap Llewelyn with that of Richard Orbec."

"Orbec?"

"Yes, my lord," said Idwal with a dry cackle. "Richard Orbec is helping to rebuild the cathedral that Gruffydd destroyed when he sacked the whole city." He became solemn. "Not that I condone the attack on a cathedral or on any place of worship, mind you. Ecclesiastical buildings of all kinds should be sacrosanct. Gruffydd was too impulsive."

"That was over twenty years ago," said Ralph. "Where are your fearsome princes now?"

"Rhys ap Tewdr is lord of Deheubarth and rules the whole of South Wales without challenge."

"King William brought him to heel in St. David's."

"Your king was on a pilgrimage to the shrine!"

"A cloak to hide his real purpose," said Ralph. "He went with an army to remind this Rhys ap Tewdr of the power of Norman soldiers. The lord of Deheubarth had the sense to become reconciled with the King. Who else can you cite?"

"Rhys holds the south, Gruffydd ap Cynan, the north." Idwal shook his head sadly. "In name only, alas. The prince of Gwynedd was imprisoned by deceitful Normans. He rules his land through the bars of a dungeon."

"It may be the safest throne on which to set him."

"His time will come again, my lord."

"But it is not at hand yet," said Ralph. "You tell me of your two most powerful men. Rhys ap Tewdr in the south and Gruffydd ap Cynan in the north. Neither is a threat to us. What of the prince of Powys?"

"Cadwgan ap Bleddyn?"

"Would he be a leader to unite your people?"

"Hardly!" said Idwal with asperity.

"Why not?"

"Because he has come to composition with the enemy and diluted the blood of his royal house."

"In what way?"

"Cadwgan ap Bleddyn is married to one of your own. The daughter of a Marcher lord, Picot de Say. His wife has taken all the fight out of him."

"Our ladies keep warm beds."

"The prince of Powys is as crafty as a fox, but he has been caged by marriage. Look for no trouble from him."

"Can you be certain of that?"

"I have met the man myself."

"Does he not have a strong army around him?"

"Yes,"said Idwal. "Brave warriors, bred for battle, but they stand idle in Powys. You will not hear a peep out of Cadwgan and his soldiers."

Goronwy led a troop of forty men down through the Black Mountains. Light armour allowed them to move fast. As captain of his uncle's *teulu*, Goronwy was a highly trained soldier who honed his military skills with unvarying regularity. Like their leader, the soldiers were expert horsemen who could use sword and spear with dexterity in the saddle. Several of them also had bows and quivers of arrows slung across their backs. As they clattered along the narrow mountain roads, nobody dared to question their purpose or obstruct their path.

They were on an important mission that brooked no delay. Goronwy had not spoken a word since they had left his uncle's court. Suffused with anger, his face squeezed in upon itself. The forehead narrowed, the eyes half-closed, the cheeks were sucked in, and the mouth became a thin strip of red amid the black hair of his beard. An invisible hammer continued to pound the anvil inside his head until his temples threatened to burst apart.

When they reached the foothills, they saw a small group of travellers coming towards them. Goronwy gave a signal with his hand and his men cantered on to surround the little cortege. Terrified by the ring of hostility around them, the travellers pleaded for mercy. Their spokesman was an ancient figure in a tattered cloak.

"Do not harm us, friends," he implored in quaking Welsh. "We are poor people with nothing worth stealing. Spare us."

"We are not robbers!" snarled Goronwy with disgust. "We are soldiers of the prince of Powys, Cadwgan ap Bleddyn."

"We did not look to find you this far south."

"North, south, east, west! We ride where we choose."

"Yes, yes," said the old man, apologetically.

"Where have you come from?"

"Caerleon."

"What did you see along the road?"

"Nothing of any note."

"Whom did you meet?"

"Nobody, my lord."

"You are lying."

"It is the truth," said the old man. "Ask any of my companions. We have ridden all the way from Caerleon and seen not a soul on the road." He stretched out an arm to point. "We came by the quieter paths through—"

"Stop lying!" interrupted Goronwy.

He enforced his command with a swish of his sword.

The outstretched arm was severed in two below the elbow and the old traveller reeled in the saddle. Goronwy kicked his horse into a canter and continued on his way. For half a mile, they could still hear the piteous howls of their victim.

Goronwy was unrepentant. "Nobody lies to me," he said with a grim smile. "I should've cut his tongue out as well."

Ilbert the Sheriff swiftly revised his opinion of the Archdeacon of Llandaff. Though everything about the man made his hackles rise, he soon came to see how useful he could be. Idwal was a calming influence on the Welsh community, moving among them to listen to their tales of woe, offer comfort, and counsel moderate action. Bellicose in theological debate, the archdeacon was also an ambassador for peace. Ilbert decided to make the best use of him that he could.

It left Ralph Delchard alone with Golde for the first time since they had quit Hereford. She was numbed by the implications of what she saw at Warnod's house and she wondered how she could soften the hard tale when she told it to her sister.

Ralph related what he had learned from Warnod's servant, but it took them no closer to understanding the motive that lay behind the attack. He turned to more personal affairs.

"You talked intently with my lord sheriff just now."

"I had many questions to put to him."

"He seemed more ready to answer them than earlier."

"Ilbert Malvoisin is a sullen man at times, but he can be brought around to a more pleasant state of mind."

"Your charms would bring anyone around, Golde."

She acknowledged the compliment with a brief smile.

"You know him well, I think?" he continued.

"The sheriff?"

"When you first met, he was peppery. When I saw you even now, he was very attentive towards you. If a man shifts so quickly between anger and reconciliation, it usually means that his heart is engaged."

"Not by me, my lord," she said, sharply.

"He was all but fawning upon you."

"Ilbert Malvoisin is married."

"You are not."

"Nor do I look to be," she insisted. "One time was enough. I have had to tell that to many who came calling."

"Including the sheriff?" he fished.

Golde was terse. "The sheriff and I meet in the way of business. I supply ale to the castle, he buys it. That is the extent of our relationship. Now and in the future."

"I see." He cast another line into the water. "Is there someone else already in your life?"

"There is, my lord."

"Oh."

"My sister. Aelgar."

"What I meant was that—"

"I know what you meant," she said, "and my answer still holds. Aelgar is my prime concern at the moment. Two days ago, she consented to marry Warnod." She rode over his surprise. "Yes, I know that he was much older and already bereft of one wife. But he was a good man. Kind and considerate. He understood our ways. Warnod would have been a loving husband."

"Did you approve of the match?"

"Aelgar is a strange girl," she explained. "Young and

still very much a child. She is at the mercy of her beauty. You have no idea what a curse it can sometimes be. For every man who looked at me, five would stare at Aelgar." She met his gaze. "Warnod is not the man I would have chosen for her, but I came to see his virtues. He wooed her for over a year. She loved him truly. I believe that he would have made my sister happy and rescued her from all that attention."

"What will become of her, Golde?"

"I do not know."

"You cannot shield her forever," he said, gently. "She has lost one husband, but there are other good men in the world. If she is even half as lovely as her sister, she will have an extremely wide choice."

Golde almost blushed. "She will, my lord."

"What of you, then?"

"Me?"

"When your role is done. When Aelgar is settled."

"That may not be for some time."

"But *then*?"

The candour of his affection was touching. She felt her pulse quicken under his gaze. A bleak purpose had brought her to Archenfield, but Ralph Delchard had breathed some warmth into the journey for her. He was a Norman lord and she was a humble brewer, but she was not abashed in his presence. She let him know it.

"I am the daughter of a Saxon thegn," she said.

He grinned. "I saw the nobility in your bearing."

"Come no closer," ordered Richard Orbec. "This is my land."

"We have a right to view it," said Canon Hubert.

"To view it, but not to trespass upon it."

"These holdings are in dispute, my lord," said Gervase Bret, reasonably. "We come to see why they have attracted such interest from three rival claimants."

"*One*, Master Bret," said Orbec.

"Did we lose two along the road?"

"Maurice Damville, as I hear, has resigned his interest."

"That still leaves you and Warnod."

"I will not be dispossessed by a handful of ashes in Llanwarne," said Orbec. "Until you show me a legal and enforceable will that bestows on someone the right to contest part of my demesne, I will not let you step onto my property."

"Then we may have to do so by force," blustered Hubert. A line of twenty men-at-arms advanced a few paces towards him. "You will not intimidate me. We are here at the king's express behest. His soldiers are at our beck and call."

"But they are in Winchester—mine are here."

"King William will be told about this."

"He is in Normandy on more important business."

"Very well," said Gervase, conceding defeat. "We will but ride along the periphery of your land. That will give us a fair idea of its worth and quality." An astringent note intruded. "But you do yourself no favours, my lord. When you are so eager to keep us away from your holdings, we are bound to wonder if you are hiding something from us."

"I am."

"What is it?"

"Myself."

Richard Orbec left half his men to form a barrier against the visitors and rode off towards his house with the others. Gervase Bret gestured to his own party to withdraw. In the shade of some trees, they dismounted to consider their next step. Canon Hubert was outraged at the turn of events. His position gave him the right to inspect any land in the county and he hated to be baulked. Brother Simon, on the other hand, was almost relieved that their passage had been blocked. He argued that it was still possible for them to ride back to Hereford before darkness completely overtook them. The prospect of a cathedral from which Idwal the Archdeacon had been exorcised was very enticing.

"Put that thought aside, Brother Simon," said Hubert. "We would be better advised to join the others in Llanwarne and seek shelter for the night in that vicinity. This murder may well have some bearing on Richard Orbec's reluctance to admit us to his demesne."

Gervase suggested a compromise. Having come this far, he did not wish to leave empty-handed. While the others rode on to Llanwarne, therefore, he would contrive some means to take a closer look at Richard Orbec's disputed land.

"*Alone?*" said Canon Hubert. "I admire your courage, Gervase, but I question your sanity. What can one man do that seven of us could not?"

"Be less visible."

For the benefit of the watching sentries, Gervase rode off with his companions on the road to Llanwarne. As soon as they were in thick cover, however, he bade farewell and doubled back in a wide circle. Orbec's land was fringed with woodland and dappled with orchards. It would not be impossible to gain access to at least some of the holdings with relative safety. Using what cover he could, Gervase picked his way along with care.

The countryside was entrancing. Rich, luscious, and rolling gently towards the horizon, it was land that any man would fight to keep. Birdsong filled the air and insects buzzed over standing pools. Gervase manoeuvred his way towards a grove of sycamores on a gentle slope. From their shelter, he could enjoy the view at his leisure. Dismounting among the trees, he tethered his horse and crept forward to find himself a vantage point. The greater part of the disputed land unfolded before him like a green carpet. Gervase could even catch a faint glimpse of Richard Orbec's house.

His survey was short-lived. He heard the crack of a twig beneath a foot, but his reactions were far too slow. Before he could even move, a wooden club struck him on the back of the head to send him tumbling forward into oblivion.

Chapter Six

AS SOON AS THEY CAME WITHIN SIGHT OF THE VIL-
lage, Canon Hubert regretted his decision to go
there. Llanwarne was no more than a scatter of mean cottages around a tiny church, but it was not the buildings
that arrested his eye. Standing on a hillock at the edge of
the village, and speaking to a dozen or more Welsh peasants, was Idwal the Archdeacon. His voice enthralled
them, his eminence impressed them, and his blend of
learning and *hwyl* kindled their spirits. Idwal held his
impromptu congregation in the palm of his hand.

"Lord save us!" said Hubert. "The Sermon on the
Mount."

"Blessed are the deaf," murmured Brother Simon, "for
they cannot hear him."

Simon's own discomfort was compounded by the sight
of Golde talking with Ralph Delchard and Ilbert the
Sheriff. Women had no place in the life and thoughts of a
Benedictine monk as unsullied as Brother Simon. When
the commissioner's work took them to Essex, he had
even been thrown into a turmoil by the presence of two
innocuous nuns. Golde's impact on his delicate sensibili-
ties was far greater. The woman had not even spoken to

him and she had done nothing specifically to earn his disapproval. She simply was.

Hubert watched Idwal toss his cloak back for effect.

"The lambskin has returned to its flock!" he observed.

The six newcomers dismounted their horses and tethered them. Hubert led his donkey across to a water trough and let it slurp absentmindedly. The soldiers went off to join their four colleagues and trade gossip. Ralph was too embroiled in his conversation to break away. It was the Welshman who became their self-appointed host.

"Welcome to Ergyng!" he said, ending his homily and scuttling over to them. "You are now in the diocese of Llandaff."

"I thought I felt a distinct chill," said Hubert.

"You came upon me preaching the Word to my people."

"A common street is hardly consecrated ground."

"I carry my cathedral with me on my back."

"What is it called? The Church of St. Lambskin?"

"Mock not, Canon Hubert," said Idwal. "Like Christ himself, I speak to my congregation on hill, on mountain, and in field. While I teach the Gospels there, it becomes hallowed ground. That is the great difference between us."

"Yes," said Hubert, "but I do not confuse idle gossip in the street with the revealed Word."

"You and Brother Simon are Christians of the closed world. You retreated into the cloister to find God and hide him away under your habits." Idwal waved a hand at the departing peasants. "I share Him with the common people. I go out—as Christ and his Disciples went out—to bring everyone closer to the wonder of God."

"Such work is admirable in itself," said Brother Simon

with a half-smile, "but only a man with your gifts could undertake it. We serve God by a life of denial."

"Then you deny His greater glory."

Hubert was waspish. "Llandaff must miss you mightily. How will the edifice stand without you to support it with these pillars of theological wisdom?"

"Sarcasm is the mark of a lowly mind," said Idwal.

Further exchange between them was cut short by the arrival of Ralph Delchard, who strolled across with Golde at his elbow. Brother Simon shrunk back a few paces and put both skeletal hands over his scrip in a forlorn gesture of defence.

"So early a return?" said Ralph with surprise.

"Richard Orbec barred us from his land," said Hubert.

"Then he bars the way for the king. Did you not tell him that in round terms and brush aside any argument?"

"Twenty men-at-arms enforced his purpose."

Ralph ignited. "Richard Orbec dared to offer violence to royal commissioners!"

"I'd have excommunicated him on the spot," said Idwal.

"He was left in no doubt about our displeasure," said Hubert. "But we were so few against so many."

"One fewer now," noted Ralph. "Where is Gervase?"

"He refused to be evicted so rudely. When we were out of sight of Richard Orbec's knights, he went back to examine the holdings privily. I advised against the danger, but Gervase was headstrong."

"He did no more than I would have done," said Ralph with gathering fury. "Bar our way! I'd have barbered his beard with my sword! When the sheriff is done here, I'll add a troop of his men to mine and cut a path to the very heart of his demesne!"

"Take me with you to care for the dead," offered Idwal with a wicked gleam. "I will enjoy reading the burial service over Norman soldiers."

"Look to your own, Archdeacon," said Hubert.

"This is beyond bearing!" said Ralph, warming to his theme. "Marcher lords have been allowed too much license. Because we let them build their little empires here on these godforsaken frontiers, they think they are above the law of the land. King William has already torn down one Earl of Hereford. He will just as easily tear down these other self-styled earls like Richard Orbec and Maurice Damville!"

Idwal beamed. "There is no sweeter music in a Welshman's ear than the sound of invaders quarreling among themselves over land they stole from us."

"Silence this dead sheep of an archdeacon!" howled Ralph.

"If only we knew how!" hissed Brother Simon.

Ralph fulminated, Idwal chuckled, Canon Hubert had an attack of pomposity, and Golde watched it all with interest. When the clamour abated, it was she who introduced a note of mild alarm.

"I fear for your companion, my lord."

"Gervase?" said Ralph. "He can look after himself."

"Richard Orbec is a strange man."

"We have seen his strangeness at close quarters."

"Your colleague is in grave danger," she continued. "If he is caught by Richard Orbec, there is no telling what might happen to him."

"He will not be caught," said Ralph, confidently. "Gervase Bret is a lawyer. And there is no more slippery breed of men on this earth. They will not catch him. Gervase will see exactly what he wishes to see."

117

When his eyes finally opened, Gervase Bret thought at first that he had gone blind. He could see nothing. His head was pounding, his mouth tasted of vomit, and he felt as if his body was being kicked simultaneously by a dozen feet. He opened his eyes wider, but still found himself staring into an impenetrable darkness. It was only when he became fully conscious that he realised where he was.

Bound hand and foot, Gervase was tied securely across the back of a horse like the carcass of a dead animal. Over his head was a sack, which, from its smell, had once contained barley. He was being dragged along at speed behind a group of riders. His stomach had revolted against the rough and indiscriminate bouncing to which it was subjected and spewed up the remains of his last meal. He was in agony.

Gervase tried to marshal his jangled thoughts. Where was he and in whose hands? The last thing that he could remember was the sight of Richard Orbec's lands rolling northeastward from the hundred of Archenfield into the Golden Valley. Was he Orbec's prisoner? Would a Norman lord dare to violate the privilege of a royal commissioner?

Buffeted unmercifully by one horse, he tried to count how many others cantered beside him. Four, at most. Voice were occasionally raised above the chaos of the hoofbeats, but the sacking muffled the sound. Gervase was trapped in a deep, black hole of pain and confusion. He could do nothing but wait, suffer more intensely, and pray.

Hooves splashed through water as they forded a stream. Gervase felt the spray on his hands. Wherever they were taking him, it was no leisurely ride. They were in a hurry.

Richard Orbec ate alone that evening. The meal was frugal and he permitted himself only one cup of wine with which to wash it down. When a servant had cleared away the dishes, Orbec allowed the waiting reeve to enter. Redwald was flushed.

"I have been told what happened a few hours ago," he said. "Was your behaviour wise, my lord?"

"It is not for you to question its wisdom, Redwald."

"Indeed, not. But I am hired to administer your lands."

"This was a case of trespass, not administration."

"The commissioners act with royal warrant."

"It carries no weight on my demesne."

"My lord!"

"I've humoured them enough, Redwald," said Orbec, quietly. "I answered their summons and replied to their questions. I even endured the unwarranted scrutiny of my private life by Canon Hubert. To what end?"

"They produced a counter-claim to some of your land."

"It is worthless."

"They had a charter."

"It belongs to a corpse."

"If someone else should inherit his claim . . ."

"What hope is there of that?" said Orbec with feeling. "I have right and title to those manors. Maurice Damville has renounced his claim and Warnod's death repudiates his."

"That is still no cause to offend the commissioners."

"My will is cause enough!"

Orbec slapped the table with the flat of his hand for

119

emphasis. His reeve backed away, trying to propitiate him with a nod and a smile. Controlling himself again, his master rose from his seat and crossed over to Redwald. An air of melancholy now hung over him.

"Forgive my anger, Redwald."

"I should beg your pardon for provoking it."

"You touch on raw flesh."

"It was not deliberate, my lord."

"I know," said Orbec. "I know. Only a Norman would understand my torment. It is the torment of loss, Redwald. The anguish of betrayal. I once held some of the choicest land in the whole duchy of Normandy. Verdant acres in the vicinity of Bayeux. Most of it was lost. Taken from me when my back was turned. That will never happen again, Redwald."

"Then do not provoke authority."

"I merely defended my legal rights."

"There may be repercussions."

"Let them come." Orbec went over to the window and looked out at the valley below. "Look at it, Redwald. The hand of God has touched this land. It is a source of continual joy to me. That is why I chose Herefordshire. It is the closest imitation of Normandy that I could find. I lost my beautiful estates near Bayeux, so I am rebuilding them here in England."

"I am honoured to be part of that work."

"Then do not question my actions again."

"I will not, my lord."

"You have been a shrewd counsellor and a faithful servant to me, Redwald, but I do not like to be crossed."

"That is a lesson I learned a long time ago."

"Never forget it," said Orbec, spinning around to face him. "A threat to my land is like an attack on my person.

120

I lash out to defend myself. Anyone who comes between me and my anger will be swept aside. Even you."

Evening shadows fell slowly across Archenfield. Ilbert the Sheriff and his men had commandeered a manor house nearby, but it was too small to accommodate more guests. Ralph Delchard and his party were therefore offered lodging a little further south in Pencoed. Though still worried about her sister, Golde permitted herself to be included in the invitation. There was much more to be learned about Warnod's death and she was, in any case, reluctant to be parted from her new friend. Golde had a Saxon wariness of all Normans, but Ralph had somehow overcome her natural suspicion.

Canon Hubert and Brother Simon were disappointed that there was no convenient religious house where they could lay their heads for the night. It was too late to return to the college of secular canons at Hereford cathedral, and the nearest Benedictine monastery was in Tewkesbury in the adjacent county of Gloucestershire. Brother Simon duly steeled himself to sleep under the same roof as a woman, while Hubert basked in the relief of escape from his theological adversary. Idwal was to spend the night in Llanwarne at the cottage of the local priest.

Ralph sent his three companions on to Pencoed with an escort of four men-at-arms. The other half of his knights remained with their master. Ralph would not even consider his own departure until the safe return of Gervase Bret.

Ilbert the Sheriff lingered with him in Llanwarne.

"Where *can* he be?" wondered Ralph.

"It is easy to go astray in Archenfield," said Ilbert.

"Gervase merely went to *look* at that land. We do not require him to measure each blade of grass on it. A sighting is all that is needed before he joins us here."

"Let us hope that he himself was not sighted."

"Gervase is too cunning for that," said Ralph. "An alert mind and a fast horse will keep him clear of trouble."

"I pray earnestly that it may."

"Why do you say that, my lord sheriff?"

"Richard Orbec is a dangerous man."

"Yes," said Ralph as he recalled the satanic face. "We saw something of his character at the shire hall. A curious mixture, indeed. Saint and soldier. Benevolent towards the cathedral yet hostile towards anyone who questions that benevolence."

"Even more hostile to those who encroach on his land."

"Why?"

"Ask directly of him. I do not know."

"But you have had dealings with him over the years."

"As few as I could," said the sheriff, ruefully. "He can be as friendly as a brother one day, but turn into your mortal enemy on the next."

"What of this private chapel of his?"

"They say it is his second home."

"He is that devout?"

"Until something disturbs him. He moves straight from altar to sword then."

"A belligerent Christian. The worst kind."

"He will not show Christian tolerance towards trespass. That is why I fear for your colleague. If he does fall into Orbec's clutches, there is no telling what might happen to him."

"No man would dare to assault a royal commissioner."

"Richard Orbec can change from man into devil."

"If he so much as touches Gervase, he'll answer to me."

"You'll first have to prove his guilt."

"What do you mean?"

"Your friend would not be the first trespasser on that demesne to vanish completely. I have pursued three such cases and found no trace of the men in question."

"Where did they go?"

"It would take you a lifetime to find out."

"Why, my lord sheriff?"

"Richard Orbec has vast estates," said Ilbert. "Only he knows where the bodies are buried. Let us hope that this Gervase Bret does not stumble into an anonymous grave."

The ride seemed endless, the pace jarring. Gervase Bret was bruised and shaken by the time they finally reached their destination. When the horses slowed to a trot, he gathered his wits about him to listen for what sound came through the sacking. He could hear water; not the slow trickle of a stream, but the deep surge of a river. Hooves went over cobbles and voices talked indistinctly. A hollow clack then told him that they were walking across a timber bridge.

His head was still aching and his whole body felt as if it had been trampled, but he tried to put discomfort aside. A series of shouts penetrated the sacking, but they came so suddenly and so fast that he could not identify them. What he did hear very clearly was the opening of two huge wooden gates. As the hinges squealed there were more shouts, then the horses went forward and met more cobbles.

Gervase decided that they must be in the courtyard of a castle. No time was allowed for more speculations. He was unstrapped from the horse and pulled from its back by two men. They dragged him without ceremony towards another door and banged on its iron studs. Bolts and a key were heard this time. When the second door swung open to admit them, their prisoner was taken down a circular staircase that seemed to burrow to the very centre of the earth. Gervase complained noisily as he scuffed the hard stone, but his captors paid no heed.

A third door was opened by a key and then a fourth. He had finally come to the end of his journey. One of the men untied the sack and lifted it from his head. The other man kicked him hard. Gervase went sprawling headfirst into a pile of noisome straw. As the door clanged shut behind him, he was back in thick darkness again.

The dungeon was damp and inhospitable. The reek of filth and excrement clutched at his nostrils like a hand. Breathing stertorously, he rolled over on his back and tried to assess his injuries. Blood was trickling down his forehead after its collision with the floor, and a few pieces of sodden straw clung to his face. His limbs and body were racked with pain, but nothing seemed to be broken.

Gervase was about to take a more detailed inventory when something was borne in upon him. He was not alone. A loud rustle in the straw made him tense. Still bound, he was completely at the mercy of an attacker.

"Who's there?!" he yelled.

"Cyfaill!" said a soothing voice. *"Croeso!"*

The hall at the castle of Ewyas Harold was filled with noise and laughter. Maurice Damville was a man with an insatiable appetite for pleasure. Seated at the head of the table, he ate voraciously and drank to excess. His knights revelled in his company. Their lord could be ruthless, often perverse, and sometimes utterly depraved, but he had a vein of generosity that made his vices seem less objectionable. When they were entertained at the castle the men were always given a lavish banquet. There were no ladies this time, no minstrels, and no dancers, but the feast was above reproach.

Damville ordered his cup to be filled with more wine.

"I will have to teach her to make this," he said before taking a long sip. "One of many things I will teach her!"

"Who, my lord?" asked Huegon.

"Who else?"

"Aelgar?"

"The fairest maid in the county," said Damville. "There is no stain on her beauty save one—she makes ale! I'll not have that Saxon piss in my castle. Aelgar will learn to tend a vineyard and make the finest wine."

Huegon was surprised. "Will she be here long enough?"

"Of course."

"Ladies enough have already graced your bed, my lord."

"They shall do so again, Huegon. Your argument?"

"It is merely an observation."

"Let's hear it. Come, man. You'll not offend me."

"Well, my lord," said Huegon, carefully. "In that case, I have to point out that your passions rarely last a week."

Damville guffawed. "They rarely last five minutes if she is just some comely milkmaid with the morning sun upon her hair!" His laughter faded. "But you are right, Huegon. Women arouse me and my interest soon wanes.

That is what makes Aelgar so different. I have wanted her for *months*. The longer she keeps me at bay, the more I respect and desire her. Aelgar is not like the others, Huegon. My passion will not be extinguished after a few nights of madness between those thighs of hers."

"What are you telling me, my lord?"

"When she moves into the castle, she stays."

Huegon pursed his lips. "Is that advisable?"

"It is what I wish."

"But the girl is a mere Saxon."

"Of noble family. You can see it in her bearing."

"Your own dear wife is due to visit Ewyas Harold in—"

"She can be stopped," said Damville. "My wife and family belong in Normandy and there they'll stay. I'll have another wife at this castle. Aelgar." He grinned at the steward. "I look to you to give the bride away. Bend your thoughts to it. I want the nuptials without the wedding itself. Charm the lady. Talk her into my bed."

"That will not be easy, my lord."

"There have been troublesome courtships before."

"Not like this one. She has a sister, Golde. Some might say her equal in beauty. A determined lady, by all accounts. It will be difficult to prise Aelgar away from her."

"Then I'll take both at once!" roared Damville. "Two sisters in one bed. We'll make something much sweeter than ale between us." A shadow of guilt passed across his face. "No, Huegon. It must not be like that. Aelgar is enough in herself. She is very special to me."

"So I see, my lord."

"I *need* her!"

Aelgar stared into the dying embers of the fire. It was only kept alight so that it could be used for cooking, but she huddled over it. On a warm evening, she was shivering. The sound of the bolt made her look up. The servant girl was shutting up the house for the night.

"Golde has not returned yet," she said in dismay. "Do not lock my sister out."

"She will not come back tonight."

"How do you know?"

"It is too dark. The city gates are closed."

Aelgar was pitched into an even greater state of anxiety. Golde was her only support. Her sister had warned her that there was a possibility that she might have to spend the night away, but Aelgar had not taken that threat seriously. It now confronted her with quiet menace.

She would have to spend a whole night alone with her grief and apprehension. Golde had nursed her until now. Her absence was devastating. Aelgar would have to lie by herself in the darkness, mourning a man she loved and fearing a man she hated. Warnod was dead, but Maurice Damville was still hideously alive. She could not hold him off forever.

Aelgar snatched up a knife from the table and hurried off to bed. The weapon was not only for her protection. As she lay brooding in the darkness, she turned its point towards her beleaguered heart.

Hours had passed. He could wait in Llanwarne no longer. When Gervase Bret did not make his way to the village, Ralph Delchard knew that some mishap had befallen him. Against the advice of the sheriff, he decided to lead a search party. He and his four knights were soon galloping hard in the direction of Richard Orbec's demesne.

They did not have to ride far across his land. It was a fine night and their torches made them visible for miles.

Word of their arrival was quickly taken to Orbec himself. As Ralph led his men into a hollow by a stream, he was suddenly met by a wide semicircle of flame.

Twenty armed men held a torch apiece. In the flickering light they were ghostly. Ralph and his men reined in their horses. Richard Orbec had a sword in his hand as he eased his horse forward. His voice was steely.

"Who is it that dares to trespass on my land?"

"Ralph Delchard."

"Turn round and ride straight back," said Orbec.

"Not until I find Gervase Bret."

"He is not here, my lord."

"I believe that he is."

"No," said Orbec. "We stopped him as we will stop you and anyone else reckless enough to tread on my land. He left hours ago with his companions."

"They came back," explained Ralph, "but he did not. Gervase is like me, my lord. He is not easily frightened. Since he could not come here by right, he came by stealth. When your back was turned, he made his way onto Orbec territory—as you well know. Hand him over!"

"He is not in my custody."

"God help you if he has come to any harm!"

"It has not been at my hands."

"Gervase is here!" yelled Ralph. "Surrender him!"

"I cannot and I would not."

Richard Orbec came close to look him full in the face.

"I speak in all honesty," he said. "Your friend is not here. If he had been taken by my men—let me be honest about this as well—he would have been punished in a manner that he would not forget. He was warned, my lord, and I do not make idle warnings."

"Neither do I!" retorted Ralph.

"Leave my land while you still may."

Ralph reached for his sword, but thought better of it.

"Do you swear that Gervase is not held by you?"

"On my honour!" vowed Orbec.

Ralph Delchard was totally bewildered.

"Then where, in God's name, is he?"

Gervase Bret forced himself up into a sitting position and turned his back so that his bound wrists were facing his companion. The man was old, but his fingers were nimble. Feeling his way to the ropes, he undid them in a minute. Gervase massaged his wrists then shook his hands vigorously in the air to restore some movement to them. When his fingers began to obey him again, he used them to loosen the bonds around his ankles. Aching in every joint, he stood up and stretched himself properly.

"Thank you," he said.

"I am glad to be of service. Who are you?"

"My name is Gervase Bret."

"I am Omri."

The old man spoke no English, but Gervase knew more than a smattering of Welsh. It had served him well during their visit to the Savernake Forest in Wiltshire, but it would be even more crucial here. The son of a Breton father, Gervase had learned his father's native tongue, a language that had a close affinity with Welsh. Conversation, though halting at times, was therefore possible.

"Where are we?" asked Gervase.

"I do not know."

"How were you brought here?"

"By horsemen. We were ambushed."

"We?"

"There were ten of us," said Omri. "Travelling north from Caerleon on an important errand. They attacked us near Raglan. We stood no chance."

"Where are the others?"

"Only two of us survived."

Omri was a tall, cadaverous, white-haired man with huge eyes that seemed to glow in the dark. Gervase could only make out a vague shape in the gloom, but the eyes told him where the long, narrow face was. Omri was a benign presence. His voice was deep and mellifluous.

"How long have you been here?" said Gervase.

"A day that seems like a year."

"And you did not see where they brought you?"

The old man laughed softly. "No, I did not."

"What is the joke?"

"It is only comical to those who know me, Gervase. In Wales I have another name. Omri Dall."

"Omri the Blind."

Gervase was covered in embarrassment and started to apologise, but the old man cut him short. He was in no way offended by the mistake.

"Besides," he said, "we meet on equal terms."

"Equal terms?"

"Both locked in a world of darkness."

"But where?" said Gervase. *"Where?"*

"It should not be too difficult to work out," said Omri. "Captured at Raglan then taken at a canter for no more than a couple of hours or so. That could put us in Chepstow."

"Chepstow Castle?"

"Though my guess would be Monmouth."

"Would it?"

"Did you not hear that river?" said the old man. "A steady flow, but nothing like the torrent of the Wye as it races towards the estuary. Our river is the Monnow. Smaller and more obedient. This castle must be Monmouth."

Gervase was slightly relieved at the news. Monmouth put them much closer to his place of capture than Chepstow, but he was still being held against his will.

"Why were you brought here?" asked Omri.

"I do not know."

"How were you taken?"

With great difficulty, Gervase pieced the story together, as much for his own benefit as for that of his companion. Omri listened intently throughout, intrigued by the reason that first took Gervase to Herefordshire.

"We have heard of this famous Domesday Book."

"It is a description of all England."

"Then I am glad that I live in Wales."

"When it is completed, it will be an extraordinary document," said Gervase. "It touches the lives of everyone in the nation."

"Perhaps that is why you are here, my young friend."

"Here?"

"Someone may not want his life touched."

Gervase immediately thought of Richard Orbec. The latter would yield nothing to the commissioners in the shire hall and it was on his land that Gervase had been attacked. Puzzled by his own presence in the dungeon, he was yet able to show an interest in Omri's plight.

"Where were you travelling?" he asked.

"To the court of Cadwgan ap Bleddyn."

"The prince of Powys?"

"I was to have sung at a banquet," explained the old

man. "And told fortunes to those brave enough to know them."

"You are a minstrel?"

"Bard, jester, and seer. Send for Omri Dall and you get all three of me. I can beguile you with a song, amuse you with a jest, or terrify you with a look into the future."

"I will settle for your friendship," said Gervase.

"A day or two locked up in here," said Omri, "and you will be begging me for entertainment. The guards were kinder to me than to you." He played a chord on a harp. "They let me keep my instrument. I take that as a good omen."

"You said earlier, I believe, that you travelled on an important errand."

"That is so. I was carrying a message."

"From whom?"

"Friend to friend."

"From Caerleon to Powys."

"My life is an endless journey around the courts of Welsh princes," said Omri. "I am known and trusted by all. Seek for me in Powys and you will find I have ridden on to Gwynedd. Ask for me there and they will tell you I am in Ceredigion. By the time you catch up with me, my songs are lifting the spirit in Brycheiniog."

"What do you sing about?"

"What else, but Wales?"

Gervase was reminded of the Archdeacon of Llandaff. Both men had a deep and loving patriotism. While Idwal was relentlessly argumentative, however, Omri was gentle and unforced. The Welsh churchman used words to batter his adversaries into defeat; the Welsh bard was more likely to lull them into agreement with a sly melody.

Under other circumstances, Gervase would have found the old man's company enchanting, but a higher priority occupied his mind. He had to escape. Someone needed him out of the way for a particular reason. His attackers could just as easily have killed him as knock him senseless. Instead, they chose to spirit him out of Archenfield. Gervase was anxious to find out why and he could not do that while he was imprisoned in the dungeon of Monmouth Castle.

One thing was certain. Ralph Delchard would be looking for him. His friend would already have initiated a search. Ralph would not rest until Gervase had been tracked down, but that might take an extremely long time. Castle dungeons were holes in the region of hell. Once thrown into them, prisoners did not often come out alive.

Escape for him meant escape for his companion as well.

"You did not tell me the nature of your message."

"No," said Omri. "I did not."

"Do you take it from one prince to another?"

"I would be a poor messenger if I could not keep a secret. Who would put water in a bucket that leaks?"

"All I wish to know," said Gervase, "is whether or not you were expected in Powys."

"Cadwgan ap Bleddyn himself awaits our arrival."

"Will he not be vexed when you do not appear?"

"Not vexed, Gervase. Moved to anger."

"And what will he do?"

The old Welshman played a few chords on his harp.

"Send someone to rescue us."

* * *

Darkness slowed Goronwy and his men, but it did not stop their punitive ride south. Travellers who had helped them were brushed harshly aside. Those with no useful information to impart were either beaten or wounded for their lack of cooperation. As warriors of the prince of Powys, they were fierce and peremptory, but Goronwy was fired by a deeper commitment. He had a personal stake in this act of revenge.

A mile from Bryngwyn, they finally picked up the trail. A shepherd boy was sleeping under a hedge near his flock. The sound of their horses brought him awake and their torches made him blink and shield his eyes. Dressed in a sheepskin, he was no more than sixteen.

"Where are we, boy?" demanded Goronwy.

"Near Bryngwyn, my lord. On the road to Raglan."

"You live nearby?"

"Our sheep graze these hills."

"And you tend them?"

"Night and day, my lord."

"Then you'll have good eyes," said Goronwy, "and a fine view of the road from on high. Help me, boy, or you'll have a lot less sheep still standing on four legs."

"I'll help you all I can," said the boy, terrified.

"We look for travellers who may have passed this way early this morning."

"How many in number, my lord?"

"No more than ten or twelve. Two people with an armed escort, riding towards the Black Mountains."

"I do not remember them, my lord."

Goronwy bent down to lift him bodily into the air.

"Think carefully, boy," he warned. "I do not want to be known as Goronwy the Sheep Killer, but I'll slaughter all your flock if it is the only way to get the truth out of

134

you. Ten or twelve travellers. One of them, an old man, tall and spare, with white hair blowing in the wind. If you saw him once, you would not forget Omri Dall."

"I saw him not at all."

"Will you lie to me?" He shook the boy and dropped him to the ground. "I ask you one more time. Did you see them?"

"Not riding north, my lord," gibbered the boy. "I saw a troop of soldiers, but they were heading south at a gallop. And there were twenty or more of them in all."

"When was this?"

"A few hours after dawn."

"On this road?"

"No, my lord. They came on the road from Monmouth."

"And where did you see them?"

"Just below Raglan," said the boy, pointing. "Some of my sheep had strayed and I went to catch them. I was up there when I heard all the noise."

"What noise?"

"Screams and shouts. It frightened me, my lord. I ran away and have not dared to go back since."

"Show us the place."

"It is dark."

"Take us there *now*!"

The boy was hauled up from the ground once more and put astride the back of Goronwy's horse. Clinging on for dear life, he was taken along the track at a brisk trot. He showed them where he had been that morning and indicated the clump of trees from which the disturbance had come.

Goronwy flung him aside and led his men at a canter towards the trees, their torches moving like a giant serpent through the night. Dismounting at the edge of the trees, they formed a line to begin their search. It was soon over.

The first body lay against the trunk of an elm, impaled by a spear. Another soldier was hanging lifelessly over a fallen log, like a rag doll. Two more had their throats cut and a third had been felled with an axe. The last three bodies were in a tight group, as if struck down while trying to defend someone.

With a torch in his hand, Goronwy kicked each body over to search his face with the darting light. Eight soldiers were accounted for, but there was no sign of the two people they had been guarding. Goronwy ordered his men to widen the search, but no more bodies could be found.

Standing amid the corpses, he let out a hiss of relief.

"Still alive!"

Chapter Seven

THE MANOR HOUSE IN PENCOED WAS A TYPICAL Saxon dwelling. Long, low, and built of stout oak, it consisted of a series of small bays which were used as rooms for family members and guests. Candles burned to illumine a house with ample space, but little practical comfort. Though the thegn offered his hospitality freely, it did not meet the standards of his Norman guests. Canon Hubert complained about the smell of animals inside the building. It reminded him uncomfortably of Idwal's cloak. There was another reason why some of them felt uneasy under its thatched roof. The house was very similar in shape and structure to the one in which Warnod had been burned to death.

Ralph Delchard was quite unable to sleep. He was too puzzled and disturbed by the disappearance of Gervase Bret. He chided himself for not being able to find his friend and vowed to resume the search in earnest the next morning. The confrontation with Richard Orbec had left him furious, but it had eliminated the obvious suspect. Gervase had not, in fact, been caught and punished by Orbec himself. Ralph was certain of that.

Recrimination made him restless. The house was far too stuffy for his lungs. Ralph let himself out quietly to get some fresh air and walked to the stables at the rear of the building. Leaning on a fence, he gazed upward and searched the heavens for the answers that he could not find elsewhere. Where was Gervase? Had he been ambushed? Injured when thrown from his horse? Attacked by wild animals? Or did he just get hopelessly lost? Was he simply spending the night elsewhere?

The more he thought about it, the more convinced he became that Gervase had met with trouble. Archenfield was no place for a lone rider. Warnod was a denizen of the area, yet he had come to grief. On the very day that Aelgar consented to be his wife, he was murdered in the most brutal and calculating way. His happiness had been snatched from him. Had Gervase fallen foul of the same band of killers? What dreadful fate would they devise for him?

Ralph was still agonising when he heard the furtive tread of feet directly behind him. In a flash, his dagger was in his hand and he whirled round to defend himself.

Golde let out a small cry of alarm and stepped back.

"It is me, my lord!" she said.

"Golde?"

"I could not sleep. I heard someone leave the house."

"It is so with me," he said, sheathing his dagger. "My mind is in turmoil. Gervase is my dearest friend, almost a son to me. I will never forgive myself if anything untoward has befallen him."

"I have prayed for his safe return."

"Canon Hubert and Brother Simon were on their knees for an hour to the same end. They blame themselves for allowing him to go off alone to Richard Orbec's demesne." He gave a grim chuckle. "If prayers have any power, theirs will batter on the doors of heaven itself.

Hubert can turn supplication into a most persuasive weapon."

"What of you, my lord?" she said. "Have you not offered up a prayer of your own?"

"No, Golde. That is not my way."

An owl hooted in the woods nearby. They were startled.

"I am too much on edge," said Ralph with a smile. "A wise old bird in a tree can make me jump. Night belongs to him and his kind. We are interlopers."

"There is nothing more you may do until morning."

"That is true."

"Be kind to yourself and try to get some rest."

"I may say the same to you."

Golde smiled quietly. "I am happy where I am."

There was a long pause. Ralph stood close in the half-dark and inhaled her fragrance. Its sweetness enchanted him. Golde had removed her wimple and brushed out her hair. He could see the outline of her tresses as they rested on her shoulders.

"I wish that we met in happier circumstances," he said.

"We have met, my lord. That is pleasure enough."

"But I am vexed by the loss of a companion, you by the death of a close friend."

"A shared anxiety gives us a bond," she said, "though I must correct one thought. Warnod was no close friend of mine. He was my sister's choice. I weep as much for her as for him. Aelgar has lost everything."

"Except you."

"Except me, my lord."

"You must love her deeply to go to so much trouble."

"I promised her to find out the truth," said Golde. "It is the only way to put her mind at rest."

"The truth might destroy her peace entirely."

"No, my lord. Aelgar has many frailties, but she also has an inner strength. Uncertainty is what will gnaw into her soul. She must *know*. Who killed her man? And why? However ugly the facts, she is ready to confront them."

"And you, Golde?"

"Me?"

"Can *you* stare the hideous facts in the face?"

She nodded. "It would not be the first time, my lord."

A wolf howled in the distance, but neither of them even heard it now. They were too locked into each other to listen to anything more than the words that were spoken between them. Ralph felt strangely coy. He wanted to reach out to take her in his arms, but he was almost tentative.

"Why did you never marry again?" he asked.

"Because that is no route to happiness for me."

"When did your husband die?"

"Three years ago, my lord."

"You have never looked at another man since?"

"I have looked at several and found them wanting."

"Did they not measure up to your husband?" he asked. "Is that why you have remained a widow? Because you are still mourning the one man who made you content?"

"No," she said, softly. "There was no contentment in my marriage. I was a faithful wife, but I could never love my husband. Companionship was the most that I could hope."

"Not love him? Why, then, did you marry him?"

"Of necessity."

"You were forced into this match?"

"It was arranged for me. I protested in vain."

"Could your father be so unkind?" said Ralph, earnestly.

"Did he have no concern for his daughter's feelings? What made him wed you to a man whom you wished to put aside?"

"You, my lord. You and others like you."

He understood. Golde's father was one more victim of the Norman occupation, a proud Saxon thegn whose wealth and position had been reduced to insignificance. Where he might have offered the hand of his elder daughter to the son of another noble house, he was instead compelled to marry her off to a brewer from Hereford. Golde was accustomed to a life of recurring loss. She was resilient enough to survive, but it had given her a slightly cynical edge.

"Thus it stands with me, my lord," she said with a resigned shrug. "I knew misery with my husband. I sometimes wonder if it is even possible to be happy in marriage."

"It is," said Ralph. "I have known that joy."

"Then I envy you."

"Perhaps I should envy you, Golde."

"Why?"

"Because you were able to put your marriage behind you and start afresh. Your life is better without your husband." He turned away with a sigh. "Without my dear wife, mine is far worse. I still grieve over the loss of that brief joy."

Ralph was astonished. He never talked about his wife to his friends, let alone to strangers. When he was standing alone in the moonlight with a beautiful woman, his marriage was the last thing he wanted to think about. Yet his words had come out so naturally. He felt no embarrassment. Golde had confided in him and produced an answering confession.

141

She touched his shoulder with the tip of her fingers. Ralph took her hand and kissed it tenderly. When he tried to enfold her in his arms, however, she held him off.

"This is not the time, my lord."

"I want you," he whispered.

"There are too many other things in the way."

"That is the only reason?"

"It is reason enough."

"Then you are not offended?"

Golde moved in close to brush her lips against his.

"No, my lord," she said. "I am delighted."

Pain and exhaustion finally overcame him. Gervase Bret fell asleep with his back up against the wall and his legs in the straw. Slumber was no escape from tribulation. His dream tormented him afresh. He was riding across Richard Orbec's land once more when rough hands fell upon him and he was bound securely. Instead of being tied to a horse, however, he was strapped to the back of a huge red dragon, which galloped along the Welsh border, breathing fire and defiance in equal measure. Gervase was helpless. The creature's spikes dug into his body. Its scales rubbed his skin raw. Its long tail curled up to thresh his back unmercifully until it ran with a waterfall of blood.

The dragon seemed to get bigger, the ropes tighter, and the pain more excruciating. Gervase had never known such agony. His grotesque mount was racing faster than ever. It suddenly stopped beside a river and rippled its whole body. Gervase was thrown high into the air before sailing down towards an outcrop of rock. He yelled in terror.

The cry and the bump brought him awake. The fiery

dragon was no more than a gentle old man, plucking at the strings of his harp. The blood down his back had been the trickling moisture that ran down the wall. Thrown from the scales of a giant beast, he had simply fallen sideways and hit the ground in the dungeon.

Gervase collected himself and sat up again.

"I am sorry if I startled you, Omri."

"Nothing can do that."

"How long was I asleep?"

"Long enough."

"Is it night or day?"

"Still night," said the Welshman. "Day will poke a finger of light in at you if you stay where you are now."

"There is a window?"

"High in the wall behind me. When they put me in here, I felt my way around every inch of the cell. If you have no eyes, you learn to see with your fingers." He put the harp aside and groped for something in the straw. "We are not alone down here, Gervase. We share this mean lodging with a tenant of much longer standing."

"A tenant?"

"Here he is."

Omri pulled the skull from the straw and offered it to Gervase. The latter shrank back for a second then mastered his fear. He took the skull and brushed the tufts of straw away from it. A beetle crawled out of one of its eye sockets.

"Who do you suppose he was?"

"Yet another nameless prisoner of fate," said Omri.

"Where is the rest of him?"

"In the far corner. I covered his bones with straw."

"Poor man!"

"He has not been very talkative," said Omri with a wry

143

smile. "That is the trouble with the dead. They do not speak Welsh."

"He was thrown in here and left to rot!" said Gervase with sudden alarm. "The same ordeal may await us."

"I think not, my friend."

"They'll let us starve to death in this hole."

"We will live. That much is very clear."

"Why?"

"Because our enemies do not need to kill us slowly when they could have done it much more swiftly on the road." He gave a chuckle. "Besides, they have fed me twice since I have been in here. Bread, water, and the remains of a chicken. This form of starvation is a tasty way to die."

Gervase was reassured. As he shook the last vestiges of sleep from his eyes, his mind cleared. His captors had gone to great trouble to bring him across the border into Gwent. Had Richard Orbec feared that Gervase might see too much on his clandestine visit to the disputed land? Or had someone else decided that the best way to halt the work of the commissioners was to remove one of them from the scene? Monmouth Castle was a Norman citadel on Welsh territory. Had it been taken? Was the red dragon on the rampage again?

Omri the Blind might hold some of the answers.

"Only two of you survived," he said. "Two from ten."

"That is so."

"Then where is your companion?"

"I do not know, Gervase."

"Locked in another dungeon?"

Omri measured his reply. "My companion is . . . somewhere in the castle. But not in such a miserable condition as us."

"How can you be so sure?"

"Instinct, my friend."

"Why were you two spared?"

"We are not soldiers. We were unarmed."

"All the easier to cut you down where you stood."

"They preferred to keep us alive, Gervase."

"For what purpose?"

"This is one," said Omri, taking up the harp again to conjure some music from its strings. "There are no bards in England but they are revered in Wales."

"Throwing you in here is an act of reverence?"

"I still breathe, I still eat, I still sing."

"And your companion?"

Omri sighed. "I am more concerned about him than about myself. Though I have sung at the courts of the great and the good, I have slept in barns and fields along the way. This dungeon stinks no worse than a stable. I can put up with it. My companion is less robust."

"Young and vulnerable, then?"

"Do not bother about him, Gervase," advised the old man. "Think only of yourself. Our case is different. We were brought here for one purpose, you for another."

"You were ambushed in Wales and brought here," said Gervase, puzzled. "Why to Monmouth? We have heard no rumours of insurrection. Can the castle be in Welsh hands?"

Omri the Blind went off into a fit of laughter.

"Alas, no!" he said. "If it were, I would not be down here with you. I would be up there in the hall, celebrating the occasion with a song of victory. Monmouth, I fear, is still a Norman castle."

"Then why do they hold me here?" said Gervase with

a burst of indignation. "Do they know who I am? *What* I am?"

"Only too well, I suspect."

Gervase became restless. Rising to his feet, he picked his way around the little rectangle of stone and accumulated filth. When his foot met the pile of bones, he laid the skull gently beside them. Omri's reconnaissance had been thorough. The window was high in one wall, set in a deep recess and slashed by thick bars. Standing on tiptoe, he could just touch the iron with his fingers. A welcome gust of air filtered in. Thin shafts of light would follow in time.

"That is not the way, Gervase," murmured Omri.

"What?"

"You will never escape through that window."

"How else?"

"Through the door."

"We could never budge it."

"They can," said the old man. "With a key. It depends on how eager you are to get free of this foul."

"I would do *anything*, Omri."

"Even take a man's life?"

Gervase hesitated. "Only if my own were in danger."

"Practice with your weapon."

"They took away my sword and dagger."

"A piece of rope can be as deadly a weapon as either," said Omri. "And they left you with two lengths of it."

Gervase stirred with excitement. There was hope.

Goronwy waited until first light before he ordered a more detailed search. He and his men had camped beside the clump of trees near Raglan. Dawn found them spread across a mile or more as they looked for more bodies.

None were found. Goronwy gathered his soldiers in the shade of the trees and assigned new duties.

Two of them rode back towards Powys to take news of the ambush to Cadwgan ap Bleddyn. Two more carried the same message along the road towards Caerleon. A burial detachment was formed and the eight soldiers from the escort were laid in shallow graves to protect their bodies from scavengers. The stench of death was already beginning to spread.

Sleep had not dulled Goronwy's rage. When he and his men rode up to Raglan itself, the young man's temples were still pulsing madly. He had found the reason for the delay and buried the victims of the attack. Rescue and retribution were now his twin aims. Raglan itself was a tiny hamlet made up of mean cottages. A mangy goat was tethered outside one dwelling. Chickens squawked outside another. Sheep ranged the hills all around.

The meagre population was dragged from its hovels to face Goronwy's stern interrogation. They were simple souls. Their testimony was honest. They had seen the soldiers come down the road from Monmouth and they had heard the sounds of the attack. Beyond that, they had little to add. Violence had locked them indoors. They had been too frightened to venture out to see the results of the ambush.

Their description of the soldiers matched that of the shepherd boy who had been questioned in the night. Goronwy at least knew one vital fact. Welsh soldiers had been killed by Norman attackers. The armed escort from Caerleon had been ambushed by men from across the border.

Brandishing his sword, Goronwy rode up and down.

"Is there anything else you can tell us?"

147

"No, my lord," said the one of the peasants.

"Did you not hear anything as they went past?"

"Nothing."

"No word? No command? No name?"

Another man edged forward. "I heard a name, my lord."

"What was it?"

"The soldiers rode past my door as I was putting the harness on my donkey. A name was spoken and they laughed."

"What name?"

"Cruel laughter, my lord. It made my blood run cold."

Goronwy knocked him over with the flat of his sword.

"The name, you idiot!" he snarled. "What was the name?"

"Richard Orbec."

Richard Orbec led the retreat at full gallop, taking his men in a wide loop before powering down the hill towards the house. Forty knights were sweating in their armour in the morning sun. Some carried spears, but most had swords in their hands. Their horses sent up a flurry of earth and grass as they descended the hill in an ordered retreat.

Orbec himself was first across the drawbridge and first to dismount inside the palisade. His men poured in through the gates and tugged their animals to a halt before jumping from the saddle. The drawbridge was hauled up and the gates were shut. On their lord's command, the knights ran to defend various points on the ramparts against an invisible enemy.

It was an impressive performance, but it did not

entirely satisfy Orbec. He pulled off his helm and beckoned his captain across.

"We are still too slow," he said, sharply.

"We can ride no faster, my lord."

"The men can be deployed more effectively once they are inside the defences. The weak point is at the rear of the house."

"Yes, my lord."

"Station four more archers there."

"I will."

"We'll have fresh timber cut to strengthen the palisade."

The captain nodded. "Is that all for today, my lord?"

"We will practice one more time."

"We are as ready now as we will ever be."

"That is what I once thought," said Orbec, crisply. "In Normandy. You can never prepare enough for any eventuality. Trouble may strike when we least expect it. The speed of our response must be decisive."

"Yes, my lord."

"Mount up again! We'll ride in from the east this time."

Canon Hubert and Brother Simon were conscientious members of the commission. The Domesday returns for Herefordshire had thrown up a number of irregularities and it was their task to look into them. One of their number had unaccountably disappeared and a second had gone in search of him. Hubert and Simon felt it their duty to press on with the allotted task on their own. The village of Llanwarne could not provide them with a shire hall, but they could still examine a witness, if only in an informal manner.

Ilbert the Sheriff was very restive under questioning.

"I am not involved in this enquiry in any way!"

"We believe that you are, my lord sheriff," said Hubert.

"The dispute is between Maurice Damville and Richard Orbec."

"It also concerns Warnod."

"His last remains are six feet below the earth."

"A legacy yet survives."

"Legacy?"

"Yes," said Hubert. "Far be it from me to prefer the claim of a Saxon thegn over that of two Norman lords, but justice must be served here. This great survey of ours is not simply an inventory of the nation's wealth. It brings to light theft, fraud, forgery, wrongful annexation, and all the other appalling abuses that have taken place in the shires."

"You talked of a legacy."

"Warnod had a legitimate claim to the land that is part of Richard Orbec's holdings. If that claim is upheld— and it lies within our power to make that judgment—then the property passes to Warnod's heir."

"He has no heir."

"How do you know?"

"He lived alone. Without kith or kin."

"That is so," conceded Hubert, "but property may be willed to close friends just as easily as to family."

"And it may be willed to the Church," noted Simon.

Ilbert Malvoisin bided his time before he spoke. He had underestimated the two men. They were shrewd and persistent. Canon Hubert was the chief inquisitor, but Brother Simon would throw in a remark from time to time to show that he had missed nothing. The sheriff looked around for a way to disentangle himself from the dialogue.

150

They had strolled to the edge of the village. The sad vestiges of Warnod's habitation could be seen in the distance. They could even pick out the mound of loose earth that had been shovelled over the red dragon.

"Did Warnod make a will?" asked Ilbert.

"Most assuredly," said Hubert.

"How can you be so certain?"

"We spoke to the priest here. He advised Warnod how the document should be drawn up. Warnod was illiterate."

"Apart from the priest, has anyone see this will?"

"Not yet."

"Is it not likely to have been consumed in the fire?"

"Warnod's claim to the land was not."

"We have that charter in our possession," said Simon.

Ilbert winced slightly. "That makes no difference," he said, recovering quickly. "The charter is useless without will, and the will is invalid without a beneficiary to urge his claim."

"The beneficiary may not be aware of his good fortune."

"That situation may remain."

Canon Hubert swatted an errant fly from his sleeve and changed the angle of attack. His tone was quite artless.

"Warnod's father was a farsighted man," he observed.

"His father?"

"A Saxon noble with several manors in this county. He did not trust Normans. He had experience of us long before the Conquest. King Edward invited many of our countrymen to this particular part of his kingdom."

"I am well aware of that, Canon Hubert."

"Warnod's father was forearmed," said the other. "When the invasion came, he knew what to expect—confiscation of his lands and a reduction of his prestige."

"The normal consequences of defeat."

"He fought to circumvent them. Rather than have his holdings taken by the state, he granted them to the Church with the proviso that he—or his heirs—might one day regain possession of them again."

"He hid his property under the skirts of religion," added Simon. "He was not alone in using this device."

"Why do you tell me all this?" grunted Ilbert.

"Because some of that land appears to have attached itself to your own holdings, my lord sheriff," said Hubert. "A few carucates here, a virgate or two there. It mounts up. Your Christian duty is to *give* to the Church, not to take from it. We see a hand in the offertory box."

"That is a monstrous accusation!"

"But not unjust."

"I made sworn statements before the first commissioners and showed them every document that was required. There was no impropriety." His voice boomed even louder. "May I remind you that I am the sheriff here, the king's own representative in this county? Do you seriously believe that a person of my eminence would stoop to the crimes that you allege?"

Hubert was bland. "I do, indeed, believe it."

"Calumny!"

"I know it to be true."

"God's blood, man!" roared Ilbert. "I am the sheriff!"

"Roger of Breteuil was the Earl of Hereford," reminded Hubert, unperturbed by the outburst. "Until he was unwise enough to join in revolt against the king. If an earl is capable of high treason in this county then its sheriff is more than capable of some astute land-grabbing."

"I was vindicated by the first commissioners."

"They did not have the full information before them."

"What information?"

"It is largely contained in Warnod's charter."

"That relates to Orbec's land," argued the sheriff with vehemence. "You said so even now. Why do you link me with this charter?"

"Tell him, Brother Simon."

The monk cleared his throat to pronounce the sentence. "Your name was written across the top of it."

A long morning in the saddle had produced no satisfactory results. Ralph Delchard and his eight men-at-arms had combed the north of Archenfield with the utmost care. They rode along and around the disputed holdings of Richard Orbec in the firm belief that he himself would have had his own land searched for any signs of an intruder. Gervase Bret was nowhere to be seen. Though they questioned everyone they passed on their way, they learned nothing of value.

They crossed the Golden Valley and headed towards Ewyas. It was conceivable that Gervase had strayed as far as Maurice Damville's land, and Ralph was keen to explore every possibility. His men fanned out across an area of a hundred yards or so, peering into ditches, searching behind bushes, and even using their swords to fish around in the water of a shallow stream. Gervase still did not appear.

Ralph tugged his horse over to the captain of his men.

"Where *can* he be?"

"I doubt that he came this far, my lord."

"He would hardly have gone back to Hereford," said Ralph. "That leaves only south and west. The curiosity that took him to Richard Orbec's land may have brought him onto Maurice Damville's estate."

"Either way he was running a risk, my lord."

"Gervase had his wits about him."

"He was still a lone man in unknown territory." He stopped his horse and gazed ahead. "The castle cannot be too far distant. We must look to receive the same welcome there that we did from Richard Orbec."

"That will not deter me," asserted Ralph. "I'll go to Damville's castle and on into Wales itself if it is the only way to track down Gervase."

A shout from one of the men directed their attention off to the left. Columns of smoke were rising steadily into the air on the far side of a wooded slope. Muffled yells could be heard. Ralph reacted quickly. Signalling his men to follow, he set off at a gallop, skirting the wood and riding down to a wide plain.

Harvesting had begun in the cornfields and the sheaves stood in rows across the fields. Five or six of the sheaves had been set alight and were blazing away. A handful of peasants were scampering around trying to move the other sheaves out of the way so that they could not be ignited by flying sparks. A few armoured knights were urging them on.

Ralph recognised Maurice Damville at once. Not content with giving orders, he had dropped from his saddle and was trying vainly to stamp out the flames that were eating one of the sheaves. Riding across to him, Ralph threw a glance at the devastation.

"Who did this?" he asked.

"Murdering Welshmen!"

"You came in time to save the bulk of the crop."

"But not to catch those devils," said Damville, turning to glare up at Ralph. "Look what they did."

"It could have been much worse."

154

"Yes. They might have butchered the rest of my sheep."

"Sheep?"

Damville pointed. "Ride over to the ditch."

Ralph and his men went in the direction indicated and found a ditch that bisected the fields. Lying on its bank was a ewe with its throat cut and its belly ripped wide open. Another animal then made a grisly appearance. Carved into the ground on the other side of the ditch, a few inches deep and three or four yards long, was a crude but unmistakeable shape. The sheep's blood had been poured into the mould and it was still lying in thick patches on the surface of the bare earth.

As the sun hit them, those vivid patches moved and shimmered with such animation that the men stepped back in alarm.

"Dear God!" said Ralph. "A red dragon! Alive!"

Night had brought her much closer to Ralph Delchard, but it had driven her even further away from the others. Canon Hubert shunned her, Brother Simon fled from her, and Ilbert the Sheriff pointedly avoided her. Golde sought the company of the one man in Llanwarne who was pleased to talk to her.

"What have you found out, Archdeacon?" she said.

"No more than I expected," said Idwal. "Warnod was not murdered by a Welshman. What would be his motive?"

"Hatred?"

"The man befriended his neighbours."

"Envy?"

He was scornful. "We would never envy the *Saeson*!"

"Malice?"

"Foreign to our nature," he said. "No, dear lady, look elsewhere for your killers. Closer to home. And when you find them, deal with them after your own fashion."

"What do you mean?"

"This is Ergyng. Welsh territory under the heel of the Normans. King William annexed this land by force, but he let us keep our customs here. Do you know how we deal with murderers?"

"No," she said. "How?"

"If a Welshman kills a Welshman, the relatives of the slain man gather and despoil the killer and his relatives, and burn their houses until the body of the dead man is buried the next day before midday."

"An eye for an eye."

"That is the custom here," explained Idwal. "The king receives a third part of the plunder, but the relatives of the slain man have the rest free."

"This is crude justice."

"Crude, but effective. It makes a man think twice before striking a blow against another."

"That custom does not apply to Warnod. He was a Saxon."

"The law differs for him. If anyone kills one of the king's men or breaks into a house, he gives the king twenty shillings as payment for the man, and a hundred shillings in forfeiture. If anyone has killed a thegn's man, he gives ten shillings to the dead man's lord."

"Warnod's death cannot be paid for with a fine."

"Which justice would you choose now: ours or yours?"

"Let us first catch the murderers," she suggested.

"Why is it so important to you?" he said, cocking his head to one side like a bird on a fence. "This is no place for a lady, especially one as gracious as you. Why are you so ready to give up the comfort of Hereford for this?"

"Warnod was a friend of my family."

"Your family?"

"He knew my father . . . and my sister."

"Ah," said Idwal, sensing a blighted romance. "That is very sad. I grieve for you—and for you sister, too. Death parts all lovers in the end, but this was a cruel divorce. It was better that you came in your sister's place. The sight of Warnod's house should not be inflicted on her."

"She will have to be told."

"Use soothing words upon her."

"I will."

"And as for you," he continued, "your duty is done. You have travelled to Ergyng and gazed upon the scene of his slaughter. Do not distress yourself by lingering further."

"But I must, Archdeacon."

"Why?"

"Until they find the killers."

"That may take days, weeks."

"I gave my solemn word to my sister."

"You have honoured it," he pointed out. "But there is nothing else that you may usefully do in Ergyng. Return to Hereford. Your sister's distress cries out to you. She needs you there to offer comfort."

"It is true," said Golde. "I must send word."

"Why send it when you can deliver it in person?" His head came upright and he scrutinised her face. "What other reason detains you here with us?"

Golde almost blushed.

* * *

They had spent the best part of a day in preparation for the event. Fed in their cell that morning, they noted every detail of the procedure. Two guards came. One unlocked the door and stood aside, leaving the key in the lock. His partner carried a rough wooden tray. On it were two cups of water and two bowls of bread soaked in milk. The tray was placed in the middle of the floor and the man departed. His colleague closed the door and locked it again.

Sufficient light striped its way into the dungeon for Gervase to pick out something of the men's appearance. The one with the tray was young and sturdy, the other was older and leaner. Their weaponry had also been noted. Both wore daggers. The older man also carried a club at his belt in case he had to subdue an unruly prisoner. They wore mailed shirts over their tunics, but both were bareheaded.

Neither of them spoke. Omri's gentle banter and Gervase's earnest pleas did not extract one word from them. They came, they fed, they went. They would come again.

"What time?" asked Gervase.

"It was mid-evening yesterday," said Omri. "About an hour or so before you arrived. They gave me time to eat my meal then cleared the things away."

They had left the tray this time and Gervase was grateful. The stout wood made a useful additional weapon. He offered it to Omri, but the old man shook his white locks.

"I am a man of peace, Gervase. I might *sing* a man to death, but that is the only assault I will offer his person."

They finalised the details of their plan and rehearsed it in the gloom. It was bold enough to work, but hazardous enough to end in disaster. They would need more than a touch of good fortune in order to succeed. Surprise was their main weapon. A blind old man with a harp would be a useful decoy.

"Supposing we do get out of here?" said Omri.

"We shall—God willing!"

"What then?"

"We leave the castle itself."

"How?"

"We'll find a way somehow."

"On foot?"

"How else?"

"I'll only slow you down."

"We'll find two horses in the town."

"Three, Gervase."

"Three?"

Omri sounded hurt. "I could never leave without my companion. We came together, we must leave together."

"But we have no means of knowing where he is."

"Leave that to me."

"Omri," said Gervase, alive to the dangers, "we cannot take anyone with us. It is out of the question."

"Then you go alone."

"Why take all that extra risk?"

"Because it is my duty," said the Welshman. "There is no other way, believe me. If I arrive in Powys alone, they will not respect my age and my reputation. I will be sorely punished for abandoning the friend who lies here."

"Would you rather stay in this fetid dungeon?"

"Yes, Gervase."

The old man was adamant. It added a new and more troublesome element to the escape attempt, but Gervase had to agree to it in the end. He turned his mind to the initial stage of their plan. Everything that followed hinged on that.

"They're not coming!" he said with concern.

"Give them time, Gervase."

"You said that it was mid-evening yesterday."

"They'll come to suit themselves," said Omri with philosophical calm. "We are not important guests. When they remember us, they'll be here."

"I hope you're right."

"Test the rope again. All depends on that."

Twenty minutes later, they heard the door at the top of the stairs open. Descent would be long and slow. They took up their positions. Omri stood beneath the window plucking his harp and singing in a deep and soulful voice. Gervase waited near the door armed with two weapons. The delay had favoured them. Light had faded badly inside the cell.

The key rasped in the lock and the door swung open. The older man who guarded it now held a lantern. The younger man entered with another tray of food, but he did not get far. As his foot caught in the taut rope that was hidden beneath the straw, he pitched forward and landed on his face, dropping tray and contents in the process. Gervase was on him at once, hammering him on the back of the head with the other tray and knocking him unconscious.

The older guard took a moment to realise what was happening. Pulling out his club, he came rushing at Gervase, but the latter was ready for him, using the tray like a shield and parrying the blows from the club. It was his second weapon that was critical. Twisted around Gervase's hand was the other length of rope. He swung it in a circle several times to build up momentum before striking with vicious force.

One blow was enough. It caught the guard on the side of the temple and sent him crashing into the wall. He slumped to the floor immediately. The human skull at the end of the rope had split on impact, but it had proved its worth. The older man would not revive for an hour.

Grabbing a dagger from the first guard, Gervase took Omri by the arm and hustled him out. He slammed the door shut and turned the key in the lock. Other keys on the same ring would take them through the doors above. They climbed slowly up the spiral staircase in the darkness. Gervase held his dagger at the ready and Omri clutched his harp.

The first stage was over. They were out.

Chapter Eight

CREEPING SHADOWS BROUGHT THE FRUITLESS SEARCH to an end. It had been a long day in the saddle and Ralph Delchard and his men were dispirited as they headed back to Llanwarne. The whole of Archenfield had now been thoroughly explored, but it yielded no clue as to the whereabouts of Gervase Bret. The Golden Valley had been traversed and they had gone deep into Maurice Damville's estates in Ewyas. Ralph had even taken his men across the Welsh border in the direction of the Black Mountains, but there was still no trace of his friend.

Canon Hubert and Brother Simon welcomed them back.

"What news?" asked Hubert, eagerly.

"Nothing good," said Ralph, dismounting from his horse. "We have not paused for one minute, but it was all to no avail. Gervase has vanished into thin air."

"Most disquieting," said Simon. "Canon Hubert and I must bear some of the blame here. We should not have left him alone to ride back to Richard Orbec's demesne."

"Gervase would not be stopped," argued Hubert.

"It was our duty to make him stop."

"Then why did you remain silent at the time?"

"I was praying for the intercession of common sense."

"There is no point in bickering," said Ralph. "I feel as

162

guilty as either of you, but the fact of the matter is that Gervase made the decision himself. And it was the right decision. He doubtless learned much of value from his secret inspection of the Orbec holdings. Unfortunately, the right decision produced an unforeseen result."

"Where did you search?" asked Hubert.

"Anywhere and everywhere. There is not a bush in Archenfield that we have not looked under. Nobody could help us and most of them could not even understand our language. I never thought I would miss so sorely the company of Idwal the Archdeacon."

Hubert flinched. "That mad Welshman?"

"We could have endured his madness for the benefit of his Welsh. Idwal would have been a quick interpreter."

"We could certainly have spared him here."

"Where else did you ride, my lord?" asked Simon.

Ralph recounted the story of the visit to Maurice Damville's demesne. They were disturbed to hear of the appearance of a second blood-red dragon and speculated endlessly on its significance.

"How did Maurice Damville receive you?" said Hubert.

"With ill grace," explained Ralph. "He demanded to know why we were trespassing on his land and urged us to leave as quickly as we had come."

"You were not invited to Ewyas Harold Castle?"

"We were not, Hubert. This Damville is a surly host. He swore that Gervase was nowhere on his estates, then sent men to escort us out of Ewyas." Ralph was simmering. "The laws of hospitality have left this benighted county untouched. Richard Orbec threatens us and Maurice Damville chases us away like boys stealing apples from his orchards. These indignities will not be borne!"

"Unleash the Celtic imbecile upon them," said Hubert. "Idwal is a red dragon in himself."

The archdeacon materialised at once out of the gloom.

"Do I hear my name being taken in vain?" he said with an amiable cackle. "That is usually an invitation to debate."

"Heaven forfend!" exclaimed Simon.

"No sign of Gervase, then?"

"No, Archdeacon," said Ralph, sadly. "None, I fear."

"Tell me all."

"When we have had refreshment. Riding through this wilderness all day is tiring business. We need food and drink to revive us. And I must first speak with someone else." He looked around for the one face that might give him solace. "Where is Golde?"

"She is gone, my lord," said Idwal.

"Gone?"

"Back home."

"To Hereford?" Ralph's heart sank. "When?"

"This afternoon. I counselled her to do so."

"Why?"

"She was needed there. Duty bade her go and I was able to strengthen its call with a homily of my own."

Ralph glowered. "You read her a homily?"

"This was no place for a lady, my lord. She should not have seen the way in which Warnod died."

"Golde came here of her own volition."

"She left at my persuasion."

"What right had you to bully her away?"

"The right that all servants of the Lord are given at ordination," said Idwal, blithely. "To help those in distress and to ease the troubled mind. Golde was greatly comforted by me. She went home to offer comfort on her

164

own account." He glowed with self-satisfaction. "Did I not do well, my lord?"

Ralph Delchard seethed with anger and disappointment. The prospect of seeing Golde again was the one bright star in an otherwise black day. Idwal the Archdeacon had robbed him of that pleasure in the name of Christian duty. Ralph became an instant apostate. He joined the long queue of people who could cheerfully throttle the little Welshman with their bare hands, seal him in a leaden casket with his homilies, and bury him in the deepest pit that could be found.

Monmouth Castle was built in a loop of the River Monnow, a narrow but fast-flowing strip of water that joined the Wye itself less than half a mile below the town. A vital stronghold that commanded the approach to South Wales, the castle was stone-built and well fortified. The gatehouse had a daunting solidity and cobbles had been set into the ground beneath it. The bailey was compact and high-walled with a mixture of timber and stone buildings.

From his hiding place in the shadows, Gervase Bret took stock of their surroundings. He could make out a chapel, a hall, workshops, stables, and a small run of farmyard buildings. What he took to be the granary also rose up at him out of the gloom. He and Omri were in luck. The bailey was largely deserted. Guards were patrolling the battlements, but they were looking outward. Crude banter came from those in the gatehouse.

The dungeons were at the lower end of the bailey. Deep and dark, hidden behind a series of heavy doors, they would smother the sound of gaolers locked in their own cells. Gervase and Omri had created time for themselves to escape.

"Where is your companion?" whispered Gervase.

"Describe what you see."

"Motte and bailey—like any other castle."

"Paint a picture," said Omri. "Give me detail."

Gervase went through an inventory, seeing more clearly as his eyes adjusted to the gloom. Omri soon responded.

"There is nowhere in the bailey to hold my friend," he decided. "Take me to the tower."

"We will never gain entry to that."

"We may not need to, Gervase."

"How, then, will you reach your companion?"

"In the way that I know best."

Gervase took his arm and guided him slowly around the perimeter of the courtyard, hugging the darkest corners and using all the cover that the various buildings offered. The motte itself was guarded by a thick stone wall, but its gates were left open to allow free access between the two parts of the castle. Gervase and Omri slipped through and flattened themselves against the cold stone.

A mound of earth now climbed dramatically in front of them. It was topped by the high stone tower in which the castellan and his family resided. No door would be left obligingly open here. Guards and guests would be inside the tower. Gervase Bret was almost ready to concede defeat.

"Take me closer," said Omri. "Up the mound."

They scrambled up the incline with great difficulty. Omri's age had taken its toll and his harp was an additional handicap. When they reached the base of the tower, the old man was panting. He needed a few minutes to get his breath back, then he tucked himself in against the stone. With deft fingers, he played a few chords on his harp.

"What are you doing?" hissed Gervase.

"Sending a message."

"You'll rouse the whole tower."

A man's head poked out of a window higher up, but soon withdrew. Evidently they were invisible from above. It gave them more confidence. With Gervase's help, Omri made his way around to the opposite side of the tower, flattening himself against its slabs before he plucked at the strings again.

This time there was more response. Two figures leaned out of one window, saw nothing, exchanged a joke, and took their laughter inside. A third figure appeared at a lower window and waved a hand. Gervase described what he could see. Omri was thrilled.

"We've found him!"

"But how do we get him down?"

"My old harp can only call him," admitted Omri. "You must do the rest, Gervase. How high is the window?"

"Twenty feet or more."

"Too high for you to climb, too long for him to jump."

"We need a rope."

Omri chuckled. "I'll wait while you fetch one."

"From where?"

Even as he asked the question, Gervase answered it. Outside the stables he had noticed a small cart, obviously used to bring provisions into the castle. When it was loaded up, it might well need ropes to secure its cargo. Gervase lay on his side and rolled swiftly down the mound until the ground finally levelled out. Running to the gate, he peered through into the bailey then stayed low as he scurried towards the stables.

Raucous laughter was still coming from the gatehouse. Nobody had yet missed or heard the two gaolers. Gervase trotted on. There were no ropes on the cart itself, but he found a coil hanging on a nail inside the stables. It was stout hemp and more than long enough for their purpose. He was about to carry it away when his eye caught something else. It was an iron bar almost three feet in length. He snatched it up and bore his booty off to the tower.

Omri was still there and the figure was still at the tower window. Gervase gestured with the rope and got a wave of acknowledgment from above. Omri was now in the way. Gervase took him gently back to the base of the mound and left him there with his harp. Ascending the incline once more, Gervase chose a point halfway up it to give himself an angle. He tied the end of the rope to the middle of the iron bar and had a few practice swings.

The figure above watched with fascination. Gervase signaled for him to withdraw into the chamber. When his target was ready, Gervase uncoiled the rope, took a firm grip on the bar, and tossed it upwards. It reached the window, but bounced off the stone. The clang brought no enquiring eyes. A second attempt also failed and made more noise. Figures appeared at two separate windows higher up the tower and looked down into the darkness for a few minutes before they finally vanished.

Gervase lay facedown on the mound until he felt it safe to look up again. The figure was back at the lower window. Something fluttered. Gervase guessed what it must be. Bedding was being placed across the stone base of the window to deaden the sound of the iron bar. It encouraged the marksman below. He waited until the space was again unoccupied before returning to his task. Holding the bar like a javelin, he hurled it straight and true. It went in through the window and landed with a muffled clink.

He was now perspiring freely with the effort and the excitement. Gervase would still have to smuggle a blind man and a youth out of the castle yard, but he would meet that problem when he came to it. Rescuing Omri's companion from the tower was his immediate concern. He lay on the mound and waited, but the window remained empty. What was causing the delay? Had the noise aroused guards in the tower? Had they rushed into the chamber where the iron bar and rope now lay?

It was several minutes before relief came. The figure returned to the window and waved. The rope dropped slightly as the iron bar was fitted across the window to act as a brace for the descent. It was not a long climb, but the figure at the window hesitated. Gervase stood up and gestured his encouragement. Every second was vital if they were to get completely away. As the body finally emerged through the window, Gervase had some idea of the age and size of their companion.

The figure was hooded and clad in a cloak. He was of medium height and lithe movement. Holding the rope in firm young fingers, he began a slow and careful descent. The iron bar was a reliable accomplice. It held the weight easily. As the youth got lower, his confidence grew. Gervase reached up to help him, his outstretched hand brushing the heels above him. There was a sudden gasp as the climber lost his nerve and let go of the rope.

Gervase broke the fall, but he was knocked over in the process. Lying across him was the sobbing figure of the youth they had come to rescue. Gervase sat up quickly to offer comfort and to still the noise, but the shock deprived him of all speech. The hood had fallen back to reveal long braided hair that fell down over one shoulder. Omri's companion was not a youth at all.

Gervase was looking into the face of a young woman.

Golde's return to Hereford brought her sister consolation and alarm. Delighted to see her, Aelgar was deeply upset by what she heard. When the death of her betrothed was a distant event in Archenfield, it had somehow not seemed quite real. Golde's visit brought it terrifyingly close. She had seen what little remained of the house in which Aelgar would have lived with her husband. Though she suppressed some facts out of kindness, Golde could not hide them all. Her sister shed many tears at the thought that the man she loved could provoke such hatred and brutality.

"Who *were* they, Golde?" she said.

"We will know in time."

"Warnod was the kindest man on earth."

"I thought him so."

"Why did they have to kill him in that way?"

"It was revolting."

"They destroyed everything that he owned."

"Not quite."

"And they destroyed me."

Golde held her close and let her cry her fill. She had been right to come back home. Her heart told her to linger in Archenfield, but her head urged a return to Hereford. It was unfair to steal fleeting joy at the expense of her sister. Idwal's advice had been unwelcome at the time, but she now accepted its soundness.

Regrets were inevitable, but her life had been strewn

with them. Ralph Delchard was merely the latest. Golde forced herself to believe that he would not, in any case, have had any time for her. With a lost companion to find, a murder to solve, and official business to transact, he could not be bothered with the widow of a Hereford brewer. Golde had good reason to see him again, but it would be on a more formal basis. Those moments alone in the moonlight at Pencoed were the sum of their happiness together.

Aelgar wiped away her tears with the back of her hand.

"Now that Warnod has gone, who will look after me?"

"I will."

"But that it not fair to you, Golde."

"Let me be the judge of that."

"I should not be such a terrible burden on you."

"We are sisters."

"You are entitled to a life of your own."

"I have one."

"Not while I am here," said Aelgar, softly. "That was why I was so pleased when Warnod asked me to marry him. Pleased for myself, of course, but pleased for you as well."

"Me?"

"You carried me for long enough. Warnod was taking the load off your shoulders. Because of you I found my way to some happiness." She took Golde by the shoulders. "I thought that when I went to live in Archenfield you would be free to seek some happiness for yourself. You deserve it." There were tears in Golde's eyes now. "Do not let my misery drag you down. I hate the feeling that I hold you back."

"I am content to share my life with you, Aelgar."

"Think of yourself for once. I did."

"You?"

"I was ready to leave you for Warnod."

"You loved him."

"Cannot you also love, sister?"

"Oh, yes," sighed Golde.

Aelgar stood up and walked around the little room. She felt reassured by her sister's presence, but she had not forgotten the visitor who came calling. As she remembered the face of Maurice Damville at her window, she trembled all over.

"He came for me again, Golde."

"When?"

"Yesterday. After you left with those men."

"What did he do? What did he say?" asked Golde with sudden anger. "Did he get into the house? Did he touch you?"

"Not with his hands," said Aelgar. "Only with words. But they were almost as bad. He said he would be back one day, and I am frightened. Warnod had shielded me from him, but Warnod is no longer here. Who will save me, Golde?"

"I will," she said firmly. "Have no fear. I will save you from Maurice Damville."

The two guards chatted quietly on the battlements. Their eyes flicked occasionally to the great black void beyond the castle. Wales seemed closer and more oppressive at night. They felt sometimes as if they could reach out and touch the mountains. The men shared a joke and laughed.

Their backs were turned to the figure who crept up the steps with a dagger in his hand. They did not hear his soft tread or see his darting movement. He chose his moment and struck. A foot in the small of the back propelled one of the guards hard against the stone wall. The other man was felled with a blow and lay flat on his back with a knife at his throat. A knee pressed hard into his chest.

"Get up!" snarled Maurice Damville, himself rising.

"Is it you, my lord?" asked the man on the ground.

"Yes, but it could just as easily have been an enemy. Some rebel Welshman or one of Orbec's men. Or even some foolish Saxon who thinks his lord works him too hard for too little." He kicked the man hard. "You were not ready!"

"No, my lord," admitted the other guard, still dazed.

"One man could have killed the two of you."

"We guarded the wall. You came behind us."

"So might your foes!" said Damville, feinting with the dagger to give the man another scare. "Guards are here to guard everything—including their own backs."

"Yes, my lord."

Maurice Damville was in a dark tunic that blended with the night. The time for feasting was over and his men had to be kept on the alert. He believed in testing his defences for himself. When they were next on guard duty, these two soldiers would not so easily lose their concentration. He had cured them of that. It was important that the castle of Ewyas Harold was securely defended twenty-four hours a day.

Both men had got up now and were dusting themselves off. One of them marched back to his post further along the wall. The other watched his master nervously. Damville put a foot up on the wall and stared out into the dark.

"We must be ready," he said quietly. "At all times."

"Will they come, my lord?" asked the man.

"Oh, yes."

"Are you sure?"

"They will come."

Goronwy overcame the barrier of language by sheer force. He could speak no English and the man could speak no Welsh, but the young captain soon made himself understood. Two of his soldiers stripped the man's tunic off so that his back was exposed. They each pulled a wrist so that the victim was in an attitude of crucifixion. Goronwy's whip took over the conversation. Six searing blows ripped the skin away and left rivulets of blood all over the man's torso. His screams echoed through the rustling trees.

They had reached the English border and crossed over into Archenfield. Their victim was a hapless Saxon freeman who was returning home late to his cottage. Goronwy's men had swooped on him and carried him away to a secluded wood. Their captain was merciless in his interrogation.

"Orbec!" he repeated. "Richard Orbec."

The man now lay writhing in agony on the ground.

"Orbec!" shouted Goronwy.

"I hope he kills you," said the man through his pain. "Every last one of you!"

Goronwy bent low to apply the whip again. The man howled and twitched even more violently. The two soldiers lifted him bodily and brought him face to face with their captain. Goronwy took a flaming torch from another of his soldiers and held it near the man's eyes.

"Orbec!" he hissed. "Richard Orbec."

He pointed at the man, then jabbed his finger in the air to indicate that they wanted directions. The heat of the

174

fire made the man cringe. Goronwy moved the torch ever closer.

"Richard Orbec!" said the man. "I'll take you!"

Goronwy smiled. They spoke the same language at last.

Rope could be a friend as well as a foe. When Gervase Bret was tied to the back of a horse, he cursed the bonds that dug into his wrists and ankles. Those same lengths of rope had enabled him to escape from the dungeon and the coil from the stables had liberated the third prisoner from her tower. There had been no time for introductions and explanations. After taking the girl down to Omri at the base of the mound, Gervase went back to retrieve the rope.

Paying it out, he cracked it like a whip to dislodge the iron bar from its position. When he cracked even harder the next time, the end came out through the window with the bar at an angle. Gervase dived to evade the missile and it sunk into the earth a few feet away. Rope and bar were gathered up and he slithered back down the mound.

Even on his own, he knew that he would stand little chance of getting away through the main gate of the castle. Encumbered by an old man and a young woman, he would be mad even to attempt escape in that direction. Rope had been their salvation so far and it might be so again.

From the top of the mound, Gervase had been able to take his bearings. The tower was enclosed by a wall and below that was a ditch. Beyond the ditch—used as a natural moat—was the River Monnow. That had to be their way out of the town. Gathering his companions, he hustled them around the tower and up the steep bank to the wall. When she looked over it, the young woman put a hand to her mouth to hold back a cry of horror.

"What is it, Angharad?" whispered Omri.

"We have to climb down the outside wall," said Gervase. "There's a ditch below. I'll tie the rope around you and lower you one by one."

Angharad understood his halting Welsh and shook her head. Descent from that height was far more dangerous than her climb from the window. Omri sensed her distress.

"I'll go first!" he said.

The old man felt for the rope and tied one end around his waist. Gervase wound the end with the bar around his waist and shoulders.

"Pull hard on the rope twice when you untie it," he said.

"Will it be long enough to reach the bottom?"

"You'll soon find out."

Angharad was moved at the sight of the blind man daring to risk such a descent. As she handed him his harp, she gave him an affectionate kiss on the cheek. Gervase braced himself and slowly paid out the rope. Omri was not heavy. They could hear his feet grating gently on the outside wall. Angharad watched until he vanished into the darkness at the base of the castle. Gervase suddenly felt all the strain taken off him. The rope had been just long enough.

"He made it."

"Is he safe?" she asked.

"Yes," said Gervase, feeling two tugs on the rope. "Safe and sound. Your turn now."

She hesitated for a moment, but the sound of commotion near the gatehouse soon swept away her reservations. The escape from the dungeon had been detected. A search would soon be under way. Gervase helped her to tie the rope around her slender waist, then lowered her as

176

gently as he could. She was lighter than Omri and her feet bounced softly off the wall.

Two more pulls on the rope told him that she had joined Omri. Gervase moved at speed. Jamming the iron bar between the battlements, he cocked a leg over the wall and grabbed the rope. It took his weight. Leaning out so that he could use his legs to brace himself, he walked and slid his way down through the darkness. Growing noises from within the castle made him rush even more. As soon as he saw the ground, he abandoned the rope and jumped, landing in the muddy ditch and falling over.

He was on his feet again at once, collecting his two companions and towing them as fast as he could along the river bank. Omri was gasping for breath within a minute.

"We need horses, Gervase."

"I've changed my mind about that."

"Why?"

"We could never outrun them on the road."

"Then how else do we get away? On foot?"

Gervase at last found what he had been hoping he would.

"No, Omri," he said. "In a boat."

Anxiety over Gervase Bret and annoyance over the unexpected departure of Golde had left Ralph Delchard in a state of dejection. Canon Hubert and Brother Simon lifted his spirits slightly. Over a frugal meal at the house in Pencoed, they explained how they had discomfited Ilbert the Sheriff.

"I wish I had been there," said Ralph. "I was looking forward to locking horns with Ilbert Malvoisin."

"His case will need to be addressed more fully at a later date," said Hubert. "But I feel that we have let him know what sort of men he is up against."

"Canon Hubert was magnificent," said Simon.

"Thank you."

"He played the sheriff like a fish."

"Since when have you been an angler, Brother Simon?"

"We are both fishers of man, Canon Hubert," said the wraith beside him, laughing tinnily at his own wit.

"Why did the sheriff leave Llanwarne?" said Ralph.

"There is nothing left for him to do," said Hubert.

"Nothing left! What of Warnod's murder? He will not solve that by sitting in Hereford with that excrescence of a reeve. Ilbert should be here."

"He has left men to continue the enquiry."

"A sheriff should lead it," insisted Ralph. "This is no random killing. It was a calculated act of savagery that was committed in part to frustrate our work. Find the murderers and we unravel all the mysteries that brought us here."

"Perhaps that is why he left," said Hubert.

"The sheriff?"

"He is reluctant to aid us in our work."

"That is not surprising, Hubert. If we nail our charges to the Malvoisin tail, he will forfeit a substantial amount of land and pay a fine in the bargain." He drained his cup of wine. "No wonder he has fled back to Hereford."

"Might there not be another reason?" said Simon, meekly.

"And what is that?"

"Speak up, Brother Simon," urged Hubert. "You are fully entitled to an opinion. Though you travel as our scribe, you can also write ideas into the ledgers of our minds."

"That was beautifully phrased, Canon Hubert."

"Enough fawning, man," said Ralph. "This reason?"

"Personal interest."

"We have just disposed of that."

"Personal interest in Warnod's death," said Simon as he enlarged his argument with diffident steps. "*Cui bono?* Who gains by the poor man's demise?"

"Not the sheriff," said Canon Hubert. "He had to ride down here to quell a feud between Saxons and Welsh."

"And when that is done, he leaves."

Ralph tapped the table with a finger. "Simon has a point. The good sheriff was far more interested in the consequences of Warnod's death than in the actual murder. Law and order had to be restored. That done, he leaves the search for the killer to lesser men."

"Your conclusion?" pressed Hubert.

"I leave you to draw that," said Simon. "I merely point out that Ilbert Malvoisin stood to profit by the death of Warnod and the destruction of his possessions. Including—or so the sheriff supposed—his charter and his will."

"The same may be said of Richard Orbec and Maurice Damville," added Ralph. "They, too, gained by the sudden disappearance of the man with a claim to their land."

"To Orbec's land," reminded Hubert.

"Yes. Damville waived his right." Ralph frowned and tapped the table again. "Now, why did he do that?"

"Not in the true spirit of altruism, to be sure."

"What does that leave us with, Hubert? Three men, all fundamental to our enquiry, all with sound reasons to kill the fourth witness." He spread his arms wide. "Who is the villain behind the murder? Orbec, Damville, or the sheriff?"

"We must first solve another riddle."

"And what is that?"

"The red dragon."

Gervase Bret rowed for the best part of an hour before he felt it was safe to rest. The boat they had stolen was one of a number of small fishing craft that had been moored upstream from the castle. Most of them were coracles, round vessels that required great skill to manoeuvre with any speed. Gervase opted for the battered rowing boat, first helping his passengers in, then wading chest-high in the river to push them along so that the plash of oars did not attract any interest. Once clear of the town, the sodden Gervase had climbed aboard and shifted the craft by more conventional and less irksome means.

They travelled with painful slowness. Gervase's back was soon aching and his hands were a mass of blisters. His passengers offered sympathy, but neither could realistically take a turn at the oars. Fearful that their voices would carry, they hardly spoke at all. Omri sat in the stern with an arm around the shivering Angharad, who eventually drifted off to sleep on his shoulder. Gervase struggled on until the pain became too great, then guided the boat into the bank. He tied it to the trunk of an overhanging willow.

"We have put some distance between us and Monmouth," he said. "So we should be safe for a while."

"You deserve the rest," said Omri. "How do you feel?"

"Wet."

"Angharad and I are eternally grateful."

"Angharad should be grateful to you," said Gervase. "For lying so convincingly. If I had known that we were rescuing a young lady, I would have thought twice about the whole enterprise."

"That is why I kept the truth from you."

"Who is she?"

"A friend," said Omri. "A friend and companion."

Angharad awoke with a start and looked around. Enough moonlight found its way through the willow fronds for Gervase to be able to see her face properly for the first time. It was arresting in its beauty. She was no more than eighteen. The long hair framed a heart-shaped face with the most luminous skin he had ever seen. Large brown eyes, a small upturned nose, and full lips enriched the portrait. Something else could be seen in the faltering light. There was an air of nobility about her. Even in her confused and muddied condition, Angharad had natural poise.

"Thank you," she said.

"His name is Gervase," prompted Omri.

"Thank you, Gervase."

"Are you all right, Angharad?"

"I think so."

"Did they hurt you?"

"No," she said. "Nobody touched me. They locked me in a chamber. That is all."

"Did they tell you why?"

"They said nothing at all."

"Did you not overhear them speaking?"

"Yes, but not in Welsh." She turned to Gervase. "Where are we?"

"I am not sure. Somewhere on the River Monnow."

"This old boat is as hard as stone," said Omri, as he

adjusted his position, "but it is better accommodation than Monmouth Castle could offer us."

"Where will we go?" she said.

"Wherever the river takes us," said Gervase. "Further north it is the border of the place where I was captured."

"What is that called?"

"Archenfield."

"Ergyng," corrected Omri.

Her face lit up. "You have friends in Ergyng?"

"Yes," said Gervase. "Good friends. They will give us food and horses." He looked down at himself. "And I can change into some dry apparel."

"You have suffered much for our sakes, Gervase," said Omri. "If I could soothe your blisters with a song or dry your clothing with a jest, I'd happily do both, but my talents are barren in this situation."

"There is one thing you can do for me."

"Ask and it is yours."

"Tell me who Angharad really is."

"A friend. No more."

"There is much more, Omri."

"Look at the dear creature," he said, "for I cannot except in my mind's eye. Angharad is a miracle of nature—a waterfall in full flow, a daffodil in bloom, a bird on the wing."

"Birds on the wing do not merit eight men-at-arms to escort them on the road." Gervase was persistent. "Who is she and why was she going to the court of the prince of Powys?"

"Tell him," she said.

"Leave this to me, Angharad."

"If you do not, then I will." She smiled at Gervase and touched his arm in gratitude. "He risked his life for us.

Why should he bother with two strangers when he could have escaped on his own much more easily? Gervase is kind. He can be trusted. Tell him, Omri."

The old man sighed and nodded. He picked up his harp and plucked at the strings to draw out a plaintive melody. His words were heightened by the music.

"Angharad hails from a royal house," he chanted. "She is the niece of Rhys ap Tewdr, prince of Deheubarth and lord of the whole of South Wales. Had he but known where we were kept, Rhys ap Tewdr would have stormed Monmouth Castle with a thousand men and left not a stone of it standing. And all the bards of Wales would have celebrated the event in song for another century."

His fingers lay still, but the music hung on the wind for a few more moments before it died away. Gervase had heard enough to be able to guess the rest.

"A dynastic marriage?"

"Even so, my friend."

"With someone from the house of Powys?"

"Goronwy, the nephew of Cadwgan ap Bleddyn himself."

Angharad tensed at the name and said something so rapidly in Welsh that Gervase did not understand it. What he did observe, however, was her evident distress.

"This match does not please the lady, I think."

"Angharad is . . . not overjoyed by the choice."

"She is not the only one," said Gervase. "An alliance between Deheubarth and Powys? They would make a powerful combination. King William himself would not be delighted with this marriage."

"It has other opponents," admitted Omri.

"Who are they?"

"The men who ambushed us on the road. I do not

183

know who they are, but they clearly had a strong reason to stop this marriage. Killing eight soldiers and abducting the bride are not very generous wedding presents."

"I do not want him," said Angharad. "I hate Goronwy."

"You have never even met him," said Omri, reasonably. "What you hate is what you have heard about him. And any man may suffer from false report."

"Who is he?" asked Gervase.

"The captain of Cadwgan ap Bleddyn's retinue."

"A soldier then. Brave and strong."

"He would not hold the position that he does without bravery and strength. They say that Goronwy is fearless—and I have heard that on a dozen tongues, so it cannot be denied." He sagged slightly. "But they say other things, too."

"I could never love this man," wailed Angharad.

"Why not?"

"He must not be my husband. I would rather spend the rest of my life in that castle than be forced to marry this Goronwy. My uncle is cruel!"

"What has she heard about this man?" said Gervase.

"He has a reputation," confessed Omri.

"Reputation?"

"It may be completely unfair to him."

"And it may be true."

"It is true!" Angharad insisted. "It is true."

"What is this reputation for, Omri?"

"Ruthless slaughter. They say that he is consumed with blood-lust. That is why Angharad is terrified of this man. When he has a weapon in his hand, he runs mad."

Goronwy slit the man's throat and left him dead in the bottom of the ditch. The Saxon guide had served his purpose. He had led them to their destination. Lying flat on his stomach in the undergrowth, Goronwy kept the house under surveillance. He was over a hundred yards away, but his position on the wooded slope allowed him to see over the fortifications. Dawn was rising and the birds were in full voice. The scene was tranquil.

When a figure came out of the chapel, Goronwy held out a hand to one of his men. Bow and arrow were passed over. This was no death to be delegated. Goronwy wanted the pleasure of execution himself. Another man came to meet the first outside the chapel. They talked in earnest. Goronwy rose up and knelt, fitting the arrow to the bowstring.

Below in the half-light, the conversation continued. The newcomer was a big, shambling man with deferential gestures. He was patiently talking with his lord. Goronwy rose steadily to his feet. Strong fingers pulled back the bowstring. The assassin waited. This was him. Goronwy was certain. This was the man who had ambushed his young bride. Revenge would be swift and sweet.

The arrow whistled through the air with the hatred of a young lifetime riding on its back. The aim was true, but its speed was fractionally too slow. Before it could strike its target, the bigger man stepped unwittingly in front of the other. The arrow hit him directly between the shoulder blades and killed him outright. He pitched ridiculously forward.

Richard Orbec caught his dead reeve in his hands.

Chapter Nine

RALPH DELCHARD WAS TORMENTED BY A DOUBLE
loss. The baffling disappearance of Gervase Bret
was always at the forefront of his mind. It gave him
another night of feverish rumination and put him back in
the saddle at dawn. Warnod's murder had been a public
event with a flaming message left behind for all to see.
Ralph was forced to consider that Gervase might have
been killed in a more private way and buried somewhere
by stealth. They might never find him. If Gervase had
met a violent end, then his death would somehow be
linked to that of Warnod. Finding one set of killers would
solve both murders.

While all his energies were directed towards hunting
for some trace of his friend, Ralph was troubled by
another loss. The hurried departure of Golde had
wounded him. She had left no message, suggested no further meeting between them. Had the shared feelings on
their first night in Archenfield been an illusion? Was her
return to Hereford a signal to him in itself? Ralph felt the
sharp pain of rejection. In the short time he had known
Golde, he had been drawn ever close to her. Had she
encouraged him in order to spite him? Was it Saxon cunning that had ensnared him in order to inflict punishment?

"I am ready for you, my lord."

Idwal the Archdeacon was depressingly bright at that time of the morning. As he mounted his horse, his eyes were glistening and his face was a mask of shining religiosity. Ralph had contained his homicidal urges in order to make use of the Welshman during the search. Mouths which had been closed to them on the previous day might open to the little archdeacon with the lambskin cloak.

"Which way shall we ride?" asked Idwal.

"To the place where Gervase was last seen."

"Richard Orbec's demesne? Will we be safe?"

"He'll not stop me this time," asserted Ralph. "Orbec promised me that he did not touch Gervase and I accept his word. But someone else may have struck on Orbec's territory. I would like to search it afresh to satisfy myself."

"Take me wherever you wish," said Idwal. "I am yours."

They set off from Llanwarne at a steady pace. Ralph's men-at-arms were refreshed by a night's sleep and as eager as their master to track the young commissioner. Having ridden with him on assignments in Wiltshire and in Essex, they had come to like and respect Gervase Bret very much. Their duty was mingled with affection, but the prospect of action kept them alert.

Ralph tried to keep ahead of Idwal, but the archdeacon was no mean horseman. He caught up to canter abreast.

"They say this Richard Orbec is a holy man."

"It is a holiness mixed with hostility."

"Towards whom, my lord?"

"Everyone. He treats his demesne as his refuge. Nobody is allowed to disturb him—on pain of death."

"A curious blend," observed Idwal. "The instincts of a monk and the impulse of a murderer. What made the man so?"

"Only he knows that."

"I would like to probe his mystery."

"He is more likely to probe your ribs with a dagger."

"Violence towards the Church? Never!"

"Richard Orbec would not scruple to kill a pope who trespassed on his land," said Ralph. "Besides, you will not be there to plumb the depths of his spirit. Orbec has Welsh subtenants on his land in Archenfield."

"Ergyng."

"Loosen their tongues for me."

"I will open their hearts and make them sing *Te Deum*."

"We want information about Gervase. Nothing more."

"I will want something else, my lord."

"What is that?"

"An explanation of this outrage."

"Outrage?"

"Ergyng is a part of Wales in the grasp of foreigners. But it was allowed to keep its old customs. Such things mean much to an ancient people like us."

"How does this affect Richard Orbec?"

"He violates those Welsh customs," said Idwal. "In every other part of Ergyng, my compatriots pay their dues in renders of honey, pigs, sheep, and so forth. It has always been so. This Richard Orbec, so they tell me, exacts rent from his Welsh subtenants in the form of money. They have no choice. Your commission should look into this abuse."

"We are already aware of it," said Ralph, "but it lies not within our jurisdiction. Landlord and tenant come to their own agreements. We only take notice when there is corruption and misappropriation at work."

"You see exactly that here before your eyes!"

"All I see is a man who prefers money to a few sesters

188

of honey and a couple of sows. Orbec commits no crime."

"But he does, my lord. He desecrates our customs."

"We talk about no more than a handful of people."

"If it was one," said Idwal with passion, "I would defend his rights. Richard Orbec is heaping the greatest shame upon people of my nation."

"How?"

"By dishonouring their *Cymreictod*."

"Their what?"

"Their Welshness."

Ralph nudged more speed from his horse and drew away. Idwal's company was taxing. He began to regret his decision to bring the archdeacon with him. There was another price to pay for his interpreter. Every time Ralph looked across at the Welshman, he was reminded of the latter's part in the return of Golde to her sister. But for Idwal's undue interference, she might well have been waiting for him on the previous night. Ralph toyed once more with the image of a leaden cask being lowered into a deep pit. He would toss the lambskin cloak joyfully in after it.

"Another matter must be raised, my lord."

Idwal was not yet ready for his removal from the face of the earth. He brought his horse level with Ralph's again.

"I could not touch upon it yesterday."

"Upon what?"

"The question of the lady."

"Golde?"

"Others were present," said Idwal. "Canon Hubert and Brother Simon are worthy jousters for me to knock from their saddles in debate, but they were raised in monastic

189

celibacy. Their flesh does not behave as that of other men."

"What are you talking about?"

"Discretion, my lord. Biding my time. Telling you alone what could not be said before your two companions for fear it might bring blushes to their virgin cheeks." He cackled merrily. "Though I share their love of God, it does not make me turn aside from all women. I am a married man."

Ralph gaped. "You have a wife?"

"Wife and children, my lord. They pine for me even now."

"Return to them as soon as you may," he urged.

"Do you not want to hear of Golde?"

"Will you ever tell the news?"

"It was written on her face for all to see," said Idwal. "Only eunuchs like Canon Hubert and Brother Simon could fail to know its import. I saw it at once."

"Saw what, man?"

"She loves you."

Work began early at the brewhouse on Castle Street. Golde was there to supervise it. Sacks of fresh barley were cut open for the day's usage. Fermentation was checked in the ale which had stood in the vats overnight. The carter arrived to return empty barrels and take away full ones. Golde tasted every consignment before she released it. Her husband had taught her well and she maintained the highest standards. Any ale which did not please her palate would be put aside. The distinctive flavour of her product had to be preserved at all costs.

After a few hours in the brewhouse, she found a moment to slip back into the house. Aelgar was sitting in front of the fire with the same sombre expression on her face.

"You must strive to get out of the house, Aelgar."

"Do you not want me here?" asked her sister.

"Fresh air may restore you. The presence of others may give you interest. It is not good for you to lock yourself away with your memories."

"They are all I have now."

"Visit the market. Buy some fruit for us."

"Later, perhaps."

"Brooding over Warnod will not bring him back."

"I know." She looked up. "Will he forgive me, Golde?"

"For what?"

"Letting him go to his grave alone."

"Aelgar!"

"I should have been there," she said, wistfully. "He was my beloved. I should have watched them lower him into the ground and said a prayer for his soul."

"You can pray as well for him here as there," said Golde. "Archenfield was no place for you. It was not his body that they buried but his ashes. It must have been a hideous sight. You were spared that. Warnod loved you truly. He would not have wanted you to witness such a scene."

"And he will not blame me?"

"No, Aelgar. Nor let you blame yourself."

The girl gestured helplessly. "I miss him."

"Of course," said Golde, squeezing her. "We both do."

"I cannot believe that he is gone."

"Time will slowly knit up your grief."

"I loved him so dearly, Golde. Yet he left so little behind. All that was to have been mine—ours to share— was burned to the ground. I have nothing save a few keepsakes, and I have been too afraid even to look at them for fear that they would make my grief overflow."

Golde's curiosity was aroused. She turned the girl to face her and knelt down to hold her hands. Red-rimmed eyes looked across at her. She kissed her sister on the cheek.

"Keepsakes, you say?"

"They are nothing much."

"Why have you not mentioned them before?"

"They were mine," said Aelgar. "Private treasures."

"And where are they now?"

"Where I have hidden them these past months."

"Even from me? Your sister?"

"Warnod made me promise."

"Why?"

"I do not know, but I obeyed. He was to be my husband."

Golde nodded reassuringly and squeezed her hands.

"May I see these keepsakes now?"

Two strenuous hours at the oars inflamed the blisters on his hands and deepened the ache in his muscles. Gervase Bret took the boat into the bank again and moored it to a small boulder. He climbed ashore and offered his hand to Angharad.

"Is it safe?" she asked.

"We are well clear of Monmouth now."

"Horses could soon catch up with us."

"We are not pursued, Angharad," he said. "Take my hand and step out. It will do us all good to stretch our legs."

"Yes," agreed Omri. "My old bones do not like boats."

They had managed a few hours' sleep in the night without daring to leave their vessel. Cramps increased their general discomfort. Leaving at dawn, they were now further upstream and able to scan the landscape all around them. Grazing sheep were the only moving figures to be seen.

Helped by Gervase, the old man clambered onto the bank. He yawned and stretched himself. Gervase guided the two of them to some nearby bushes which offered them complete cover and protection from the stiff breeze. Secure in their hiding place, they settled down on the grass.

Angharad was embarrassed to be seen in such a sullied condition and tried to tidy her hair with hands that flitted like butterflies around her head. Gervase was far more conscious of his own bedraggled state. The dignity of a royal commissioner had been stained and soaked quite beyond recognition. He could feel the muck on his face and smell the stink on his attire. He was hardly in a presentable state to meet a lady from one of the royal houses of Wales.

Omri seemed to read his mind. He gave a rich chuckle.

"Adversity makes strange bedfellows," he mused. "What else but a malign fate could have thrown we three together?"

"Gervase saved us," said Angharad, simply.

"Indeed, indeed. I will compose a song to thank him."

"Do not mention the mud and the water," said Gervase.

"My music will cleanse you from head to toe. I will tell of a hero with golden lustre." He sniffed deep and chuckled again. "And my song will have to put a peg on the noses of my listeners. Heroes do not stink of a night in a dungeon and a dip in the River Monnow."

Angharad laughed nervously, then looked around with frightened eyes. She drew her cloak around her shoulders.

"You are sure we are safe, Gervase?" she said.

"For the time being."

"Why have they not come after us?"

"Because that was not their task," said Gervase. "Their job was merely to hold us at the castle. They had no remit to organise a search if we chanced to escape."

"What of the men who took us to Monmouth?" she said.

"They have long gone."

"How can you be certain?"

"We would have heard from them by now," decided Gervase. "The road from Monmouth never strays too far away from this river. I heard a cart go past in the night and a drover took his cattle past at dawn. We were hidden from them by the banks of the river, but travellers were not hidden from us. A posse of soldiers at full gallop is a sound that we would surely not have missed."

"My ears would not have missed it," said Omri. "I have heard every insect that crawled, every blade of grass that stirred. I have listened to the conversation of the fishes and the complaints of the frogs. No soldiers."

"Other enemies still linger," said Gervase. "We must take no chances. When we have rested, I will search for food. There may be berries to sustain us and clean water to drink."

"Find a tree that grows dry clothing," said Omri. "And some bushes that yield spices to sweeten our persons."

"Clothing must wait, but flowers may give us scent."

Angharad looked increasingly uncomfortable. She bent to whisper into Omri's ear. He nodded understandingly and hauled himself to his feet.

"She would be alone awhile," he said, feeling for Gervase's hand and pulling him up. "Let's stand aside. This is no place even for a blind man."

They left her to satisfy the wants of nature and found more cover behind the trunk of an elm. Its spreading branches dipped and creaked in the breeze. Gervase was grateful for a moment alone with Omri. Strategy needed to be decided.

"What will you do with her?" Gervase asked.

"Take her to Powys."

"Even though she does not wish to go?"

"I obey the command of her uncle."

"Does he know how much she resists this match?"

"Rhys ap Tewdr has only spoken to the girl once or twice in her entire life. Power falls to the man with the strongest arm. A Welsh prince is always too busy guarding his territory against rivals. Even Rhys ap Tewdr must fight off foolhardy pretenders. He does not have much time for his wider family."

"Until they can be used as pawns in marriage."

"That is your judgment."

"Is it not yours?"

"I am hired to sing and crack a jest."

"And tell fortunes at the courts of the great."

"Only to those who will hear me."

"I will hear you, Omri."

"You?"

"Can you see into the future for us?"

"I have already done so," said the old man, with a sly grin. "Why do you think I agreed to escape with you? It was because I foresaw success. I knew that you would put us both on your back and fly over the walls of the castle."

"Was the river part of your prophecy?"

"I deal in generalities, Gervase. Do not pin me down."

"What lies ahead for us now?"

"Trouble, sorrow, and threats to our lives."

"And then?"

"My vision becomes blurred."

There was movement in the bushes. Angharad came to join them with a posy of flowers in her hand. She inhaled their fragrance then held them under Omri's nose. The scent revived him.

"I will pick some of my own," he said, moving away.

"Let me help you," offered Gervase.

"I would go alone."

It was the old man's turn to relieve himself. Gervase watched him grope his way towards the bushes, then he turned his attention to Angharad. She looked even more beautiful by daylight. The glow on her skin was captivating. Gervase basked in its glory. Angharad studied him carefully. After making sure that they were not overheard, she moved in close to whisper to him.

"You have friends in Ergyng?"

"If we can reach them."

"What will happen to me, then?"

"We will arrange an escort for you," said Gervase. "Omri will take you on to Powys."

"No!"

"Your uncle has decreed it."

"My uncle does not have to marry that pig!" she said with quiet ferocity. "Goronwy is an animal. I will not share my bed with him. He frightens me."

"You only know him by report, Angharad."

"There are too many tales. They all say the same thing about him. I want to please my uncle, but I will not tie myself to a madman for the rest of my life." She clasped his hands. "Goronwy is strong and brutal. Think what he could do to me. Would you hand any girl over to a man like that?"

"No," he said. "But this is not my concern, Angharad."

"It is now."

"What do you mean?"

"Omri is sweet and kind, but he is afraid to disobey. You are not bound by any orders from my uncle." She clutched at his chest. "You have rescued me once, Gervase, and you must do it again."

"Rescue you?"

"From Goronwy. You are the only hope I have."

"It is not my place."

"I *need* you," she begged. "Do not force me to go to Powys. I will do anything to avoid that. Marriage to this ogre would be like suicide. Help me, Gervase." She flung herself at him and clung tight. "Help me. Please, help me."

They rode for another mile or more and still there was no challenge. Indeed, their presence seemed to frighten people away rather than rouse their interest. Expecting an armed resistance, they instead sent peasants scurrying away from their fields, and fishermen abandoning their nets to seek the nearest refuge. Ralph Delchard and his men continued their search in a state of bewilderment.

"Why do they run away from us?" said Ralph.

"The sight of Norman armour unsettles them," said Idwal.

"Then they must quake with fear every day of their lives because Orbec's men-at-arms are everywhere."

"Not this morning, my lord."

"Why?"

"Let me find out for you."

They were moving up the Golden Valley now and he

spotted the first of the mills on the River Dore. While Ralph and the others waited, Idwal rode on down to see if his religion and nationality would reassure. They saw him meet two men beside the mill and fall into animated conversation with them. Idwal, for once, seemed to be doing most of the listening. One of the men pointed up the valley and the archdeacon nodded. He was soon cantering back to his companions.

Watching the lambskin cloak approach, Ralph spared a thought for the man's wife. What creature of flesh and blood could endure his unremitting volubility? Was she not crushed in bed by the sheer weight of words? By what weird process had their children been conceived? Ralph had a vision of their progeny as tiny sermons with arms and legs. The woman herself was a martyr. Marriage to the gushing urgency of the archdeacon was surely a giant step towards sainthood.

"I spoke with them," said Idwal, halting his mount.

"Do they think we have leprosy?" said Ralph.

"They fear all soldiers. The manor house was raided."

"By whom?"

"Nobody knows," said Idwal. "That is what makes it so alarming. But Richard Orbec's reeve was killed with an arrow and soldiers were seen galloping away."

"When was this attack?"

"At dawn this morning. Word has spread like wildfire."

"Let's find out more about this."

Ralph abandoned the search and led his men in the direction of Richard Orbec's manor house. The intruders might possibly have some connection with Gervase's fate. It was important to learn all that he could about them as soon as possible. Ralph had seen at first hand the forceful way in which Orbec shielded his land from visitors. It would require courage and daring to launch an assault on the man's house.

When the building came in sight, they could see the strong military presence at once. The drawbridge was up and the palisade was manned. Helmets glinted on all four sides of the manor. Richard Orbec would not be caught unawares again. They were fifty yards from the gate when a voice ordered them to stop and state their business.

"I am Ralph Delchard and I seek immediate conference with your lord. We come as friends. If there is danger, we will gladly lend what help we can."

"Wait there."

A message was sent up to the house. When the drawbridge was lowered five minutes later, Richard Orbec himself came out on his horse. He was in full armour.

"What do you want?" he demanded.

"To hear details of this attack," said Ralph. "It cost you a steward, but the same men may also have deprived me of my dearest friend. Who were they?"

"Raiders from across the border."

"Welshmen?"

"Never!" howled Idwal.

"Who is this?" said Orbec.

"I am the Archdeacon of Llandaff, but I speak for the whole of Wales. You are deceived in your judgment, my lord."

"I pulled the arrow out of my reeve's back," said Orbec. "It came from a Welsh bow."

"But not necessarily shot by a Welshman."

"Keep out of this," snapped Ralph. "Let's hear the tale in full before we rush to judgment."

"You have heard it," said Orbec. "I left the chapel just after dawn. Redwald, my reeve, met me and chanced to step in front of my body. He presents too large a target to miss. The arrow killed him instantly."

"You say that he stepped in front of you?"

"Accidentally and foolishly. Had he stayed where he was, Redwald would now be telling you how Richard Orbec was picked off by a Welsh archer."

"I refuse to believe it!" said Idwal.

"Did you give pursuit?" said Ralph.

"We were after them within minutes, but they got clear away." Orbec gestured with his hand. "Since then, I have looked to my defences, as you see. This was a small party. We saw the marks of their hooves in the wood above the house. A larger force may come next time."

"Why?"

"To kill me."

"For what reason?"

"That has yet to be disclosed."

"Have hostile soldiers come over the border before?"

"Not for several years."

"Did you do something to provoke their ire?"

"Nothing."

"There is the questions of the renders," said Idwal. "If you had respected Welsh customs in Ergyng . . ."

Orbec blinked. "What is he babbling about?"

"Ignore him, my lord," said Ralph. "Have you informed the sheriff of this attack?"

"No."

"What of your neighbour, Maurice Damville?"

"I send no messages to him."

"But a Welsh raid must surely be of concern. The castle of Ewyas Harold is first in the line of attack. If a larger force did come, Damville would bear the brunt of it."

"That is his problem."

"Will you not unite in the face of an enemy?"

"I look after my own," said Orbec, sternly. "One man has been killed. I will not lose another so easily."

"I, too, have lost a man," said Ralph. "I came here this morning to look for him. You have problems enough of your own, as I can see, but we must talk. If we try, we may help each other. I would appreciate a word in private."

Richard Orbec stared at him with a mixture of curiosity and disdain. The green eyes flashed, but Ralph was equal to their glare. The long perusal eventually came to an end.

"Follow me," said Orbec.

"Thank you."

Ralph nudged his horse forward and Idwal followed suit.

"Alone!" insisted Orbec.

Idwal protested in both languages, but his words bounced off the backs of the two departing Norman lords. When they had ridden over it, the drawbridge was lifted and secured. The Welshman and the eight men-of-arms were left outside.

"These are sad tidings, my lord," said Ralph, falling in beside Orbec. "We met your reeve. He seemed a sound man."

"Redwald was an excellent reeve."

"Cut down by a stray arrow."

"Not stray, my lord. It was meant for me."

"Do you have any idea who could have shot it?"

"Yes," said Orbec, "but I did not wish to name a name in front of your companion. He could be an intelligencer."

"Idwal? He is an archdeacon."

"Religion might be a convenient disguise. It allows him to pass among you and gather information freely. Why has he attached himself to you when he has no official place in your commission? This much I do know. Somebody led those Welsh soldiers to the one place from which an arrow could be fired. What does that suggest?"

"A spy."

"I treat all the Welsh as such. And most Saxons."

"You said that you knew the assassin?"

"I can guess at his identity."

"Who is he?"

"A wild man from the house of Powys," said Orbec. "You have seen the way I drill my men and marshal my defences. How would you plan an assault on me?"

"With a substantial force or a very small one."

"A very small one argues cunning and valour. To come this far across the border is no light matter. They took grave risks." He gazed up at the wooded slope from which the arrow was discharged. "I know of only one Welshman who would dare to insinuate himself this far into my land."

"Who is he?"

"The prince's nephew."

"What is his name?"

"Goronwy."

Goronwy and his men had retreated across the border and camped beside the road to consider their next move. The Black Mountains were at their back and the castle of Ewyas Harold was a couple of miles in front of them. Goronwy was pleased that he had made his presence felt, but angry that he had killed the wrong man. Ever since the name of Richard Orbec had been put into his ear, he had a target for his rage. He would not rest until he had cut out that man's heart with a dagger.

Angharad was alive. Of that there could be no doubt.

They would not have killed her train and taken her off to murder her elsewhere. His bride was, he believed, held by Richard Orbec. He did not even speculate on the motive. Whether it was lust, spite, or the seizing of a hostage in order to exact a ransom, it did not matter. Angharad, his Angharad, a lovely young girl, destined for his bed, had been taken by force. Orbec would be taught to rue his outrage.

While his men lit a fire to roast the chickens they had stolen from a nearby farm, Goronwy took one of his men with him and rode towards Ewyas. It was another commote which had been cut ruthlessly away from Wales by the Normans. The castle of Ewyas Harold was a token of that ruthlessness. When they got within sight of it, they reined in their horses and assessed its strength. Its site had been chosen well. Approach from any direction would soon be seen. The ditch was deep and the high walls looked impregnable. Even from that distance, they could see figures on the battlements.

Goronwy's companion mixed valour with discretion.

"Richard Orbec's house is an easier target."

"This one would test our mettle more."

"We do not have men enough."

"We will," said Goronwy.

"Why waste time here?" argued the man. "Our business lies in the Golden Valley."

"Sack this castle and we ride straight through into Orbec's territory. He will not look for us to come from this direction. Besides," said Goronwy, "my blood is up and I will kill any Norman I can find. We will start here. Ewyas Harold Castle will whet my appetite."

* * *

Maurice Damville was called up to the battlements by his guards. Two figures had been sighted in the distance, but they were too far away to identify. Damville ran up the stone steps to look for himself. He was just in time to watch Goronwy and his companion leave. Their light armour denoted them as soldiers. Here was no casual observation of his stronghold. The castle had been studied with a view to attack.

"They are coming," said Damville. "Double the guard!"

"Yes, my lord."

"Alert the whole garrison."

"Yes, my lord."

"They are coming," he said, almost gleefully. "At last!"

Damville went back down the steps at speed and into the bailey. He summoned his captain and barked orders. The castle was soon alive with activity. Shouts came from the gatehouse. A messenger was approaching. The doors were heaved open so that the horseman's gallop could take him on into the centre of the courtyard.

He brought his steaming horse to a halt in front of Damville and leaped from the saddle. The parchment was taken from his belt and handed over at once.

Maurice Damville broke the seal and read the missive. His grin soon turned to a sneer of contempt. He scrunched the letter up and hurled it back at the messenger. The captain's orders were countermanded.

"Saddle up. Take a dozen men."

"Are they not needed here, my lord?"

"Do as I say!"

"Yes, my lord."

"Ride hard and this may not take long," said Damville. "You will return here well in time. Have the men waiting and I will give instruction."

The messenger picked up the discarded letter from the ground.

"Is there any reply, my lord?"

"Yes," snarled Damville. "Here it is."

He knocked the man to the ground with his forearm.

Gervase Bret rowed intermittently for a few more hours before exhaustion obliged him to ship his oars and drift into the bank. He chose a place where the Monnow cut deep and the banks were high enough to conceal them. Gervase had torn strips of material from his tunic to bind around his hands, but the blisters still burned like hot coals. He was fit and strong, but no boatman. The effort of rowing three of them along the winding course of the river took him close to total fatigue. His whole body was now one continuous ache and perspiration was streaming down his face.

"Where are we?" asked Omri.

"I do not know," said Gervase, "but we still have some way to go, I am sure. That fisherman we met a little way downstream said we had four or five miles yet before we reach Archenfield. Or Ergyng, as you all insist on calling it. We have come nowhere near that distance since then."

"You would be quicker on foot," said Omri.

"I might be, but what of you?"

"We could hide somewhere while you went for horses."

"No," said Angharad. "I will not leave Gervase."

"Then the two of you must go," suggested Omri. "I will only slow you down. My walking days are over. And I am hardly fit for catching horses."

"I think that we should stay together," said Gervase.

"And break your back at those oars?"

"I will be fine again after a little rest."

"We are right out in the open here," said Angharad. "It does not feel safe. I do not want to leave Omri, but it is only for a little while. We will come back for him."

There was conviction in her voice, but none in her face. Gervase sensed that her predicament was far more important to her than the old man's welfare. Once free of her companion, he felt certain, Angharad would want to press on without him. Fond as she was of Omri, she would rather abandon him in order to secure her own escape from the journey to Powys. Gervase was in a cleft stick. He liked the wry old bard and was enchanted by Angharad. One of them would have to be disappointed.

"We stay together," he decided.

"No," she protested, "that is foolish."

"I will not be alone," said Omri. "I have my harp."

"We must go, Gervase," she urged. "It is our only hope."

He felt sad at her readiness to leave the old man to his own devices. Omri would be quite defenceless. His instinct told him that he should somehow protect them both, but that would consign him to more misery at the oars. He was still agonising over the situation when the decision was taken for him. The faint drumming of hooves could be heard in the distance. Omri was a swift interpreter.

"They're looking for us!"

"We will be caught!" cried Angharad. "They will see us."

"Hold still," said Gervase.

He jumped from the boat and scrambled up the bank to peer over the top. There were a dozen or more of them. They were still some way off, but their search was systematic. As some stayed on the road, others fanned out on each side. Three of them were picking their way along the river.

Gervase slid back to the boat. They seemed trapped.

The search party was thorough. They came at a steady trot and swept along a front of over a hundred yards. Their quarry would not be difficult to spot. A white-haired old bard, a girl, and a young man in the garb of a Chancery clerk were unfamiliar sights. Sooner or later, they would find a trace of them or meet someone who had seen the trio. It was only a question of being patient and methodical.

Their leader held to the road and directed the others.

"What do we do with them?" said his companion.

"Let us find them first."

"They say the girl is very fair."

"No hands must be laid upon her!" said the other.

"Not even in sport?"

"You can have the old man instead."

"What pleasure lies in that?"

An answering voice came singing through the air.

"Mehefin ddaeth, fugeiliaid mwyn . . ."

The harp was a small instrument that could be tucked under Omri's arm, but its strings produced a sound that reverberated between the banks of the river. As the horses quickened their pace, the song increased in sweetness and volume. The leader signaled to his men and all converged on the source of the melodious sound.

Two men and a frightened girl were no match for thirteen armed soldiers. The men grinned as they made their way along the river. Their search had borne fruit and they would be rewarded by their lord. Meanwhile, there

207

would be the satisfaction of feasting their eyes on a Welsh beauty.

"Mor wyn a'r oen, ni wnawn ei fam . . ."

The boat was around the bend in the river at a point where the bank was steepest. Picking their way through the trees, they arrived in a group directly above the vessel.

"Croeso!" said Omri.

The Welsh beauty was an old man with a harp. There was no sign of the others. The leader dismounted and tried to question Omri, but no common language existed between them. The soldiers split up and looked all around them.

Half a mile away, Gervase and Angharad were running for their lives.

The visit to Richard Orbec's fortified manor house changed their plans. Not even Idwal's glib tongue could explain away the presence of a Welsh arrow between the shoulder blades of Orbec's reeve. Ralph Delchard dismissed the archdeacon's earlier assurances that there would be no incursions from across the border. Redwald's death was indisputably the result of an attack by a Welsh raiding party. Warnod's murder and the red dragon carved in Maurice Damville's cornfield were further evidence of a hostile Welsh presence.

"You are safe as long as you are with me," said Idwal.

"I would rather not put that to the test," said Ralph.

"No Welshman would attack you when I am here."

"One is already doing so. With words."

"I offer you wise counsel."

"Save it for the Bishop of Llandaff."

"But I am your talisman, my lord."

"You would not stop me getting an arrow in the back."

208

"I still have doubts about the archer."

"Redwald doesn't."

Ralph took his men back in the direction of Llanwarne. If a more serious onslaught was to come from across the border, he was singularly ill-prepared to cope with it. Eight men-at-arms and a loquacious churchman were an inadequate defence against light-armoured Welsh horsemen who could move at speed and shoot their arrows with deadly accuracy. Ralph needed additional soldiers. Only then could he resume the search for Gervase Bret.

The sheriff had left a handful of men in Llanwarne to continue the investigation into Warnod's death. Ralph would despatch one of them to Hereford at full gallop to spread word of the danger and to collect reinforcements. Canon Hubert and Brother Simon could also be sent back to Hereford for their own safety. There was little more they could achieve by staying. If, as Orbec predicted, the Welsh did come in greater numbers, there would be far too many dragons in Archenfield for anyone's comfort.

"Let me go to them, my lord," offered Idwal.

"It is too late for that."

"I can act as an envoy. To calm them down."

"You are more likely to inflame them to greater wrath."

"Blessed are the peacemakers . . ."

"Unless the Welsh are actually winning the battle."

Ralph spurred his horse into a gallop that left Idwal well behind. He was vexed that the search for Gervase had been temporarily abandoned, but there was no virtue in making themselves easy targets in open country.

When they reached Llanwarne, they were met by Canon Hubert and Brother Simon. They came running

209

out to see if the premature return of the search party meant that Gervase had been found, hoping that he would still be alive, but fearing that his dead body might be strapped across a horse. Their faces crumpled when they realised that their companions were empty-handed.

"What happened?" said Canon Hubert. "Why come back?"

But Ralph Delchard did not even hear him. He had seen another figure nearby and she blotted out every other sight and sound in the vicinity. Golde was standing there with a fond smile that washed away all his recriminations. Ralph was almost tongue-tied in his excitement.

"I am delighted to see you again, Golde."

"The pleasure is mutual, my lord."

"Why have you come?"

"To bring you a gift."

"I have it when I gaze upon your face."

"It may make you smile even more," she said, handing him a thick scroll that was secured with a ribbon. "Take it."

"What is it?"

"Something that Warnod gave to my sister."

"Warnod?"

"Yes, my lord," she said. "His will."

Chapter Ten

THEY RAN UNTIL THEIR LUNGS WERE BURSTING AND their legs were threatening to give way beneath them. Gervase Bret and Angharad staggered to a halt and fell against the trunk of a gnarled tree for support. Omri had been a valuable decoy. The old man and his harp bought them crucial minutes to make their escape into the woods. By the time the soldiers gave chase, the couple were the best part of a mile away.

The headlong race through the trees had been costly. Neither of them was dressed for sprinting over uneven ground. Catching on bushes, their clothing had been torn to ribbons. Unfriendly brambles had lashed at their arms and ground ivy had snatched at their feet. They were more dishevelled than ever. Gervase was deeply concerned for Angharad. Shuddering with fatigue, she was bent almost double as she took in huge wheezing breaths. He reached down to pluck a twig from her hair and to brush some strands of bracken from her cloak.

Voices in the distance intensified their panic.

"They're coming!" she gasped.

"We'll have to hide."

"They'll find us."

"Not if we're careful."

"I can't run any farther, Gervase."

"Lean on me."

"My legs . . ."

"Shhhh!"

He touched her lips with gentle fingertips to still her voice. Silence was vital if they were to elude the pursuit. Slipping an arm around her waist, he half-carried her deeper into the woods. Gervase hoped they would not see the strips of material that had been ripped away from their attire.

The soldiers would have split up again to continue their search. No help could be beaten out of Omri. He was plainly unable to tell them in which direction the couple had fled. That limited the number of men who would be combing the woods.

The voices were coming nearer. Twigs were snapping under hooves, and branches were being broken off by armoured shoulders. Sound was magnified in the stillness of the woods and played tricks on their ears. Voices seemed to be all around them. Gervase dragged Angharad towards the thickest undergrowth and forced his way through the shrubs. The soldiers could now be heard quite clearly, reporting to each other as they crashed their way forward. There were three of them and they sounded angry.

Gervase reached a shallow ditch half-hidden by an outcrop of holly. The ditch was filled with stagnant water and the holly leaves scratched at their hands and faces, but the choice of refuge was forced upon them. Gervase crawled in under the bushes and lay on his back so that he was partly submerged. He pulled Angharad on top of him using her cloak as a blanket to hide the two of them.

Their hearts were pounding. They felt the helpless fear of hunted animals. Angharad's cheek was against his. He could hear the anxious short breaths and smell her terror. The horses came ever closer. Long, prancing legs stopped within touching distance of them. Angharad saw them from the corner of her eye and stifled a scream. Gervase held her more tightly. He could feel her hot tears coursing down his cheek.

"They won't have come this far," said one voice.

"It depends how much of a start they had."

"They're on foot. The girl would slow him down."

"I'll slow *her* down when we catch her."

Ribald laughter bounced off the trees and sent animals scurrying and birds flapping. A third man joined the others and ordered them to press on. The search moved slowly away from the fugitives. As they lay entwined in the ditch, they could hear swords hacking a path through the undergrowth. With an excuse to relax slightly, they stayed exactly where they were.

Gervase was at once moved and guilt-stricken. Stirred by the presence of a beautiful young woman in his arms, he was yet distressed that she was not his beloved Alys. Even in their desperate situation, he could take a momentary pleasure from being Angharad's protector. It felt like a form of betrayal. At the same time, however, it seemed so gentle and natural. Angharad was not nestling into him with the eagerness of a lover. She was a girl in torment, taken from her family to marry a man she loathed, ambushed on her way to Powys to meet her unsought bridegroom, imprisoned in Monmouth Castle, and now chased like a wounded doe through the woodland. Comfort in the arms of someone she trusted was all she desired.

Voices, hooves, and slashing swords faded to the margins of their hearing. They dared to embrace hope. Angharad lifted her head and peered around with care.

"Have they gone?"

"Stay here until we are sure."

"And then?"

"We press on."

"This is a nightmare, Gervase. Where are we?"

He wanted to reassure her somehow, but honesty won through.

"Lost."

Ralph Delchard was too caught up in the welter of activity to attend to Golde immediately. He first sent a messenger to Hereford to inform the sheriff of the killing of Orbec's steward and to alert him to the prospect of danger on the Welsh border. Urgent reinforcements were needed. Ralph then took command of the remainder of Ilbert's men, arguing that they were more likely to find Warnod's killers among the raiders than from the indigenous population. The murder would not be solved by staying in Llanwarne, but by returning to that part of the Golden Valley where Goronwy and his men had penetrated with such effect.

Canon Hubert and Brother Simon agreed to go back to Hereford with two men-at-arms by way of an escort. Idwal's role next came up for discussion. Opinions varied.

"I think I should ride with you, my lord," he said.

"No!" refused Ralph. "Return to Hereford."

"The archdeacon might be more use here," said Canon Hubert, horrified at the prospect of travelling once more with the contentious Idwal. "He speaks Welsh."

"He also speaks Latin," said Ralph. "You, he, and Brother Simon will be able to quote the scriptures at each other."

"My place is here," avowed Idwal. "Among my people."

"Then remain," urged Hubert.

"I will."

"No!" protested Ralph.

"Yes!" said Hubert.

"Perhaps there is a middle way," suggested Simon. "A *via media*, as you might say. We will return to Hereford. You, my lord, will ride back to Richard Orbec's demesne. And the good archdeacon will stay here in Archenfield."

"Ergyng!" corrected Idwal.

"Among your flock," added Hubert. "Thank you, Brother Simon. An admirable compromise. We will then each be allowed to pursue our imperatives in our own way."

"My imperative is to defend my country," said Idwal.

"Do it from Llanwarne," decided Ralph.

"Take me to the heart of the action, my lord."

"It will be no place for long-winded homilies."

"What if there *is* armed conflict?"

"There will be if you insist on following me."

"Before the two opposing sides clash," said Idwal with a grand gesture, "I could interpose myself between them."

Hubert was scathing. "They would take you for a stray sheep and ride over you."

"At least I would be mistaken for a ram!" retorted the other. "And not for a pair of sanctimonious geldings like you two!"

The argument waxed on and Ralph left them to it. He took Golde aside for a quiet word. The chosen place could not have been more apposite. They were standing beside the tiny churchyard in which the last remains of Warnod lay buried.

"A thousand apologies for keeping you waiting, Golde."

"I would wait any length of time for you, my lord."

"That thought excites me." He looked at the document in his hand. "Tell me in more detail how this will came into your possession."

"It was given to Aelgar by her bethrothed."

"Why?"

"She thought it a keepsake," said Golde, "but I feel he had another purpose. Warnod knew that she would guard it like a secret treasure. He wanted it kept safe."

"A secret treasure is what it may turn out to be," said Ralph, fingering the scroll. "Did you sister not read it and understand its import?"

"She is illiterate, my lord. It was from Warnod. That was enough for her. She held it to her at night like a letter of love." Golde smiled. "She was not misled."

"You have studied the document?"

"Aelgar is the sole beneficiary. Warnod could not write himself, but his character comes through in every line. No man could pen a more loving tribute to a woman. Warnod leaves everything to her." She heaved a sigh. "Except that there is nothing now to leave."

"There may be," he said. "Warnod has claim to a thousand acres of land here in Archenfield. We have the charter that enforces that claim. So there is hope yet."

"When will your business be concluded, my lord?"

"It will take some little time yet."

"Will I, then, see you in Hereford again?"

"Nothing would keep me away."

"I would be honoured if you called upon me."

"That is the least that I will do, Golde."

Their eyes met and their hands touched. It was too public a place for any more intimate exchange of vows. Enough had already happened. A commitment had been

216

made on both sides. Ralph glanced across at the grave nearby.

"Your sister may yet have something of Warnod's to cherish," he said. "All will depend on the charter."

"You must judge its legality."

"I am more interested in its origin, Golde."

"What do you mean?"

"Someone sent it to the Exchequer at Winchester," he said. "Not Warnod himself, to be sure, but someone with his interests at heart." He leaned in close to watch her reaction. "Can you suggest who that might be?"

Golde was uneasy beneath his scrutiny. She seemed to be torn between confiding completely in him and denying all knowledge of the document's existence. Her answer was brief.

"Ask the sheriff, my lord."

Ilbert Malvoisin was alarmed by the news. He hoped that the slaying of Richard Orbec's steward was an isolated example of Welsh aggression, but he doubted it. Two red dragons had now appeared in Herefordshire and the arrow in Redwald's back was further proof of stirrings across the border. If the sheriff was alarmed, the reeve was almost driven to hysteria. His bulky frame shook with trepidation.

"They will not reach the city, will they?"

"No, Corbin. Hereford is safe."

"It has fallen to the Welsh before."

"That was a long time ago, Corbin."

"It is within living memory," said the reeve. "May I remind you that both a sheriff and a bishop of Hereford were killed in one battle with the marauders."

"We have improved our defences since then."

"The best defence against the Welsh is a degree of amity with them. That is what we sought. We came to terms with them and peace was guaranteed. Until now."

"Do not fly to the worst conclusions, Corbin."

"Then offer me reassurance."

"One Welsh arrow has been fired," said Ilbert. "That is not even a skirmish."

"It may be the prelude to one," argued the reeve. "Add that one arrow to the burning of Warnod's house and the scale of the danger is enlarged." Corbin gestured with both hands. "What are we to say?"

"As little as possible."

"Should we not ring the alarm bell in the city?"

"No," said Ilbert. "The problem will be contained before it grows any larger. I will double the guard at the castle and on the city walls, but do so in no spirit of anxiety. These are merely sensible precautions."

"What of you, my lord sheriff?"

"I will take men and join Ralph Delchard." A grudging note sounded in his voice. "Though I do not relish the idea of meeting the man across a table in the shire hall, I would rather be with him in the event of trouble than with anybody. He is a true soldier."

"Which way are they coming?"

"Calm down, Corbin. We do not know that they *will* come."

"But if they do?"

"Ewyas is the most likely point of entry."

"Maurice Damville."

"He stands between them and us," said Ilbert. "They will not get past the castle of Ewyas Harold, I assure you. Damville will see to that."

* * *

The castle had been in a state of readiness for several hours. No further sightings of Welsh soldiers had been made from the battlements, but that induced no false sense of security. The enemy might still be there, unseen. Guards patrolled with extra vigilance. Down in the courtyard, other men-at-arms practised their swordplay. The armourer's hammer had not paused all day.

Maurice Damville was in a state of high excitement. For him, the prospect of a battle was like the anticipated conquest of a new woman. All would be resolved in one ecstatic embrace. As he tested his skill with a spear, the weapon felt alive in his hands. Damville feinted, moved in quickly, and swung the blade of his spear. It caught his opponent a glancing blow on the side of his helm and knocked him flying. The victor laughed and pulled the man back to his feet.

A cry from the gatehouse alerted them, but it was no danger signal. The search party was returning. Damville ran to the end of the bailey as the gates swung open to admit the returning soldiers. They drew up in a penitential line before their lord. On the back of their captain's horse was a white-haired old man, clutching a harp.

"Where are they?" bellowed Damville.

"They slipped through our fingers, my lord."

"Again!"

"We lost them in a wood. They went to ground."

"Did you not stay to find them?"

"For an hour or more, my lord. Without success."

"Idiots!" roared Damville. He jabbed a finger at Omri. "And who, in the name of the devil, is this?"

"A bard, my lord. They call him Omri the Blind."

"Then he is in good company with you sightless dolts!"

"He was Angharad's companion."

219

"I want the girl herself, not this old fool. Can you not perform a simple task? I asked for Angharad and that young commissioner, Gervase Bret. And who do I get in their stead?" He pulled Omri from the horse. "This! A blind old man with a harp. What use is he? Lock him up!"

Omri was taken away by two guards. Damville glowered.

"Get back out and find them!" he ordered.

"Yes, my lord."

"They are out there somewhere. Get them both."

Gervase Bret and Angharad struggled on up the hillside. They had no means of knowing how far they had walked or in what direction. After their narrow escape in the wood, they had continued on their way at a brisk, but not reckless, pace. Gervase estimated that they had covered several miles, but the overcast sky blocked out the compass of the sun. He had the dreadful feeling that they might be traveling in the very direction from which they had first fled.

Angharad was a brave companion. Brought up in the sheltered domesticity of her father's house, she was used to being waited on and cared for at every hour of the day. To be chased across rough countryside by hostile soldiers was nerve-racking. Coming as it did on top of the ambush, the experience was devastating. As she strode along gallantly at Gervase's side, she hardly said a word. She was far too dazed.

Gervase kept hold of her hand, more for reassurance than guidance. His eyes scanned the landscape for signs of danger or hopes of assistance. None appeared. Whenever they did pass an isolated cottage or a remote mill, the occupants closed their doors to them. Gervase could understand their fear. After the soaking in the river and the additional drenching in the ditch, he was a disturbing sight. Their flight through the wood had not improved Angharad's beauty. Her face was spattered with mud, her cloak torn and blotched, and her hair tugged loose from its braiding.

Angharad came out of her reverie and turned to him.

"What will become of me?"

"I do not know."

"They must not send me to Powys."

"I will do what I can."

"Omri was a friend, but he would not save me."

"He had his duty."

"We had to leave him," she said, trying to justify their actions. "There was no other way. I hope they did not hurt him when they found him down by the river."

"They had no cause."

"That would not stop them."

Gervase had tried not to think about Omri. He was still troubled by pangs of guilt about the old man. In assisting their escape, Omri had put himself at the mercy of the pursuing soldiers. They might well have tormented him.

"Who are they, Gervase?"

"I do not know."

"Why do they want to catch me?"

"To keep you from going to Powys."

"But *why*?"

"They have their reasons, Angharad."

Hoofbeats sounded in the distance and they crouched down at once. The hillside offered little cover. Movement would only attract attention. It was better to lie flat in the hope of not being seen. Gervase pressed her to the ground and kept a hand in the small of her back as they lay side by side. Horses reached the crest of the adjoining hill and the riders paused. Gervase counted a dozen of them.

He lay quite still, but they did not evade notice. One of the riders pointed in their direction and the others looked towards the hill. The soldiers set off again at a canter. Gervase and Angharad had been seen.

"Quick!" he said, jumping to his feet and helping her up. "Run, Angharad!"

"The horses will catch us!"

"Run!"

The nearest cover was a clump of bushes at the top of the hill, but they had to race up a steep incline to reach it. Gervase was hampered by her fatigue. Though he tried to pull her along by her hand, Angharad kept stumbling and slowing him down. The thunderous hooves climbed up towards them and the soldiers yelled for them to stop. Gervase would not give in, forcing himself on and making one last effort to reach some sort of cover.

But their luck finally ran out. The good fortune which had attended them at the castle and in the wood now deserted them. Angharad twisted her ankle and fell. Gervase tried to pick her up, but was kicked to the ground by the first soldier to arrive. He rolled over and reached for his dagger, but he was too late. A spear was already at his throat to pin him where he lay.

He looked into stern eyes separated by an iron nasal.

"Who are you?" said the man.

Goronwy kept the castle of Ewyas Harold under observation, but remained out of view himself. He had had time to rest and take refreshment now, but the food had not satisfied the hunger for revenge that still clawed at him. He wanted more action. Having tasted blood on Richard

222

Orbec's land, he was ready to wade triumphantly into it. Norman castles were well-built, but they had been stormed before. To leave Ewyas Harold a smoking ruin would be to send a signal the length of the whole border: Wales was rampant once more.

It had started as a search for his stolen bride, but the contest had taken on larger proportions now. Goronwy would not settle for the safe return of Angharad. And he would certainly not pay any ransom for her. Her abduction was a profound insult to him and to the house of Powys. It could only be answered in one way.

His captain came scrambling up to the vantage point and lay beside him in the bushes. Ewyas Harold castle was a bleak citadel under a lowering sky. The captain appraised it.

"How many men will it take?"

"A hundred."

"Five times that number are on their way."

"The messenger has arrived?" asked Goronwy.

"Your uncle has responded to your request."

"He is sending five hundred men?"

"No, my lord," said the man. "He is bringing them."

Golde rode back towards Hereford with Canon Hubert and Brother Simon, but her presence still hovered in Archenfield. Ralph Delchard was deeply moved. In the space of a few minutes, he and Golde had made solemn decisions that called for days of serious meditation. Time had not been needed. Simply to see her again had lifted him out of his anxieties and preoccupations. Warnod's will would be a mighty weapon in the forthcoming duels with Richard Orbec and Ilbert Malvoisin. Both men had assumed that it had been destroyed in the blaze at the

223

house. Its appearance as a piece of evidence in the shire hall would astound them.

Even more pleasing than the will itself was the fact that Golde had brought it. It could just as easily have been sent by messenger, if not retained in Hereford until the commissioners were ready to resume their work there. Golde had taken precious time away from her business to deliver the message in person, even hiring an escort to ride with her. That action brushed away any doubts that Ralph might have had about her feelings towards him.

He chuckled to himself as he recalled what Idwal had said to him. The archdeacon had finally got something right.

"Where do we meet them, my lord?" asked his captain.

"At the next village," said Ralph.

"How long will they be?"

"My message urged all speed."

"Will the sheriff respond?"

"As fast as he may," said Ralph. "Unless I am very much mistaken, Ilbert Malvoisin looks to be Earl of Hereford one day. He will not gain the title by skulking in the city when there is trouble on the border. He will respond."

They were riding northwest in the direction of Richard Orbec's holdings for a rendezvous with the sheriff and his men. The reinforced party could then ride on with confidence to widen the search for Gervase Bret and to hunt for the killers of Warnod and Redwald the reeve. Ralph would be doing what he liked best—taking his men into action with a sword in his hand—but he did not feel the usual thrill of anticipation. Golde kept intruding gently into his mind. He had never met a woman who had so easily and so painlessly taken up lodging in his heart.

It was baffling. Golde was everything that would normally have rebuffed his interest. She was a woman of Saxon birth, the widow of an unloved husband, and the brewer of a liquid that Ralph regarded as a species of poison. Yet he wanted her. There was a sense of independence about her that drew him ineluctably to her side. His main goal was still to track down his dearest friend. If Gervase were to be found alive, however, Ralph would celebrate the joyous event by racing off to be with Golde.

"He is still trailing us, my lord," said the captain.

"What?"

"The archdeacon."

"Can we never shake him off?" moaned Ralph.

"He is like a burr—he sticks."

Ralph turned in his saddle and saw the diminutive figure a quarter of a mile behind them. Forbidden to ride in their company, Idwal was following in their wake. His whole life was a verbal confrontation between Wales and England. If a real battle was to take place, he did not wish to miss the opportunity to be involved in some dramatic way.

"Shall I frighten him off?" offered the captain.

"It would be a waste of time."

"What does he *want*, my lord?"

"Listeners."

They reached the meeting point, but had a long wait before the sheriff finally arrived with fifty men at his back. He thanked Ralph for sending the warning and gave him an account of the precautionary measures he had taken in Hereford itself. The two men rode together at the head of their troops. Ilbert wanted more detail about events on the Orbec demense and Ralph obliged him. The latter then took the opportunity to broach another matter.

"You know Golde, I see."

225

"She is a presence in the community."

"She would be a presence wherever she went," said Ralph. "But you seemed to have a closer acquaintance with her."

"That is all past," said the sheriff huffily.

"Then there *was* something?"

"A private matter of no account."

"It must have some weight if it still troubles you."

"I have put it behind me, my lord. Ask no more."

"But I do," pressed Ralph. "The lady interests me. If you have anything to say against her, take care. You will find me ready to defend her name against all slander."

"Then I will hold my tongue."

"Why?"

"The truth might cause offence."

"What truth, my lord sheriff?"

"As I have said, it is all done. We are reconciled."

"You cannot leave me in the air like this," complained Ralph. "There is a charge against the lady's character, I can tell. When I saw the two of you together, I sensed a tension between you. What was its cause?"

"Golde is a thief," said the sheriff bluntly.

"Never!"

"I speak but as I know, my lord."

"Then speak no more falsehood of her or I will not be answerable for my temper. The lady is abused here. I know it."

Ilbert let Ralph sulk in silence for a while then raised the topic that had been exercising his mind. Ralph and he were riding shoulder to shoulder as comrades. The sheriff attempted to build on that relationship.

"Your help is much appreciated, my lord."

"I harry the Welsh in order to regain a friend."

"Whatever your motives, it is comforting to have such an experienced soldier at my side. Neither of the men we ride towards would support me as they should. Richard Orbec is too bound up in his own concerns and Maurice Damville is too ambitious to take orders from any man."

"Ask the favour," said Ralph.

"What?"

"I know when I am being licked into a giving vein."

"That is not the case at all."

"Ask the favour and let's have done with it."

"It is not a favour, my lord. Merely a request."

"Put it to me."

"I simply wish to say that I hope we can come to some amicable agreement with regard to your work here."

"Of course," said Ralph. "We'll dispossess you and fine you as amicably as we can."

"Is there not another course we could pursue?"

"Do I detect the odour of bribery?"

"No," asserted Ilbert, colouring under his helm. "All I ask for is a balance between justice and practicality. If something works well, why change it?"

"If a man beats his wife well, why stop him?"

"I have to go on living in Hereford, you do not."

"In view of what we have uncovered, I am very grateful." Ralph clapped him on the shoulder. "Save your breath, my lord sheriff. This is one battle. The shire hall will be another."

"I am sure that we can come to an understanding."

"We already have."

"All it takes is a little effort on both sides."

Ralph chuckled as he thought of the document that was safely tucked away in the satchel that Brother Simon had borne off to Hereford.

227

"Yes, my lord sheriff," he said, cheerily. "Where there's a will, there's a way."

Richard Orbec watched impassively as they came into the room. Still in full armour, he was standing in the hall of his manor house with an armed soldier on either side of him. Gervase Bret and Angharad had been allowed to wash and change before they faced his interrogation. The men who had run them to earth had been from the demesne in the Golden Valley. Instead of being recaptured by enemies, they were in the hands of a putative friend. At the moment, however, there was nothing friendly in his manner. Orbec kept them on their feet while he fired questions at Gervase.

"Who is she?" he snapped.

"Angharad, my lord. Niece of Rhys ap Tewdr."

"The prince of Deheubarth?" His interest kindled. "What were you doing with the lady?"

"It is a long story."

"Tell it in full without prevarication."

Gervase related all that had happened to him since he had been ambushed on Orbec's demesne. Not understanding a word, Angharad waited quietly with her eyes downcast and her hands folded. She was wearing a man's tunic and mantle. They were much too large and hung in folds about her, but they did not diminish the regal quality that she bore. Listening attentively to Gervase's account, Orbec never let his gaze leave Angharad.

"Who is this man she rides to Powys to marry?"

"Goronwy, nephew of the prince."

"A murderer!"

Orbec's explosive denunciation made Angharad jump and she looked to Gervase for comfort. He put a hand on her arm. In a clean tunic and mantle himself, Gervase felt restored and renewed. He was not going to be browbeaten by their host.

"There is no need to frighten your guest," he chided. "We did not ask to come here, my lord. If we offend you in some way, lend us horses and we will happily quit your land."

"You have been far too happy to trespass on it," said Orbec. "This is the second time that you were caught here without licence for your visit."

"We strayed onto your land by mistake."

"And the first time?" He rode over Gervase's gabbled apology. "Yes, my friend. Another mistake." He turned to Angharad once more. "Does she know she is to wed a killer?"

"Only too well, my lord."

"Oh?"

"That is why she resists the match. All the time we have been together, she has implored me to save her from this Goronwy. The man's reputation puts the fear of God into her."

"His reputation does not deceive," said Orbec.

"You know of the man?"

"He paid me a visit—and killed my reeve."

"This same Goronwy?"

"It had to be him," insisted Orbec. "He put an arrow in Redwald's unprotected back. And now I know his reason for coming here. There she stands. He thought that I held his bride in captivity. Now I do."

Angharad begged for a translation of the words that had darkened Orbec's face even more. Gervase gave her an edited version in Welsh of what was said. She began to tremble.

"Tell her that I will not harm her," said Orbec.

Gervase relayed the message. She replied to it.

"She begs you not to hand her over," said Gervase. "She knows that Goronwy is a bad man and will have none of him."

"In that, at least, she shows some taste."

Orbec looked at her strangely for a long while. Dismissing the two soldiers, he summoned food and wine. When he waved his guests to seats, they sank down with the utmost gratitude. Gervase had never been so pleased to see a tray of meat brought in. The wine tasted like nectar. Angharad ate more sparingly, but emptied her cup within minutes. It seemed to enliven her. Colour returned to her face and animation to her manner.

"It was not her fault, my lord," argued Gervase.

"Fault?"

"The murder of your reeve. She is hardly more than a child, caught up in the politics of an alliance. If Goronwy did come here in search of her, you should forget Angharad herself and ask another question."

"Which is?"

"*Why* did this assassin come? What gave him the idea that his betrothed was in custody here?"

"I have no idea."

"Then let me put one into your head, my lord," said Gervase. "Someone told him. Whoever ambushed her escort on the road left your name as the culprit. The same men wanted me out of the way as well, so I was captured on your land. That, too, threw suspicion on you and no doubt brought Ralph Delchard hammering noisily on your door."

"Twice," said Orbec with a faint smile.

"Does any name suggest itself?"

"It does."

"We both agree on that at least," said Gervase. "It has been a long day for me, but it has given me ample time to reflect on events. In different ways, Angharad and I were weapons to be used against you. Blame the man who forged us."

Angharad leaned across to whisper in Gervase's ear.

"What does she say?" said Orbec.

"She asked if you were married, my lord."

He recoiled slightly and shook his head. She spoke again.

"In the chamber where she changed, Angharad saw the gown of a lady. They would not let her put it on."

"It is not to be worn," said Orbec, softly.

"She took it for your wife's attire."

"And so it would have been."

Richard Orbec fell silent. The green eyes were fixed on a spot in the air. Neither of them dared to intrude on him. Gervase was touched to see a vulnerable side to an otherwise hard and unyielding man. Angharad needed no translation. The man's grief was all too visible and it was bathed in a deep guilt. His mind was years in the past.

A tap on the door brought his introspection to an end. In response to his call, a servant entered with deference.

"Visitors at the gate, my lord."

"Who are they?"

"Ilbert the Sheriff and others besides."

"I'll see what they want."

Orbec left the hall and Angharad immediately aimed a flurry of questions at Gervase. He made her speak slowly so that he could understand her.

"What will he do with me?" she asked.

"I do not know."

"Will he hand me over to Goronwy?"

"No, Angharad," said Gervase, wanting to put her mind at rest without telling her about the deadly visit of her intended. "That is the last thing he will do. He has a personal score to settle with Goronwy."

"Then he will hold me as a hostage?"

"I think not."

"He is a strange man," she said. "I cannot tell if he likes me or hates me. His eyes say both things at once."

"He will not harm you, Angharad."

"When you asked him about a wife . . . ?"

"Yes?"

"Why was he so sad?"

"Memories."

Angharad plied him with more questions and he did his best to answer her. Having been with her only in the most trying circumstances before, it was a joy to sit in comfort and enjoy her company. Footsteps interrupted them. They came running into the house and approached the hall. The door was flung open and Ralph Delchard stood framed in it.

"Gervase!" he exclaimed. "You're alive and well."

"Half-alive." The two men embraced warmly. "But what are you doing here?"

"My tale can wait," said Ralph, dismissively. "How came *you* here? And who is your charming companion?" He bowed to Angharad then gave Gervase a knowing wink. "Is this lady the reason that you went astray?"

"In a manner of speaking, she is."

"I long to hear this story, but first embrace me again. I thought we'd lost you forever, Gervase."

They embraced a second time, then sat down opposite Angharad. Gervase recounted the salient points of his adventures at speed. When the narrative reached Orbec's demesne once more, Ralph became serious.

"One hand is at work behind all this," he said. "Our villain is the castellan of Ewyas Harold."

"Maurice Damville."

"He had Warnod murdered to stir up hatred against the Welsh. He had Angharad here waylaid in order to heat up the blood of her bridegroom." Ralph stood up and paced the hall. "Damville is clever, I have to hand him that. The red dragon in Archenfield pointed the finger towards the border. The same dragon in his own cornfield pointed the finger away from him."

"We arrived in this shire at the wrong time," said Gervase, "just as his plans were coming to fruition. No wonder he was so quick to drop his claim to Orbec's land. He did not want us prowling around the margins of his own land in case we jeopardised his scheming."

"So you were removed from the scene."

"And the work of the commission ground to a halt."

"Not quite," said Ralph. "More news on that front anon. Let's stay with Damville. I see why he wanted to stir the Welsh into a fury then set them on Orbec. But why have Warnod murdered so cruelly?"

"He needed the poor man out of the way."

"Why?"

Gervase shrugged. "Warnod must have had something that Damville desperately wanted. That charter, perhaps."

"It was in our hands."

"True."

"And Damville did not even know of its existence until we told him of it." Ralph was thoughtful. "Besides, he waived his right to that land as soon as he realised it might bring us poking around too close to his own estates." He stopped beside Gervase. "There must be something else he wanted from Warnod. What on earth was it?"

Aelgar brought the cup across to her sister and offered it to her. It was her turn to provide the consolation. Since she had come home from Archenfield with the others, Golde had been moody and withdrawn. The ride had patently tired her, yet she would not rest. Aelgar pushed her gently onto a stool and held the cup out to her.

"Drink it, Golde. It's only water."

"Later."

"Drink it."

Aelgar held it to her lips and made her sip it. Once she had tasted the water, Golde realised how dry her throat was and quaffed the whole cup. She looked up in thanks.

"What is his name, Golde?" asked the other.

"Whose name?"

"You did not ride all that way simply to deliver the will. It was an excuse to see somebody. One of those commissioners, I think."

"It was," admitted Golde.

"Does he like you as much as you obviously like him?"

"I think so."

"Then be happy."

"I cannot, Aelgar."

"Why not?"

"Because of who I am and who he is."

"You are as good as any Norman lord," said Aelgar, with a show of spirit. "We were born into a noble house. Does he know that? Our father was a wealthy thegn. This man has no right to look down on you."

"He does not do that."

"Then what is the problem?"

"*We* are, Aelgar." Golde stood up to face her sister with an air of resignation. "My home is here and his is far away in Hampshire. My work is here and his takes him wherever the king sends him. My place is with you and . . . that is that."

"Your place is where your heart takes you."

"Then I have to stay here."

"No, Golde."

"I have foolish thoughts, I admit, but they fall apart when I examine them. How could I leave you? How could I walk away from the brewhouse when I have devoted myself to it all these years? How could I even dream of leaving Hereford?"

"I did."

"That was different."

"No, Golde. I put my feelings first, as you must do." A resilience was now showing. "Do not worry about me. The brewhouse will not fail because you are not here to run it. I work in it just as much as you."

"That is so."

"Ask but two questions and all else follows."

"What are they?"

"Do you want him?"

"Yes, Aelgar!"

"Does he want you?"

"I am not sure. I believe so."

"Find out for certain. Go to him now."

"I cannot," said Golde in despair. "That's what grieves me most. He has ridden with the sheriff to Richard Orbec's estate. Welsh raiders crossed the border and killed a man. They fear a larger army will come. Ralph will have to fight them if it does." She grabbed her sister's hands. "I would hate to lose him just as I have found him."

"Have faith, sister. He will come back."

"What if this army masses on the border?"

"We have heard such rumours many times before," said Aelgar. "We are at peace with the Welsh. There is a truce. They have no just cause to break it."

Cadwgan ap Bleddyn, prince of Powys, led his men down from the Black Mountains. They clattered along a narrow, winding road between hedges of hazel and thorn. The mountains were olive green in the evening sunlight. Five hundred men came out of them like a silver avalanche and rolled inexorably towards Ewyas Harold. The soldiers were armoured, their weapons sharpened, and their purpose heightened by a speech from their prince. They were lusting for battle.

Down below them, waiting impatiently with his men, was Goronwy. They heard the noise of the hooves first, then saw the banners dancing above the host. Five hundred warriors to wreak a terrible revenge. Goronwy was inspired.

He would mount the red dragon and ride it to victory.

Chapter Eleven

THE COUNCIL OF WAR WAS HELD IN THE HALL OF Richard Orbec's manor house. Angharad had retired to a chamber on the floor above while the men discussed tactics and contingencies. Orbec himself was on his feet, constantly on the move as the argument became louder and more intense. Ralph Delchard, Gervase Bret, and Ilbert Malvoisin sat around the long table. Of the four of them, the sheriff was the most anxious to sue for peace.

"Give them what they want," he said, "and this battle is concluded before it has even started. Hand over the lady and let them have their wedding in Powys."

"No," said Orbec, bristling. "That I cannot do."

"Angharad refuses to marry this man," reminded Gervase.

Ilbert was contemptuous. "Her refusal is neither here nor there. She will do what her uncle orders her to do. We need trouble ourselves no further about her feelings in this matter. God save us! If women were allowed to choose their husbands on their own account, the better part of mankind would be forced to remain celibate."

"It is not the lady's feelings I consider," returned Orbec, advancing on the sheriff. "It is my own. Goronwy killed my steward. That death must be answered. I will not appease a Welsh murderer."

"Then this marriage is doomed," observed Ralph with a wry grin. "They want the bride, but you pursue the bridegroom. The couple are divorced before the nuptials even start."

"Goronwy is mine!" insisted Orbec.

"Not by surrender," said Gervase. "They would never exchange him for Angharad."

"Then she stays here."

"That only invites attack, my lord," said Ilbert.

"Let it come. We are prepared."

"Not if Goronwy's uncle becomes involved. Even your defences would not hold out long against the full might of Powys."

"Cadwgan ap Bleddyn is bound by terms of peace," said Gervase. "He will not be drawn into this."

"He has no choice," argued the sheriff. "An affront has been offered to the house of Powys. It cannot be ignored. The men who ambushed this lady did so to enrage these fiery Welshmen."

"And bring them down on this manor," added Gervase.

"Only if we are foolish enough to keep her here," said Ilbert. "One woman can end this whole business. Throw her out and let's have peace again in this shire."

"Goronwy must pay for his crime," asserted Orbec, "or I'll keep the lady here in perpetuity."

"Your hospitality need not be that overgenerous," said Ralph. "But I agree. She stays."

"It is madness!" yelled Ilbert.

"Expediency."

"We are stoking up a conflict."

"No, my lord sheriff," said Ralph. "We are risking a

skirmish in order to prevent a war. Angharad and the madcap Goronwy are not two young lovers pining for each other. They are merely links in a chain. Join them together in the forge of matrimony and you join Deheubarth with Powys. Is that what you want? A chain that runs almost the whole length of the Welsh border?"

"Ralph counsels well," said Gervase. "It is in our interests to keep these two apart."

"My interest is to keep myself alive!" hissed Ilbert.

"Then return to Hereford," said Orbec with scorn. "We will fight without you and send you news when it is safe to venture out of doors again."

"Why fight at all?"

"Goronwy slew my reeve."

"Are we all to be put in jeopardy over the death of a Saxon?" said Ilbert. He turned to Ralph. "I do not fear this marriage as much as you. It need not bode ill for us. It is a way to reconcile Deheubarth with Powys, that is all. If we let them have amity between themselves on that side of the border, we will not have hostility on this side."

Orbec was resolute. "The lady stays!"

"I agree," said Ralph. "We would be poor hosts to turn her out so rudely. Angharad remains."

"And brings the red dragon into this shire again."

"It need not be so, my lord sheriff," said Gervase. "We are arguing only about possibilities. How can we know what is in the mind of the Welsh unless we treat with them? This Goronwy is wild and impulsive, but his uncle is more politic. Cadwgan ap Bleddyn took a Norman wife in the name of peace. When they are weighed in the balance, his own marriage will always tip the scales against that of his nephew."

"What are you advising, Gervase?" said Ralph.

"That we first find out exactly what danger we face. I side with my lord sheriff, but for a different reason. Peace is our first concern. Use words before weapons."

"A weapon has already been used against my reeve," said Orbec. "I will not let that pass."

"Nor need you, my lord," said Gervase, "but your quarrel is with Goronwy alone. Not with the whole house of Powys. One more thing. Angharad must be shown to them. They must see that she is unharmed and not held against her will."

"I'll not yield her up!" asserted Orbec.

"You do not have to, my lord. But we must prove that she is alive and well. We cannot do that if she is locked away here. Angharad is our flag of truce. Let us wave her before them."

"Gervase talks sense," endorsed Ralph. "Instead of hiding behind these walls, let's ride out to know their purpose. And take the girl with us. I'll lead the embassy."

Orbec was still unpersuaded but made no protest.

"You'll need a good interpreter," warned Ilbert. "The Welsh use words as other men use ropes. They'll bind you hand and foot with lies and false promises."

"Not if we speak their own language," said Gervase.

"You are fluent enough in Welsh?"

"Not me. My knowledge of their tongue is not sufficient for this purpose. We need someone whose voice was schooled in Wales itself. Someone who can talk a bird out of a tree. Someone who is as proud and as devious as they themselves."

"Where would we find such a person?" said Orbec.

"He waits at your gate, my lord."

"Saints preserve us!" said Ralph in horror. "Idwal!"

* * *

Cadwgan ap Bleddyn gazed at the castle of Ewyas Harold with an amalgam of hatred and respect. It was a despised monument to Norman occupation of Welsh land, but its effectiveness could not be denied. The prince of Powys had been forced to admire the marcher lords. Ewyas Harold was one more citadel to defend the border and taunt those who lived beyond it.

Goronwy was impatient. His pugnacity brooked no delay.

"Let us attack at once, my lord!" he urged.

"Control your haste, Goronwy."

"I have taken inventory of the castle's weaknesses."

"You should have made more note of its strengths."

"We have men enough to storm it, my lord."

"They are *my* warriors," reminded Cadwgan. "They answer to my command and not yours."

"Why bring them if not to engage in battle?"

"A show of force can often achieve as much as force itself, Goronwy. I will not spill blood if I can secure our purpose by another means. We'll parley."

"Destruction is the only parley they understand."

"It would only come at a terrible price."

"I'd pay it willingly to get Angharad!"

"You may still have her," said Cadwgan, "but not by violent means. Our quarrel is not with this castle. Though I would love to see it wiped from the face of Ewyas, I will not lay siege without more cause. You tell me that Richard Orbec is the man we seek. Let's ride around this stronghold in a wide circle and confront Orbec instead."

Goronwy glowered. "Is my uncle afraid of battle?"

"No!" snarled the other. "But I have fought too many. You are still young, Goronwy. You think that everything can be settled with a sword and spear. I have learned to

241

conserve my strength for the moments when a man has to strike."

"Such a moment is at hand."

"I do not see it here."

"Will you let them watch you walk tamely away?" cried Goronwy, pointing at the castle. "Will you let them jeer at us from the battlements? They cower behind their walls in fear. We have only to mount one assault and they will be glad to surrender."

"There is no chance of that!" said Cadwgan, grimly.

"Look at the size of our army. They are terrified."

A loud whistling noise took their eyes towards the castle. A huge boulder had just been catapulted over its walls in their direction. It fell fifty yards short of them, but its challenge could not be denied. The whole army rumbled with anger and pulled back slightly.

"Does that look like fear, Goronwy?" said Cadwgan.

"They *want* a fight, my lord. Let them have it."

"No!"

"They fired at us!"

"A warning shot only. I will fire one back."

Cadwgan gave a signal and one of his soldiers brought his horse trotting forward. The prince gave him his orders and the man went off in the direction of the castle. He stopped when he was within hailing distance and translated Cadwgan's questions into a language they could understand.

"Who speaks for you?" he boomed.

"Maurice Damville!" yelled the castellan, appearing on the battlements. "Who dares to threaten my castle?"

"Cadwgan ap Bleddyn, prince of Powys."

"Send him back to his mountains."

"We come in peace to search for a missing bride."

"She is not here. Ask of Richard Orbec."

"We have only your word that the lady is not within your castle. Let us search it to satisfy ourselves."

"Away with you!" roared Damville. "I am not such a fool as to let marauding Welshmen through my gates. If you wish to fight, then do so with your army."

"Do not provoke us, my lord. We have five hundred men."

"Five thousand would not take us!"

Damville waved an arm to unseen soldiers in the bailey below and the catapult was fired again. The boulder went high over the messenger's head and landed much closer to the waiting soldiers. They backed away with gathering fury and looked towards their prince for the excuse to retaliate. Cadwgan ap Bleddyn had seen enough. Recalling his messenger with a wave, he passed a command through the ranks.

The soldiers divided into four groups and surrounded the castle. Dozens of them dismounted and took their bows from across their backs. Some of the arrows in their quivers were bound with rags beneath the heads. Flasks of oil, which had hung from pommels, were uncorked and used to soak the rags. Fires were lit and the material set alight. The air was suddenly filled with blazing fire as flights of arrows descended from all sides. Some bit harmlessly into the ground and others bounced off stone, but a number landed in the thatched roofs of the timber buildings; flames crackled. Men rushed to put them out with wooden pails of water.

Horses neighed and bucked in the stables at the sight of fire, but it was soon brought under control. A second flight of arrows followed the first and with more effect. One man fell from the battlements as his eye was

243

pierced. Two others were burned to death as the skin of oil beside them was set instantly alight and exploded with rage. More roofs blazed and one of the storehouses began to smoulder. Once again, however, water was on hand to douse the worst of the anticipated attack.

The taunting figure of Maurice Damville appeared again.

"Thank you," he shouted in the direction of Cadwgan. "Now that you have warmed our hands for us, let us warm your arses for you." He let his arm fall. "Fire!"

Archers on the battlements sent volleys in reply. The Welsh bowmen turned to run out of range, but a number of them were wounded or maimed. Damville shook with laughter. Battle had been engaged and blood drawn on both sides. He was confident of success. The advantage of Welsh numbers was outweighed by the strength of his defences. Soldiers in light armour were vulnerable targets from the battlements. Without siege engines and scaling ladders, the men of Powys were no match for him.

His laughter soon died as a new factor entered the fray. Riding north along the border road came another army of Welsh warriors, no more than a hundred strong this time, but with a weapon that made Damville take their threat far more seriously. Four carts had been commandeered from nearby farms and lashed together in a line. Keen axes had felled a massive oak and sharpened one end to a gleaming white point. Resting on the four carts, it was towed by a dozen horses and pushed along from behind by the willing hands of Welsh peasants. Word of the ambush had at last reached Angharad's father. He had come in search of his daughter.

Cadwgan ap Bleddyn rode to meet the newcomers and friendly greetings were exchanged. The prince of Powys recalled his men from around the castle so that they stood on a ridge with their backs to Wales. Maurice Damville was allowed to see the full power of the force that threatened him. Six hundred men with a battering ram of such size were a different proposition. The soldiers along his battlements grew uneasy and loud muttering began. Damville bullied them into silence with yells and threats then looked out at his enemy.

A stillness had fallen on the attackers as well. They were drawn up in a long line to await the signal to attack. Cadwgan conversed quietly with Angharad's father, then he pointed towards the castle. The messenger rode out again and stopped within hailing distance.

"Is Angharad within your castle?" he called.

"No!" shouted Damville.

As his defiant bellow faded away, it was replaced by a more haunting and melodious sound, faint at first, but growing in volume and intensity as it wafted through a window in the tower. Behind the song was the plaintive note of the harp and every Welshmen on the ridge knew who was playing it.

"Omri Dall!" said Cadwgan. "They are inside!"

Goronwy was manic. "He holds Angharad prisoner!"

"We have heard enough."

The prince of Powys gave the command and six hundred men came trotting down from the ridge towards the castle in a menacing line with the battering ram pulled along behind. It was a daunting sight and even Maurice Damville felt the icy touch of apprehension. It was ironic. They were attacking his castle to release someone who was not even in there. Ready to provoke their ire before, he now wished that he had calmed it.

Discomfort ran along the battlements, but he enforced discipline at once, marching along with a sword in his hand and ordering his archers to have their arrows ready. The oncoming surge rolled ever closer and the battering ram slowly gathered speed. Goronwy was at the head of the charge with his temples throbbing violently and a vision of his bride before his eyes. It seemed as if nothing could stop a savage battle that would bring hideous casualties on both sides.

Then she came. Dressed in white and escorted by four men, Angharad came riding around the angle of the castle. She was an arresting sight. She wore a white gown with elbow-length sleeves over a white chemise. Her mantle was edged with gold braid and a gold belt hung at her waist. Her head was uncovered so that her face could be seen by all. Angharad held herself like a true princess—proud, dignified, and unafraid.

She and her companions drew to a halt between the castle and the Welsh battle line. Archers on the battlements lowered their bows. The cavalry reined in their horses. The battering ram was slowed and stopped. An eerie stillness fell. All eyes were on Angharad. She did not look like a helpless prisoner now. Her father burst into tears with relief. Goronwy stared at her with his heart on fire.

Ralph Delchard and Gervase Bret waited on one flank. Richard Orbec and Idwal the Archdeacon on the other. She said nothing, but held the two sides at bay with the sheer magic of her presence. Angharad gestured her spokesman forward. His cadences rolled towards his countrymen.

"I am Idwal of Llandaff," he chanted. "A man of your own nation with your own values and ambitions. I speak as an envoy of peace. Lay down your weapons. There is no longer any reason to fight. Angharad is safe, as you see. She is here with us of her own free will. She was ambushed and held in captivity, but she was rescued by this man." He pointed to Gervase. "He risked his life to save hers. She was brought to the Golden Valley and taken in by this man." He indicated Orbec. "He fed her and clothed her even though one of your number murdered his reeve. His name is Richard Orbec and he makes one demand through me."

Idwal was not allowed to make it. As soon as Orbec was identified, Goronwy broke from the line and galloped towards him with his sword flailing. Too much hatred was boiling inside the Welshman to be dispersed by a few conciliatory words from the archdeacon. The name of Orbec was lodged in his mind like a spike. Killing the man was the only way to pluck it out. It was also the only way to claim his bride.

With a blood-curdling cry, Goronwy closed on his quarry. Concerned for her safety, Gervase took the reins of Angharad's horse and led her a little distance away. Idwal bombarded the oncoming rider with warnings of eternal damnation, but they bounced harmlessly off. Ralph Delchard held his ground, but drew his sword as a precaution.

Richard Orbec also had his weapon out of its scabbard. He nudged his mount forward and kept it prancing on its toes. Orbec and Goronwy were starkly contrasted, the one a dignified figure in full armour on a huge destrier, the other a reckless warrior in light armour on a much smaller horse.

Power confronted passion. Ambition faced revenge. As the two men clashed, it seemed as if the conquest of Wales was about to be played out in miniature. Goronwy's wild assault was easily rebuffed. Orbec simply deflected the blows from the Welshman's scything sword and swung his horse in a quick loop to confuse his assailant. Goronwy roared with fury and came in again, but every slash of his sword was parried with expert ease.

The Welsh horde was strangely silent, admiring Goronwy's courage in launching the attack, but disapproving of his folly in riding within range of the archers on the battlements. Those in the castle or in front of it also watched without a murmur. As the swords met time and again, only the clang of metal echoed across the grass.

Goronwy's frenzy robbed him of all control. He simply hacked away repeatedly with his weapon. Richard Orbec was a more complete soldier. He had greater strength and vastly better technique. It was clear to all that he could knock his man from the saddle at will, yet he chose not to do this. Orbec contented himself with a defensive role, letting Goronwy expend his energy in a series of futile attacks.

The Welshman's frustration became too great to bear. When he next closed on Orbec, he flung himself at the Norman and tried to buffet him to the ground, but his adversary was ready for him. Moving his horse sharply away and smashing a forearm against Goronwy's chest, Orbec sent him sprawling to the ground. Once again, he had held back. When he might have finished his man, he allowed him to get to his feet again.

Goronwy was fired by a sense of indignation. He had been humiliated in combat in front of his own men. He vowed to cut out Orbec's heart and hold it up on the point of his sword. He let out the most ear-splitting war cry yet. Before he could strike again, however, the plaintive voice of Angharad was heard.

"Goronwy!"

He froze and turned to look up at her. That moment of immobility was his downfall. Up on the battlements, Maurice Damville took a small axe from his belt and hurled it down with vicious power. It came spinning through the air with gathering speed to strike Goronwy full in the face and to split his head in two like a cleft apple. Blood spurted everywhere. The Welshman fell backward with a thud.

Angharad screamed and was immediately shielded by Ralph Delchard and Gervase Bret. Orbec glowered up at Damville in disgust. The archers drew their bows on the battlements. Incsensed by what they had seen, the Welsh host was ready to charge again.

Idwal the Archdeacon bravely interposed himself between the two forces and raised his voice to full volume.

"Do not be roused to battle!" he shouted in Welsh. "This death will be paid for in full. The man who ambushed a beautiful young bride has just murdered her bridegroom. You all saw him—Maurice Damville, castellan of Ewyas Harold."

Hearing his name, Damville acknowledged it with a cheerful wave. His old defiance had returned. He pointed down at Goronwy's body and laughed derisively.

"*He* is the true enemy here," continued Idwal in his own tongue, "and has many crimes to answer for. It is not your task to bring him to account. He will pay for this cowardly murder. The sheriff will arrest him and he will stand trial."

"He will stand trial now!" ordered Cadwgan. "He slew my nephew. That crime cannot be settled in an English court of law. Move aside that we may raze his castle to the ground."

Idwal extended both arms. "Why kill so many men on both sides to get at one?"

"Move aside, I say!"

The prince of Powys began to marshal his men again and the battering ram was retrieved. Angharad would not be able to halt them this time. Seeing the sudden change of mood, Ralph Delchard took control. He rode up to the castle walls alone to address Damville directly.

"This slaughter will serve nobody's purpose," he said. "Your plans have gone awry, my lord. You killed Warnod and set an ambush for Angharad in order to sow the seeds of enmity along the border. But she escaped and we divined your purpose. You will be arraigned by the sheriff and held for trial in due course."

"The sheriff will have to take me first."

"I may leave that to this army here, if you wish. They are but the first wave you will have to repulse. More will surely follow. Is that what your men seek?" he said, raising his voice so that the whole castle could hear. "Will you throw away your own lives for this murderer you serve?"

Damville's soldiers looked out at the battle line and the battering ram. If the Welsh were held at bay, there would be the sheriff and his men to follow them. If they were beaten off, the king himself would send a larger army to know the reason why. The castle of Ewyas Harold was doomed. That realisation showed in every face but one.

"We will fight to the last man!" yelled Damville.

"You are he," said Ralph.

"I will never give myself up to the sheriff."

"There is no need. A simpler procedure may be followed here. It will resolve the matter forthwith."

Damville glowered at him. "What simpler procedure?"

"Trial by combat," said Ralph. "Against me."

To subdue the tumult in her mind, Golde threw herself into her work. When she was busy in the brewhouse with her assistants or taking further orders from her customers, she had no time to fret about her future. It was only when she watched some casks being loaded onto a cart that he slipped back into her thoughts. The casks were destined for the castle and it was there that she had first met Ralph Delchard. Seeking a sheriff whom she resented, she had instead been shown kindness by a man she had come to love. She smiled as she recalled his opinion of ale. Of all the men she might have chosen, she picked one who despised the brew with which she made such a comfortable living.

"Are we finished for the day, Golde?"

"I think so."

"Shall we eat together?"

"I am not hungry."

"He will not thank you for starving yourself."

"Leave me, Aelgar. I would not be teased."

But her sister had come to renew her earlier advice. The death of her own beloved had awakened her to the readiness with which she had planned to walk out of the house in Castle Street. Golde had not been consulted at any stage, but she did not complain about that. She had shared in Aelgar's happiness and that was enough for her.

The roles were now reversed. In her despair, the younger sister could pluck comfort from Golde's happiness. The problem was that the latter was still reluctant to bask in the pleasure herself. Doubts continued to assail her.

"You love him, Golde. He loves you. What else matters?"

"The truth, Aelgar."

"What truth?"

"There should be trust and honesty between us."

"Is there not?"

"Up to a point." Golde looked across at her. "How much did you confide in Warnod?"

"Everything."

"You held nothing back? No little secrets?"

"Of course not."

"Did you tell him all your faults?"

"I have none."

"That is one of them," said Golde with a smile. "To think you are perfect. Was there complete trust between you and Warnod? On both sides?"

"On both sides," said Aelgar. "To share a man's life properly, you have to commit yourself to him. I trusted Warnod utterly. If he had not trusted me, he would never have given me that will to keep."

"It is not the will that worries me."

"Then what is it?"

"His charter."

Aelgar was surprised. "Have you not told him yet?"

"I am not sure that I should."

"He may find out by other means."

Golde sighed. "That's my fear. All would be lost."

"Tell him, sister. He will understand."

"It may make him think ill of me."

"Not if he loves you, Golde. Put him to the test."

"I am afraid to do so."

"Then let me do it for you," volunteered the other. "I can praise you in ways that you would not. I am involved

252

here. It was I who first told you of the charter. I should be the one to explain to him in full."

"No," said Golde, reaching a firm decision at last. "You are right. He must be told. But not by you. It is my duty and I must not shirk it. Since I have been blessed with the chance to meet this man, I must have the courage to speak openly with him. I will tell all. It is the only way."

Maurice Damville bowed to necessity. He had no alternative. His carefully laid plot had been sundered by the escape of Gervase Bret and Angharad. With them safely in custody in Monmouth Castle, he could have controlled events with ease and directed all the hostility at Richard Orbec. That was no longer possible. He had been overtaken by events and his own men had now revolted against him. Lured by the promise of lavish gains, their ambition waned in the face of six hundred men with a battering ram. Their lord must fight on alone.

The contest took place outside the castle on the land facing the Welsh border. Cadwgan ap Bleddyn and his men formed a wide circle around the combatants. The body of Goronwy had been discreetly moved from the scene and lay under sacking in the back of one of the carts. Reunited with her father, Angharad did not dare to watch the duel. She had at least been rescued from the ordeal of marriage to Goronwy and that was a big consolation. Omri had been released from the castle to join his compatriots. Though he could not view the contest, he would later celebrate it in song.

Idwal did all he could to stop the bloodshed, shuttling between the Norman and the Welsh onlookers with bilingual excitement, but finding no support. Richard Orbec wanted to take Ralph's place against Damville, but the challenge had already been thrown down. Ilbert Malvoisin and his men had also arrived to witness the event.

Gervase Bret made a final attempt to dissuade his friend.

"This is not your fight, Ralph," he argued.

"I have made it so."

"If anyone should meet him, it should be me. I was the victim of Damville's machination. Let me confront him."

"He is too fierce an opponent for you, Gervase."

"I can use a sword."

"Damville has chosen a lance first," said Ralph. "It needs a trained soldier to go up against him. Leave this to me. I'll meet him on even terms."

"Five years ago, perhaps."

"What's that you say?"

"You are not quite as young as you once were," said Gervase with tact. "Time slows a man down. That could be fatal."

"I am as strong and lusty as ever I was," said Ralph, hurt by any suggestion of weakness on his part. "I'll fight three Maurice Damvilles, one after the other."

The sheriff called the men to order and Gervase moved reluctantly away. Maurice Damville deserved the ultimate punishment, but he was an expert soldier at the height of his powers. Sitting in commission with Gervase and the others was not the best preparation for Ralph Delchard. The latter would have to draw deep on his experience if he were to survive the duel.

Ilbert Malvoisin reminded the two men of the rules of combat, then withdrew to the edge of the circle. Ralph Delchard and Maurice Damville mounted their horses, put on their helms, and took the long, oval shields that were handed to them. Their left arms went through the two vertical straps on the back of the shield and gripped the reins. From shoulder to shin, they were now covered on the undefended side. The spears came next to be used as lances for thrusting. Ralph adjusted his grip as he searched for the right balance.

Maurice Damville had supreme confidence that he would rip his opponent apart at the first charge. There would be immense satisfaction in that. But for the arrival of the royal commissioners, Damville's plans would have succeeded. Single combat might frighten some, but he embraced it gladly. In killing Ralph Delchard, he would escape trial at the hands of the sheriff. Exile would follow, but at least he would live to rebuild his shattered dreams of power. All he had to do was disappoint his audience by destroying their champion.

The sheriff gave the signal and the contest began. After prancing on their toes, the high-spirited destriers were at last released into action. They cantered towards each other at a steady pace that allowed their riders to sit firm in the saddle. Dipped lances rose to strike and shields were held ready to parry. Ralph watched his man every inch of the way, banking down the exhilaration of combat with the cool judgment of experience. There was no margin for error. Damville would be an extremely difficult opponent.

Immediate proof was given of his expertise. There was a resounding clash as the two men closed and thrust hard with their weapons. Ralph's spear was easily deflected upward by his opponent's shield, but his own defence was not quite as sound. Damville's lance chose a sharper angle and a lower point of contact, striking the shield with such force that Ralph was knocked off balance and unseated. A gasp came from the watching throng as he was dragged along the ground with one foot still caught in the stirrup.

Kicking himself free, he rolled over to meet the attack that would certainly come. His spear had been knocked from his hand on impact, but the shield was still on his arm. He used it with more care this time, watching the lance that now came hurtling towards him, taking its point in the centre of his shield and parrying it away. Damville's speed took him past Ralph and gave him time to pull out his sword. As his adversary swung his horse around again, Ralph had a means of attack as well as defence.

Damville came in more slowly to pick his spot, jabbing with the lance as he circled his quarry. Ralph swung his sword at the swirling shield, but his attacks were met firmly. The spear kept him at bay. He simply could not get close enough to land a telling blow on body or limbs. As he dodged another vicious thrust, therefore, Ralph changed his tactics, feinting to lash at the body, but taking his sword down sharply in the opposite direction instead. Damville's spear was severed in two, its head rolling in the dust.

They were now on equal terms. Hurling the stump of his spear at Ralph, his furious opponent leaped from the saddle and pulled out his own sword, unleashing such a barrage of blows that Ralph was driven back several yards by the onslaught. He recovered enough to hold his ground, but Damville was getting the better of the exchange. When their shields met with a clatter, it was Ralph who was finally pushed away. Sensing victory, Damville came after him with renewed energy.

Ralph fought well and parried the iron whirlwind with his own sword. His temper was up now. Maurice

256

Damville had committed terrible crimes and he was the chosen executioner. Such a man could not be allowed to live. Ralph came back at him with a flurry of blows and put him on the defensive. For the first time, Damville was forced to give ground. It hurt his pride. Ralph now had the surge of strength, but Damville had more mobility. The ankle which had caught in the stirrup was burning. Ralph found it increasingly painful to put his full weight on it.

Damville took advantage of the weakness, giving more ground to make Ralph lurch after him, then dodging and weaving to put more strain on the twisted ankle. As Ralph lunged in again, Damville parried his sword blows, then dropped to a knee to slash at his feet. The blade passed beneath the bottom of the shield and caught the damaged ankle a glancing blow. Ralph yelled in pain and danced on one foot. When Damville pounded away at his shield, Ralph was knocked to the ground.

Even in such disarray, he had the instincts of a survivor. He heard the roar of triumph and saw the open-mouthed grin. His opponent was coming in for the kill. Ralph was ready for him. As Damville discarded his shield and used both hands to bring the weapon straight for the unprotected heart, Ralph rolled quickly to the side. One sword sank several inches into the ground, but another found its target with deadly accuracy. Thrusting with every ounce of energy he could muster, Ralph drove the weapon through the open mouth and up into the brain.

Maurice Damville let out a gurgle of pain and collapsed on top of Ralph Delchard. Blood was still gushing from his mouth as they lifted him off. Cheers of congratulation rang out on every side. In one gruesome death, many debts had been paid. English and Welsh hearts were reconciled at last.

Gervase Bret was the first to run to the aid of his friend. As he was pulled to his feet, Ralph was jocular.

"Thanks, Gervase. I'm not quite as young as I once was."

Richard Orbec was sorry to bid farewell to Angharad. When he was introduced to her father, he was very touched by the kind things that she said about him. He was unused to compliments and awkward in his replies. Idwal was their interpreter.

"She asks about the clothing, my lord."

"Tell her to keep it."

"But she said it was very special to you."

"That is why I give it to her as a gift." He looked into her smiling face. "It becomes her so well and takes away memories that I should have outgrown long ago."

Idwal translated and Angharad nodded gratefully.

Orbec groped for another compliment. "Tell her that she is the first lady ever to enter my house. I could not have met a more charming guest. Apologise for my being so stern at first. My anger soon melted." He managed a smile. "If she ever wishes to visit me again, she and her family will always be most welcome."

Father and daughter were both delighted with the offer. Gervase came up to claim his share of gratitude. Angharad kissed him and her father embraced him warmly. He had heard the full story of the escape from Monmouth. Omri, too, was part of the leave-taking.

"Will you ride back with Angharad?" asked Gervase.

"No," said the old man. "I'll follow the others home to Powys. When they've buried their dead and put all this behind them, they'll need a song and a jest to brighten up their court. I'll not want for employment."

"I hope we meet again."

"Anywhere, but Monmouth Castle."

They shared a laugh. Omri then departed with Cadwgan ap Bleddyn and his host towards the Black Mountains. Angharad and her father headed back towards South Wales with their soldiers. The reason that had brought the two families together no longer existed. Goronwy lay dead in the back of a cart along with the alliance between Deheubarth and Powys.

"Where will you go now?" asked Orbec.

"Back to Hereford," said Gervase.

"Evening draws in. You will not get back until well after dark." He glanced after Angharad then shifted his feet. "You may stay the night at my house, if you wish, and set off first thing in the morning."

"I accept your invitation, my lord," said Idwal with a cackle of pleasure, even though it had not been directed at him. "I have looked forward to meeting you and to seeing this chapel that you told me about."

"You, too, will be welcome, Archdeacon," said Orbec. "You helped to avert a battle this afternoon. That deserves a good meal and a warm bed at the very least. Gervase?"

"The meal and the bed sound too good to resist."

"The invitation includes Ralph Delchard."

"I will have to refuse on his behalf, I fear."

"But he must be exhausted," said Orbec. "His ankle is injured and he is bruised all over. Riding a horse will be agony for him. He needs to rest."

"I know," agreed Gervase, "but you will never persuade him to do so. He must ride with the sheriff to Hereford to attend to urgent business."

"What can possibly drag him back through the night?"

"Ale."

Golde was about to retire to bed when he knocked. When she realised who it was, she was thrilled to see him again, but embarrassed that he had caught her at the house. Aelgar's presence made any privacy impossible and Ralph detected the faint aroma of ale. It was enough to change the venue of their meeting. He escorted her to the nearby castle, walking gingerly on the twisted ankle and telling her about events at Ewyas Harold. She was alarmed to hear about the duel, but relieved to see that he had come through it alive. Ralph felt it appropriate to enjoy a gentle boast about his prowess with the sword, but she was more concerned about his injury.

Before she knew it, Golde had been conducted into the apartment which Ralph had shared with Gervase. His manner changed at once. Guiding her to a chair, he sat beside her.

"We must talk, Golde."

"Yes, my lord."

"And that is the first thing we must talk about," he said. "My name is Ralph. Call it me from now."

"If you wish."

"I do," he said, kissing her lightly on the lips.

"Thank you, Ralph."

He took her hand. "I have thought much about you."

"And I about you."

"Good things, I hope?"

"For the most part, my lord . . . Ralph."

"Oh? Bad things, also?"

"Not bad, perhaps. But worrying. Doubts, fears."

"Put them aside," he said, lifting a hand to kiss it. "I

260

am here, Golde. I endured a hellish ride and the even more hellish company of Ilbert the Sheriff to return to you. Have no more doubts about me."

"The doubts are about myself."

"In what way?"

She bowed her head. "I am not sure that you will think me worthy of you."

"No woman could be more worthy of me, my love."

"You do not know me."

"I know you as well as I need, Golde."

"There is more."

"Explain."

She hesitated.

"Warnod's charter, is it not?"

"Yes."

"*You* sent it to Winchester."

She was shocked. "How did you know?"

"By your eagerness to become involved," he said. "Part of that could be put down to your sister's grief, but her future interests were also served. You knew about a charter which gave him a legal claim to part of Orbec's land. If he was going to marry your sister, it was natural that he should show such an important charter to you."

"But he did not," she said.

"In that case, he gave it to your sister for safekeeping. Along with the will."

"That is not how the document came into my hands."

"Then how did it?"

She braced herself. "I stole it from the sheriff."

Ralph froze. He remembered the earlier ride to Orbec's demesne when Ilbert Malvoisin had conversed with him. The sheriff had called her a thief. Ralph would hear no criticism of her then and put the notion straight

261

from his mind, but here she was now, sitting before him confessing frankly to the same crime. His hands gently disengaged themselves.

"I felt that you should hear the full story," she said. "It is only fair to you. I would not like your interest in me to be based on a false assumption."

"Stealing from that oaf of a sheriff is no sin," he said, trying to laugh it off. "Do not let it trouble your conscience so."

"If I do not tell you, Ilbert Malvoisin may."

"Is his version of events different from yours?"

"Very different."

"I'll hear both and be the judge."

Golde was hurt when he stood up and moved away from her. It was painful enough to have to tell him her secret, but that pain would have been lessened by his proximity. Instead, he was standing a few yards away and watching her with a mixture of suspicion and mild distaste.

"The sheriff had the charter," she said, plunging in. "Aelgar told him of it. She is a good girl, but a little naive at times and too impressed by status. Warnod had talked often of a claim to some land in the north of Archenfield, left to him by his father and confirmed as his by charter. When the first commissioners came, he wanted to show it to them to see if they would uphold his claim."

"But the charter had gone."

"Into Ilbert's possession."

"How?"

"When Aelgar boasted of the document to him, he rode to Archenfield himself and asked to see it. Warnod could hardly refuse such a request from the sheriff. Ilbert promised to take it away to make sure that it was not a forgery." She gave a shrug. "He never gave it back. When your predecessors came to assess all the holdings in the shire, Warnod had no charter to produce. The sheriff refused to see him."

"Wait one moment," said Ralph, sifting through her story with great care. "There is something I do not understand. Your sister *told* him of the charter? How could a young girl like that even come into contact with Ilbert?"

"He came to the house."

"Why?"

"I supply the ale for the castle."

Ralph tensed. "Is that all you supply, Golde?"

"My lord!"

"The sheriff would not bother with matters that his underlings would handle. I buy wine for my cellar, but I send another to make the actual purchase."

"Ilbert grew fond of me," she said, quietly. "Against my wishes, I assure you, and without any encouragement from me. But I cannot control a man's feelings."

"You spurned him, then?"

"Every time."

"Then nothing occurred between you?"

"No." There was a long pause. "Except that once."

His tone was glacial now. "Go on. Except that once?"

"That charter was everything to Warnod," she said. "If his claim could be enforced, he and my sister could live in happiness and comfort instead of scratching a living on his land in Llanwarne. I did it for *them*. For Aelgar."

"Did what?"

"Secured the charter from the sheriff."

"How?"

"I took it, my lord."

"Yes, but how?" he pressed. "There's more besides. *How?*"

"I agreed to come to him one night."

"To that pig of a sheriff?" he said in disgust.

"Hear me out in full and you may not be so harsh on me. I did it to gain access to his chamber here. His wife sleeps at their house in Leominster. He often stays at the castle when business keeps him here."

"I am sure that he does!"

"I knew that the charter would be here," she said. "If I spent the night in his chamber, I would have a chance to find it. It was our only hope."

"So you slept with that ogre first."

"No!" she protested. "I did not and could not do that!"

"The two of you alone all night in his chamber?"

"We were not alone." A faint smile showed. "I brought some ale with me. A very special brew. The sheriff preferred wine, but learned to drink my ale to please me. I knew that he would take this potion if I offered it."

"Potion?"

"I have been brewing for many years," she said. "There is little I have not learned about the trade. I can make an ale that tastes like honey, but has the kick of a donkey. One sip of it would send the strongest man to sleep."

"He drank it down?"

"The whole draught."

Ralph began to laugh. "What happened?"

"He did not wake up until noon the next day."

"By which time you and the charter had long gone."

"Yes," she said. "My absence he noticed at once and realised he had been duped. The theft of the charter he did not discover till later. He is certain that I took it, but has no means of proving it."

"And is this the full extent of your crime?" he said as he came back to her. "Teaching a lecherous sheriff a lesson that he will never forget?"

"I thought it would turn you away from me."

He grinned. "Has it?"

"It did at first."

"You have my deepest apology and profoundest thanks."

"Thanks?"

"Yes, Golde," he said, taking her in his arms. "Without that charter, we should not have come to Hereford with such haste. Warnod was abused. You brought it to our attention. There were other matters that arose from the returns of the first commissioners, but that piece of land in Archenfield was the main one." He hugged her then laughed aloud. "I would love to have seen Ilbert the Sheriff snoring away like that! No wonder he was blunt with you."

"It was not only the charter that I stole from him."

"Something far more precious was taken away from under his greedy nose?"

"Ilbert has not touched ale since. He sticks to wine."

"Let's forget Ilbert," he said. "There is no place for him here. I came back to be with you, Golde. You have been honest with me and I respect you for that." He pulled her close. "I merely wish to ask one question of you."

"What is that?"

"Will your sister expect you back tonight?"

Golde looked at him and all her doubts fell away.

"She will have to learn to manage without me."

The events of the day had exposed a vein of conviviality in Richard Orbec which had been hidden for some years.

He was a generous host. In the hall of the manor house Gervase Bret and Idwal the Archdeacon were treated to a delicious meal and offered a choice of fine wines. The dishes set before them were so tempting and so plentiful that the Welshman fell on them with a vengeance, gormandising with such relish that he actually stopped talking for a while.

Orbec himself was a revelation. He joined happily in the banter and led the laughter. The death of Maurice Damville seemed to have lifted a huge rock from his back. He was no longer pressed down into a life of frugality, self-denial, and defensiveness. Orbec ate more during that one meal than during the whole of the week. Wine brought out a gentle mockery in him.

"Are you telling us, then, that God was a Welshman?"

"Probably," said Idwal.

"Do you have any Scriptural basis for this claim?"

"It is something I feel in the blood and along the heart, my lord. We are a nation with *hwyl*. Not a spiritless people like the *Saeson*. Not a gloomy race like the Normans. We love our religion with a passion unlike any other. God put that passion there for a purpose."

"We have noticed," said Gervase with a smile.

"What, then, is your ambition?" asked Orbec.

"Ambition is a sin," said Idwal, waving an admonitory finger before using it to pop another eel into his mouth. "The quest for personal gain is unchristian. What I have is not the sneaking lust of an ambition, but the soul-enhancing joy of a mission in life."

"And what might that be?"

"To become Archbishop of Wales!"

"Your country has no archbishop," Gervase pointed out.

"We will, my friend, we will. My mission is clear.

When it pleases God to choose me, I will become Bishop of St. David's without—I hope and pray—having to be consecrated by the Archbishop of Canterbury. That will make me nominal head of the Welsh Church. I can then don my lambskin cloak and go to Rome for an audience with the Pope himself."

"What will be your request?" said Orbec.

"It will be a demand," corrected Idwal. "To recognise that we are a separate people with our own spiritual identity. To appoint me Idwal, Archbishop of Wales."

He reached across the table for another piece of bread and almost fell from his seat. Rich food and heady wine had overtaxed a constitution that was accustomed to simpler fare. Idwal began to sway dangerously.

"I must take my leave of you," he said with an air of maudlin contrition. "Thank you for your hospitality, my lord. I must now beg the use of your chapel so that I can get down on my knees and ask a pardon for my gross indulgence."

Orbec called a servant to help the Welshman out. They bade him good night, then finished the last flagon of wine. Gervase was ready to retire to his bed, but Orbec wished to talk a little longer. The latter's joviality fell away. A more soulful mood gripped him.

"Idwal was right," he said. "Ambition is a sin."

"That depends on the nature of the ambition, my lord."

"Mine was based on a craving for power. I fought to acquire this demesne so that I could surround myself with a vast moat of land and hide here within my citadel." He gave a bleak smile. "Not all that land was acquired honestly."

"We have taken note of that, my lord," said Gervase.

"Maurice Damville was partly to blame," continued

Orbec. "As long as he was my neighbour, I could not rest for one second. I had to patrol my estates like an army of occupation lest he steal them away as he stole so much else. Now that Damville is gone, my imperatives have changed."

"You were the victim of his malice, my lord."

"There was more to it than that, Gervase. He did not devise his plan simply to spite Richard Orbec and bring the fury of the Welsh down on me. He had a wider ambition than that."

"What was it?"

"To become Earl of Hereford."

"By inciting violence on the border?"

"Precisely by that means," said Orbec. "Why do you think he spent so much time on his fortifications? Ewyas Harold was the bulwark against the Welsh. If they had ridden around it and laid waste on my estates, Damville would then have sallied forth and harried them back across the border. He would have been given the credit for ending a Welsh incursion that he himself had provoked."

"And thereby strengthened his claim to be made earl."

"The shire has lacked a controlling hand since Roger of Breteuil was disgraced and imprisoned. The king has been careful not to appoint another earl. Welsh hostility along a sensitive border might well change his mind. He would need a powerful man with a stronghold in a strategic position."

"Maurice Damville."

"Yes, Gervase," said the other. "Warnod was killed to set the plan in motion. Angharad was captured to unsettle the Welsh and you were abducted to stop a royal commission from straying too close to Ewyas at a crucial time. And all to serve one overriding ambition."

"To be the Earl of Hereford."

"And to hold the whiphand over all of us."

Gervase was grateful for the insight into Damville's designs, but there were questions about Orbec himself that had still to be addressed. His host seemed to read his mind.

"You are wondering why, Gervase."

"Yes, my lord."

"Why do I lead the life of a hermit when I have such wealth and position? Why do I skulk away?"

"Maurice Damville is only part of the explanation."

"She was the rest of it."

"She?"

"Cecilia."

"Your betrothed?"

"Yes," said Orbec, staring into his wine. "It was because of Cecilia that I came to England to start anew and build afresh. My problem was that I brought her with me. In my mind and in my heart. I even kept the apparel she would have worn to our wedding."

"The white gown and mantle that Angharad put on?"

"Now they are gone and Cecilia has at last left this house." He drained his cup then rolled it between his palms as he relived his story. "I had everything, Gervase. Power and standing. Fine estates near Bayeux. A beautiful woman to share it all with me. But good fortune always produces envy. And it came from the one place I did not expect."

"Within your own family?" suggested Gervase.

"My half-brother, Stephen. I gave him so much, but he wanted far more. While I was away in England, he took it all by force. Including my beloved Cecilia."

"Could she not resist him?"

"Four men-at-arms held her down while he raped her.

269

She could not live with the shame of it, Gervase. By the time I got back to Normandy, Cecilia had taken her own life and I had lost everything in Bayeux that I held most dear."

"What did you do?"

"I turned into a devil. I visited the horrors of hell upon Stephen and those four men. I made them suffer such pain that they begged me to kill them."

The cup fell from his hands and bounced to the floor with a hollow clack. Gervase watched it roll across the flagstones and stop in front of the fireplace. Orbec was staring down at the hands which had been responsible for the slaughter.

"I now understand why you fled to England," said Gervase. "And why you built that chapel in your house."

"I pray for the souls of those five men every day," said Orbec. "They deserved to die, but not in that hideous way. They released something inside me that I have tried to keep locked away ever since. Damville came close to setting it free again, but I held it in." He looked up at Gervase. "I pray for Cecilia as well. The chapel is dedicated to her memory. But I pray, above all else, for forgiveness."

Richard Orbec's gifts to the cathedral now took on a new light. They were self-imposed acts of penance. The new ceiling for which he was paying would be an epitaph to the woman he loved and the five men he slew. The tiny chapel was at once a house of God and a cage for the Devil.

Epilogue

CANON HUBERT WAS IN SUBLIME FORM AT THE SHIRE hall the next morning. His spirits had been lifted by the news that Gervase brought with him from the Golden Valley. Idwal the Archdeacon had decided not to return to Hereford before continuing his journey around his native country. Hubert felt like a besieged castle that had just been providentially liberated. His good humour was further increased by Ralph Delchard's willingness to hand over the business of the morning to him without let or hindrance.

An exhausting day and a joyously long night had persuaded Ralph to yield pride of place to his colleague for once. Gervase, too, was happy for the canon to undertake the searing examination of Ilbert the Sheriff.

"I hold in my hand a charter," said Hubert.

"I see it well," grunted Ilbert.

"Have you set eyes on this document before?"

"Never!" he lied.

"Did you know of its existence?"

"Only by rumour."

"Can you guess at its import?"

"I believe that it relates to the carucates of land in the

north of Archenfield, at present in the hands of Richard Orbec."

"It touches on a few adjacent manors as well," said Hubert, pointedly. "At present in the hands of Ilbert Malvoisin."

"Can this document have legal substance?" blustered the sheriff. "If it is so important a charter, why have we not been allowed to view it before?"

"Some of us *did* view it," Ralph said, wickedly.

"You are fully entitled to peruse it now," said Hubert. "Along with all the other charters that relate to your land. Did you not think to be shearer by occupation, my lord sheriff?"

"A shearer?"

"Your fingers are so nimble with a pair of shears. You have snipped away some of the richest wool in the county. And done it so skilfully that the rest of the fleece looks almost untouched." Hubert held up another document and smiled benignly. "Let us begin with your work among the sheep of Leominster . . ."

Ilbert Malvoisin was destroyed by a combination of sardonic wit and legal charter. His subtle seizures of property had been concealed from the earlier commissioners, but laid bare by the unremitting searches of Ralph Delchard and his colleagues. It was Hubert who turned shearer now, clipping away merrily until several carucates of land, three mills, two churches, and a small castle lay on the floor to be returned to their rightful owners.

The sheriff shivered in the cold air like a shorn ewe.

"You look distressed," teased Ralph. "May I send for a tankard of ale to revive you?"

It was a humbled sheriff who limped out of the shire

hall. His rank did not save him. Abuse of his position encouraged the commissioners to confiscate with severity and fine with compunction. They would also relay details of his malpractices to the Exchequer at Winchester where they would fall under the eye of the king himself. The sheriff might even lose his shrievalty.

Brother Simon had made copious records throughout, but he now threw aside his quill to congratulate his companion.

"You were magnificent, Canon Hubert."

"I did no more than my duty."

"You exposed the ugly face of corruption."

"We must root out abuse of power wherever we find it."

"Simon is right," agreed Ralph. "You were fearless."

"That is not entirely true," admitted Hubert. "One nagging fear was always at the back of my mind. I was afraid that a certain archdeacon might take it into his mind to pay a final call on me. When may we *leave* this confounded place, my lord? It makes me feel uncomfortable."

"We shall soon be quit of it," said Ralph.

"Yes," added Gervase. "Richard Orbec will not detain us long. The turn of events has changed his attitude towards the acquisition of land. He will cede all that we ask without argument or delay."

"That thought contents me," said Hubert. "Winchester beckons. I will be more than happy to bid farewell to that fire-breathing Idwal and to all the other dragons of Archenfield."

Gervase Bret could not resist correcting him.

"Ergyng," he said.

Two more hours in session brought their business to a most satisfactory conclusion. Richard Orbec was anxious to set matters right and he put up no defence against the confiscation of part of his land. It would now pass to Aelgar, along with some of the manors reclaimed from Ilbert the Sheriff. She would become a wealthy young woman.

Ralph Delchard and Gervase Bret collected their baggage from the castle then waited at its main gate with the men-at-arms. Having gathered up their things from the cathedral, Canon Hubert and Brother Simon joined the rest of their party. Everybody was anxious to be on the way, but Ralph would not budge. He held them all back.

"Why this delay, my lord?" complained Hubert.

"Be patient, man."

"We should be on the road to make best use of daylight."

"Then ride off on your own," said Ralph, testily. "I will catch you up in no time at all."

"What keeps you here?"

"My own affairs."

"Come," said Gervase, taking charge. "We'll set forth. Our presence here intrudes upon Ralph's wishes."

The cavalcade moved off with Canon Hubert in the lead, his chubby legs urging his donkey forward. He took a last look at the cathedral over his shoulder and quivered at the memory of the little archdeacon whose florid argument had set them all by the ears. Winchester would be a safer haven. Even Idwal could not claim *that* city as part of Wales.

Left alone at the gate, Ralph Delchard waited with growing irritation. He had sent word to Castle Street and expected a swift response. None came. A bargain which had been struck in the long reaches of the night was being repudiated. Irritation was supplanted by doubt. Did he make too great a demand on her? Had he taken Golde for granted? Was she having second thoughts in the light of day?

He waited until the uncertainty could be borne no longer. His horse took him to the house within a minute. Ralph wanted to hammer on the door, but his knock was instead timid. It was Aelgar who answered his summons.

"Good day, my lord," she said.

"Is your sister within?"

"No. Golde went out some time ago."

"To the brewhouse?"

"Into the city. I do not know where."

"Did she not leave a message for me?"

"None, my lord." Aelgar smiled. "But I must thank you for the message which you kindly sent *me*."

"Oh, yes," he said absently. "The terms of Warnod's will were upheld. You will inherit all his land in Archenfield."

"This has saved my life. Golde was so happy for me."

"Did she speak of no happiness for herself?"

The girl grew embarrassed. Wanting to offer him good news, she could only distress him with bad tidings. Golde had left the house without explanation.

She had not come to Ralph. What further upset him was the likeness between the two sisters. As Ralph looked at the beautiful Aelgar, he saw a younger version of Golde. His sense of loss was acute.

"I wish you good day," he said.

"God speed, my lord!"

Ralph did not look back. His horse trotted along the streets until it came to the city gate. He went through it and quickened the animal's pace to a canter. When it came to the moment of decision, Golde would not

275

surrender her independence. A night in his arms had been merely a token of her affection. He had been foolish to build so much hope on it.

The others would be a mile or more ahead of him now. He was about to spur his horse into a gallop when he saw her. Golde was waiting beneath an apple tree beside the road. Dressed for travelling, she sat astride her palfrey. A packhorse was loaded with her belongings.

Ralph was overjoyed. He cantered to her and reined in his horse. Golde gave him a welcoming smile. He put an arm around her waist. The kiss she offered him was frank and uninhibited. It made him feel ashamed of his doubts about her.

"Your sister said that you left the house."

"I have."

"Did you not tell her where you were going?"

"I had no time."

"But Aelgar will wonder what has become of you."

"No, Ralph," she said. "My sister does not need me now. She is well provided for. I may ride away with a clear conscience." Golde gave him another kiss. "She will understand."

Don't miss the other books in the Domesday
Chronicle series...

**THE WOLVES OF SAVERNAKE
THE RAVENS OF BLACKWATER**

❖⚬❖

...and for a taste of murder in Elizabethan
England, follow the chronicles of Nicholas
Bracewell and Lord Westfield's players in:

**THE QUEEN'S HEAD
THE MERRY DEVILS
THE TRIP TO JERUSALEM
THE NINE GIANTS
THE MAD COURTESAN
THE SILENT WOMAN
THE ROARING BOY**

by
Edward Marston
Published by Fawcett Books.

Edward Marston

Published by Fawcett Books.
Available in your local bookstore.